The Second Time Around

Contemporary Fiction/Western Romance/Adult Content

The Second Time Around

Book One
of the
Belanger Creek Ranch Series

by
Gloria Antypowich

Gloria Antypowich

Copyright@ 2014 by Gloria Antypowich
Library and Archives Canada Cataloguing
Antypowich, Gloria, 1943-
The Second Time Around / Gloria Antypowich.
(Book I of the Belanger Creek Ranch series)
Originally published under title: **Hearts at Risk**.
Issued in print and electronic formats.
ISBN 1511533692 (pbk.).--ISBN 9781511533690 (ebook)

PS8601.N878S43 2015
C813'.6
C2014-908320-3
C2014-908321-1

All rights reserved. No part of this book may be reproduced or transmitted in any form or by any means, electronic or mechanical, including photocopying, recording, or by any information storage and retrieval system, without permission in writing from the copyright owner.

This is a work of fiction. Names, characters, places and incidents either are the product of the author's imagination or are used fictitiously, and any resemblance to any actual persons, living or dead, events, or locales is entirely coincidental.

NOTE: This book has undergone an extensive rewrite since its first publication as *Hearts At Risk, Book one of the Thompson Family Trilogy.*

Published by *Gloria Antypowich*

***
5 stars! Reviewed By Gisela Dixon for Readers' Favorite

The Second Time Around (Belanger Creek Ranch Book 1)... by Gloria Antypowich is an intense, realistic love story that is not the usual boy-meet-girl type. I loved reading about life on the ranch and the outdoors lifestyle that goes with it. I also found Frank's character to be superbly portrayed, and hopefully a book like this will open up the discussion about mental health and mental illnesses and how devastating they can be. I actually liked both of the central protagonists and found myself rooting for them. A great new novel in the romance genre and a fun read!
***
5 stars! Reviewed By Faridah Nassozi for Readers' Favorite

The Second Time Around by Gloria Antypowich is an enthralling contemporary romance story with a captivating plot and fresh characters, set against the serene and enchanting background of a beautiful ranch. Gloria Antypowich's incredible writing brought out the characters and their inner wars and wounds perfectly. Frank and Colt brought out a whole mixture of feelings in me; sometimes I wanted to give them each a hug and ease their pain, and at other times they were so infuriating I felt like smacking them on the head. Their story is a perfectly portrayed example of how fear of being hurt again can get in the way of true love
***
4 stars. Reviewed By Tina Gibbons for Readers' Favorite

Gloria Antypowich has created a world with vibrant characters in The Second Time Around. Frank - a very interesting name for a lead female character - can do anything a male ranch hand can do and better. She's been hurt and she's vulnerable, but she's strong and independent at the same time. Her attraction to Colt sizzles and their chemistry is undeniable. They both make their share of bad decisions trying to find the right path. Painful moments brought tears to my eyes, and the stubborn streak in that cowboy, well, it's what kept me reading. Shauna Lee is also a multidimensional character. I wanted to dislike her for being in Frank's way, but I couldn't. Part of the second book in the series was included. I look forward to reading that installment to continue Shauna Lee's story and find out more about her.

***

5.0 out of 5 stars A Great Read!

Amazon.com Review By Kathleen Ball
I love a book full of emotion and The Second Time Around is such a book. One minute I was hopeful and the next I was near tears. Gloria Antypowich has written a winner!! Her characters are flawed and true to life. The story is complex with the right mix of action and emotion. This book is a keeper- the type you'll want to read again!

***

5 stars By Juliette Douglas

Loved It! Author Antypowich pulled me in gently and before I knew it, finished the book in 3 hours. Just a delightful, wonderful afternoon read! The two main characters fought their feelings for each other like they were fighting the plague. Lots of tugs, tension and pulls. I like a book with good descriptions and this author did that for me. I love the author's writing style...and well...hummm...will have to read her others now…. Well done!

***

5 stars review By Picky

What an absolutely charming read. As my name states, I'm very picky about what I read. I start books and if they don't grab me within moments, I shut them. I started this book and was amazed to find myself drawn in almost without even realizing. And the key was dialogue. This author writes dialogue like nobody's business. The exchanges are crisp, each voice distinct, and—most importantly—it sounds authentic.

Speaking of which, this author also knows her way around a rodeo/ranch/farm. The rustic setting (rustic to this city gal, anyway) was perfectly drawn, the details rendered without bogging me down with vocab I didn't understand, and woven in seamlessly

***

5 stars By Cathy Poole
Gloria Antypowich delivers an amazing story!! A fast moving story, that is most definitely a page turner! Once you pick up this book, you cannot put it down until you are done. I promise the story will

leave you with a smile on your face and a song in your heart. Well done Gloria!!!!

***

4 stars By Frank Daley

Gloria Antypowich...demonstrates a good knowledge of human nature in this take of a woman who has suffered three devastating losses in a short period, something most of us have also experienced. Her central character is a feisty, ex-tom-boy named Frank, who is a vet and, having gown up on a ranch, a pretty good horsewoman and stable hand. She meets a guy whose opinion of woman is pretty low and she straightens him out right smartly. My main interest was in how she handled Frank's depression and although, she does not belabor the issue, Frank's attitudes and behaviors reflect the condition well. Ms Antypowich also writes cleanly and clearly and the story develops smoothly.

***

5 stars from By mbsgreg

Really sweet story with characters you would love to have as friends. I read it quite quickly and stayed up into the wee hours to see what would happen next.

I really love stories with strong independent women and the character Frank Lamonte fit the bill to a tee. She, yes I said she, is bright and gutsy and while she is obviously attractive to the male population, she never comes across as conceited, but more as a wholesome country girl. However, bear in mind that even though I used the word 'wholesome' never fear, this book is not lacking in the spice department, but the author still knows how to titillate the reader without going over the top, so don't expect full on erotica..

In the book, Frank suffers from depression... I appreciate that the author touched on the subject of mental illness, as it is so prevalent nowadays and we all need to be able to talk about it just like any other illness without feeling as if it is something we should be able to snap out of, or be ashamed of having.

I also loved the chemistry between Frank Lamonte and Colt Thompson. While it wasn't quite love at first sight (without giving too much away) it was really sweet how the relationship unfolded slowly but surely even though due to past hurts on both their parts, they were both guarding their hearts

***

TABLE OF CONTENTS

- DEDICATION 11
- OTHER BOOKS 13
- ACKNOWLEDGEMENTS 14
- CHAPTER ONE 16
- CHAPTER TWO 27
- CHAPTER THREE 39
- CHAPTER FOUR 45
- CHAPTER FIVE 53
- CHAPTER SIX 63
- CHAPTER SEVEN 77
- CHAPTER EIGHT 91
- CHAPTER NINE 103
- CHAPTER TEN 114
- CHAPTER ELEVEN 126
- CHAPTER TWELVE 139
- CHAPTER THIRTEEN 150
- CHAPTER FOURTEEN 165
- CHAPTER FIFTEEN 172
- CHAPTER SIXTEEN 181
- CHAPTER SEVENTEEN 193
- BOOK TWO CHAPTER ONE 201

BOOK TWO CHAPTER TWO 210

BOOK TWO CHAPTER THREE 220

ABOUT THE AUTHOR 233

DEDICATION

This book is dedicated to the many people who struggle with depression, whether in its mildest form or in its darkest, most debilitating way. Millions of people, in all walks of life, experience it in varying degrees.

I strongly believe that mental illness is a subject that needs to be talked about honestly and openly. Shining the light on it makes people aware and, hopefully, more willing to seek help.

People don't hesitate to go for treatment when they have a physical illness, like heart disease, cancer or diabetes. *Depression is no different.* Sadly, some people still feel there is a stigma attached to being diagnosed with a "mental illness." That is often the biggest obstacle to seeking help. I believe that early professional diagnosis is important. Today, medication is only one of the tools available to aid long term recovery. If you suffer from symptoms of depression, please go to your doctor. If you recognize those symptoms in someone else, please encourage them to get help, even though they may be resistant to the idea. Most importantly, don't try to ignore the symptoms, thinking they'll go away.

I am not a stranger to depression. I have experienced it twice. The first time it happened, I justified what was happening as being the result of stress. The happy, cheerful person I had been, disappeared. I became tearful and overly emotional. I worried constantly. I had insomnia and was always tired. I had trouble concentrating, and it became difficult for me to believe in myself, to trust my decisions. The asthma, which I had dealt with for years, went off the chart. After a time, my employer became concerned for my well-being and encouraged me to seek medical help. Once I did that, my life started to improve, but recovery didn't happen overnight. The second time, I recognized the symptoms and went to my doctor immediately. Once I started taking medication, I got back on track quickly. Today, I am a happy person who loves life, but I maintain an awareness of how I'm feeling.

In The Second Time Around, Frank Lamonte has dealt with a series of traumatic personal setbacks, and experienced feelings that she has thought of as "the blues" for several months. Frank's boss is concerned for her well-being. He insists that she get help and places her on an indefinite leave of absence. This action is the impetus for the rest of the book. This is a work of fiction and I did not go into great depth about depression.

OTHER BOOKS
by Gloria Antypowich:

Full Circle, Book Two, of the Belanger Creek Ranch Series
The Hand of Fate, Book Three, of the Belanger Creek Ranch Series
Second Chances, Book Four, of the Belanger Creek Ranch Series

ACKNOWLEDGEMENTS

I want to express heartfelt appreciation to the following people who read and reread this manuscript, edited it and seeing it through fresh eyes, have made unbiased suggestions: Monicka Gregory, Sharron Hynes, Darlene Bell, Diane Maureen Pleasance, Cathy Hoy, and Donna Wassenaar Rezansoff. There were times when I struggled; this project would have been much more difficult without your support. You are all very special to me.

Monicka Gregory is a Social Media maven. She is the owner Bizz~Linkzz Social Media Services. She also has a successful web page of her own; Kids Goals at http://kidsgoals.com/

Sharron Hynes is a longtime friend, who is very creative in her own right. She designs and sells beautiful all-occasion cards and business cards. She is a musician and singer. She and her husband, Mel, sing and play with their band the Kootenay Legends. Their CD's are enjoyed by many people around the world.

I also want to say a big Thank You to Steve Caresser and *the team at ePrintedBooks*- (http://eprintedbooks.com/)

Steve Caresser and I have worked together before, and I appreciate the quality of work that he produces. It is a pleasure to work with him again. ePintedBbooks offers a wide range of author services, as well as a virtual bookstore. Steve is also the author of five books. I have read the *Sacred Crow, What Every Married Woman Needs, and Five Gallon Bucket*. He has produced several audible poems and he is in the process creating "The Whole World News" Reality is what you make it. Steve and Jason Sinner are the newscasters for this production.

Jason Sinner is a talented copy editor and proofreader at ePrintedBooks and I had the privilege of working with him on one of my husband's book before he edited this series.

Laura Wright LaRoche, at LLPix Designs, (http://llpix.com/) designed the covers for the Belanger Creek Ranch Series. She was a pleasure to work with. I'm convinced she can do anything—that she has magic in her fingers! I also discovered that Laura is an author and her creative imagination shines in that field too. I have read *both Black Woods and Black Woods Revealed.* They have a touch of paranormal, along with mystery and horror. I thoroughly enjoyed them and the image of the "beast" lingered with me for days! *Broken Soul* is on my Kindle, waiting to be read. Her books are available on Amazon.com.

I also want to thank *Jen Blood* for evaluating the four book series in the first draft. She gave me terrific input, suggestions, and encouragement. Since then, she has established a successful editing service (http://jenblood.net/adian-enterprises/) and has become a bestselling author. It was a once in a lifetime opportunity for me and I would never be so fortunate now. (I cannot claim that she is a close friend) I am a big fan of her writing, and I have read all of the books in the *Erin Solomon Pentalogy*. Look for them on Amazon!

And last, but not least, my husband Lloyd Antypowich (a prolific author who has published six books at this time: *A Hunting We Did Go, From Moccasins to Cowboy Boots, Horns and Hair of the High Country, A Chip off the Old Block, Louisiana Man and Grasshopper McLain and Gotleep the Frog*); also my children and their spouses, my grandchildren and the great-grandchildren that I'm blessed to have—I love you all. I appreciate the times you have encouraged me, ragged on me for spending too many hours sitting at the computer and asked when the books were going to be published –after two years, you must have wondered if it would ever happen!

CHAPTER ONE

Thank God it is Friday!
Frank Lamonte sighed when she completed her last patient's file and clicked save. Ruger was an adventuresome Yellow Lab, who managed to get out of his kennel and disappear for a few days. When he limped home that morning, his concerned owner had brought him to the clinic. Frank had assessed him before she cleaned his deep lacerations and stitched them. When the dog and his owner left an hour later, she had been confident that Ruger would be as good as new in a few days.

She turned off the computer and grabbed her coat from the rack behind her. It was closing time, and she sighed with relief, knowing that she had managed to get through one more week at the clinic without falling apart.

Before she left, she decided to check on the new foal they'd delivered that morning. There had been complications before the mare arrived and the foal was unsteady and sluggish. They'd decided to keep them both at the clinic over the weekend.

All day, Martin Cole, her co-worker and fellow veterinarian, and the receptionist at the clinic, Coleen Nutlatch, had been giddy with anticipation. They were leaving right after work to spend the weekend skiing in Banff. Usually they kept their relationship low-key at work, but today their excitement, their happy, carefree laughter, the little looks and suggestive comments had no restraint, and Frank had to fight to keep her fragile composure intact. She hoped they would be gone when she got back from checking the foal. Then she wouldn't have to put on a happy face and wish them a good weekend.

She lingered with the horses, but she didn't stay quite long enough. When she came back into the office, she heard Dr. Winters say "Have a great time on the slopes, you two." As the back door closed, Martin and Coleen's laughter hit her like a tsunami. Her stomach clenched and her chest tightened. She struggled to keep her composure, but it crumbled in spite of her efforts. Desperate, she slipped into the utility room, confident that she wouldn't be found there. Her knuckles whitened as she clenched the edge of the stainless steel counter. She leaned forward and rested her head against the cupboard, eyes squeezed closed, trying to force back the tears that wanted to spill down her cheeks. Her breath came in harsh hiccups as she fought to stifle the ragged sobs that threatened to explode from her throat. *No*, she thought. *I can't do this now. Dr. Winters has to leave first. Then I can cry my eyes out.*

She listened to her boss's movements as he drew the slatted blinds in the waiting room. He checked to make sure the front entrance was locked and turned out the lights. He whistled cheerfully as he walked through the operating theater to the stall where the mare and foal were resting. On the way back, he stopped in his office and called his wife to ask if she wanted him to pick up anything on his way home. Then Frank heard his footsteps when he walked passed the utility room to the back entrance. When she heard the door slam shut, she sagged against the counter and gave in to the dark cloud of sadness that had overshadowed her life for the past four months.

Her shoulder length auburn hair fell forward, covering her face as anguished sobs shook her body and she let the tears flow. Minutes later she didn't hear the utility room door open. She wasn't aware that anyone else was there until Dr. Winters' fatherly arms enveloped her. He turned her into his chest and held her close. She leaned into his comforting strength and let the storm of emotion run its course. When the sobs subsided, she pushed away; embarrassed that he'd witnessed the collapse of the façade that she presented every day, as she valiantly tried to act like her world was still intact.

"I'm sorry about that," she murmured. "I thought you were gone."

"I saw your car in the parking lot. I came back to see what you were doing."

"I'm alright."

He shook his head and guided her out the door.

"Let's go into my office. We need to have a talk."

She shook her head. "You should go home. Sadie is expecting you."

He gently led her into his office. "Sit down." He pointed to a soft chair. As she sank into it, he walked behind the desk and sat in his office chair. He looked directly at her, but she refused to meet his gaze. He extended an arm across the dark surface of the desktop and reached out to her.

Dr. Winters' voice was filled with concern. "Look at me, Frank."

When she glanced up at him, her dark brown eyes were blurry from the storm of emotional tears. Her look met his, and then quickly darted away.

He sighed. "Frank, you are not okay. I've known you since you were knee-high to a grasshopper. I've watched you grow from a chubby-cheeked princess in your daddy's arms, into a gangly, adolescent tomboy who was always at his side. I watched you learn to ride and team rope, and I was as proud of you as he was.

"Then you started coming here to help me on weekends and school holidays. I watched you grow into a feisty, confident young woman and when you decided to go into veterinary medicine I was damned proud of you. When you graduated and came back here to practice, I couldn't have been happier if you were my own daughter.

"I hired Martin because he came with you. He's a good vet, but I never felt he was the right man for you. Sadie said I was prejudiced; I wanted to protect you like I would my own kid. But when he dumped you and hooked up with Coleen while you were staggering from your dad's accident and the sale of the ranch, I knew I was right."

Frank twisted her hands in her lap. "That's all in the past now."

"It isn't, Frank. You see them together every day. It has to be like constantly rubbing salt into a raw wound. I've struggled with it. I know what you've been through these past nine months." He shook his head. "And, Martin had no compassion. He dumped you and took up with Coleen, right in the middle of everything that happened." He picked up a pen and slammed it on the desk in frustration. "I couldn't believe how insensitive he was. I wanted to tell him what a jackass he was; I wanted to tell him to leave. But he's a good vet and what he did to you had nothing to do with his work here at the clinic. Sadie warned me. She told me it was a personal matter between the three of you, and from a business point of view I didn't have a leg to stand on.

"But I've watched you struggle. I've seen the light fade out of you. You've tried to get on top of things, but you haven't been able to. You've just kept sliding deeper into a hole of despondency." He cleared his throat. "I've meant to talk to you for a while, but I've put it off because this is hard for me.

"I've thought about this a lot. Martin is a good vet and I have no reason to ask him to leave, except to protect you. If I ask him to leave, I'll lose Coleen too. I'd accept both of those things if I thought it would help you, but I don't think it would. You'd still be here with all the memories, all the pain. You need to take a break; you need to get away from Stettler for a while."

Frank's head shot up. "Are you telling *me* to leave?" Disbelief and anguish filled her voice.

He got up and walked around the desk to crouch beside her. "Frank, your mom, and dad are in Arizona for the winter. Your dad still has a lot of healing to do, but so do you. I'm asking you... no, I'm telling you, to take a leave of absence. I'm not a medical doctor, but I know enough to recognize that you are slipping into depression."

"Jeez! I admit I've been feeling down and I haven't exactly been a ray of sunshine lately, but don't you think I might have a few reasons to feel blue? My dad almost died, we had to sell the ranch I grew up on, the man I've spent five years with, the man I was engaged to marry, dumped me for the secretary in our office." Her eyes flashed with anger. "I'm not sick. I'm not depressed. I'm trying to get my feet under me."

"Honey, that's a classic response. But feeling blue shouldn't last for months like this has for you."

"Damn it. I am not some weak person who got depressed because things didn't go my way."

"Frank, please listen to me. You are one of the strongest people

I know, and people don't get depressed simply because things don't go their way. Often, they are strong people who have struggled against the odds for too long: they try to shoulder their burden, no matter how crushing it is. That's what you've been doing, and I'm not surprised that you're emotionally exhausted and overwhelmed. To be honest, if I was in your place, I couldn't have dealt with the situation here at the clinic. Given time, I know that you'll get past all this and the black cloud that is hanging over you will lift. But staying here, in the mire of your hurt, is not conducive to getting better. So, as of now, you are on an indefinite leave of absence."

Frank's eyes blazed with anger when she stood up. "I can't believe you're doing this to me. You've been like a second father to me, and now you are turning on me too."

He placed his hands on her shoulders. "This is the first real emotion I've seen you express in months. I hate that it's taken this, but get mad at me. I'll bear the brunt of your anger it if it helps to shake you out of the lackluster state you've been in.

"This is tough love, sweetheart. Go to see your doctor and get some medication: then get out of town. Take a few months off. Go to Arizona and spend some time with your folks—or get a job doing something totally different. Go work on a cattle ranch in B.C., or wait tables in a restaurant in Nova Scotia. But get away from all the painful reminders here in Stettler."

Frank pushed away from him. "You just want to wash your hands of me because you're uncomfortable with the three of us working here together. If you force me out of the picture, you'll only lose one member of your staff."

"That's not true, Frank. I'm...."

"I can't believe you'd do this to me. You know I'd go nuts in Arizona, and can you see me waiting tables? I'm a vet. I work with animals and I that's what I love doing."

"Frank! I'm not washing my hands of you. And, I'm not forcing you out." He pulled her against his chest again. "I'm doing this for your own good. A raw sore won't heal if it is constantly picked at, and that's what is happening to you here, in this clinic, in this town."

"Don't." She tried to push away again.

He held onto her arm. "Frank, do you have any friends in Stettler? Who do you hang around with? Who is your support system? Who do you talk to and share your feelings with?"

She glared at him.

"I know you. I've watched you grow up. You never were a giddy schoolgirl. You spent all of your time with your dad. You were named after his father and you became the son he knew he'd never have. You worked around the ranch, rode horses, and learned to rope with Clint Roberts. You never hung out with the girls. I doubt if you dated when you were a teenager. You and Clint were best buds and you hung out with him and his friends, just like you were one of the guys. On weekends and holidays, if you weren't at a rodeo with your dad and Clint, you were here at the clinic. I wondered about it at times, but your family seemed happy. In hindsight, it was a damned selfish way for him to raise you."

"Don't you dare criticize my Dad. You're supposed to be one of his best friends."

"I'm still one of his best friends, but I'm not blind either. Maybe if he hadn't guarded you so closely, maybe if you'd spent some time being a girl, maybe if you'd dated when you were younger...maybe you wouldn't have fallen so hard for Martin. You had no awareness, no experience, no reference points...."

His phone rang. "Damn," he muttered as he retrieved it from his pants pocket. "It's Sadie. I have to answer this, but we're not finished here, Frank."

He gave her a stern look, as he spoke into the phone. "Hi, hon. I got side tracked here. Frank and I have had that long overdue conversation." He listened for a moment, and then said, "She's not very happy with me right now." He was silent as he listened to his wife, and finally said, "I'll let you talk to her."

He handed the phone to Frank, who automatically took it.

"Hi, Sadie."

"Frank, please come to our place for supper tonight. Going to your apartment to sit alone isn't a good idea. I know you're upset, but the three of us need to talk. I know where Jason is coming from and you need to understand that he has your best interests at heart."

Frank didn't answer right away.

"Frank," Sadie implored. "Let us be there for you."

"Okay," Frank whispered and handed the phone back to Dr. Winters. Her eyes were full of tears.

The oppressive cloud that overshadowed Frank's life seemed to grow even darker and heavier as she followed Dr. Winters to his house. Sadie met her at the door with a warm hug, but even though she tried to show some enthusiasm, she couldn't find it.

Sadie was a registered nurse. After dinner, she sat down with Frank and told her about her own sister, who had become deeply depressed. Like many people, Valerie had refused to admit that she was mentally ill, and she hadn't gone for help as soon as she should have. The family had watched her languish in depths of despair for years.

Sadie said that it wasn't uncommon for the illness to manifest after a person had gone through traumatic experiences, such as Frank had during the past nine months. She insisted that she go to see her doctor before she left town, impressing upon her that it was crucial for her long-term mental health.

Half an hour later Jason entered the kitchen. Sadie motioned for him to sit down at the table and join them. "Frank and I have been talking about what's been happening to her. She says you told her to leave town."

He grinned, ruefully. "I didn't mean she should leave permanently. I think she needs to get away and give herself a chance to get on top of things. I told her to do something totally different for a while. She doesn't have to tell anyone that she's a vet. That could raise expectations and put more pressure on her, and she definitely doesn't need that.

"She says she'd go crazy in Arizona, and the idea of waiting tables in a restaurant doesn't appeal to her. But it's calving time and I'm sure there must be a ranch looking for a hand that has her experience. It would be a total change of pace for her."

He looked at Frank. "I'd give you a good reference. You worked with animals for years before you became a vet and you've always been good with them. You understand animals; maybe better than you actually do humans."

Frank leaned her elbows on the table and closed her eyes while she massaged her temples with her slender fingers.

Sadie frowned and reached out to touch her shoulder. "Do you have a headache?"

Frank looked at her sadly. "Headache, heartache, body ache, brain ache…I have it. How do I deal with all of this?" She sighed. "I love my apartment and I waited so long to get one in that area. But if I go away, I'll have to give it up. And what would I do with my furniture?"

Dr. Winters leaned back in his chair and stretched out his legs. "Let's think about this, Frank. The bigger ranches pay decent wages and board and room is usually included. You wouldn't have a lot of other expenses. You could keep your apartment: you'll have your job at the clinic when you are well and ready to come back. All I ask is that you take enough time to get back on your feet. I want to see the twinkle in your eyes again and that beautiful smile on your face. I want to see a bounce in your step and hear your laughter. You need to take long enough to get over Martin, and come to terms with what happened to your dad."

Frank chewed her lip. "That's a tall order. Do you really think that in three or four months, I can get over losing the man I spent five years with? The man I was going to marry?"

"Then take six months or a year. I think you'll realize that he wasn't right for you in the first place. I know you'll eventually meet a man who will appreciate you; someone you can count on through thick and thin."

"This is too much for me to absorb right now. I need to go home and think." She stood up and looked at Sadie. "Thanks for supper… and the talk too. I guess I needed that."

She turned to the man who had been her boss. "Doc, are you sure you meant it when you told me I have to take a leave of absence?"

"Positively," he replied without hesitation.

"I… I feel lost. What will I do if I don't go to work at the clinic?"

"You'll find another job. I'll help you. Tomorrow, I'll start looking online. Something will come up. The more I think about it, the better I feel about you going to a ranch. You'll be working with animals, and you'll be able to use some of your skills. I'll check out the owner." He grinned. "I don't want to send you off to work with some lecherous old man who'll try to take advantage of you when you're stuck in the back of beyond."

"He'd only try once!" she said heatedly.

Dr. Winters smiled. "Things are getting better; you've shown real emotion twice in the past four hours. You're making progress already."

She didn't sleep much that night and she was still tired when she got up the next morning. As she wandered through her apartment, she railed against her situation, angry with Doc, Martin, and even at her dad for getting hurt.

She grieved again for the loss of the ranch that had been her childhood home. That afternoon she went for a drive and was filled with resentment when she saw the new sign at the driveway. It was no longer *Lamonte's Paradise.* The new sign read *The Holloways.*

She drove to the vet clinic and parked at the back, where she always had. Despair washed over her. She still couldn't believe that Dr. Winters had arbitrarily put her on a leave of absence. She stared at the building where she'd spent a large part of her life. Finally, she put the truck in gear and drove away: she began to accept that there was nothing to keep her in her hometown anymore.

She slammed the door when she went into her apartment. She looked around the place she loved. She wouldn't give it up! She had money in the bank; she would continue to pay the rent while she was away. She vowed that it wouldn't be long until she came back to work at the clinic.

She stalked into the kitchen and made herself a cup of coffee. As it brewed, she could hear Dr. Winters voice. *Get mad. That's good. You're showing some emotion.*

"Yes!" she stormed. "I'm feeling tons of emotion. I'm damned mad about everything! Doc was right about Martin. He's an insensitive jerk. The way he dumped me proved he isn't the man I thought he was: he can't be depended on in tough times. He's not worth the heartache. And, Dad is alive and getting better. I'm grateful for that. And, as much as I hate to admit it, Dr. Winters did the right thing last night; I do need to get out of here. I need to get away from the constant reminders, the painful memories. I need to heal. I like the idea of working on a ranch for a while. I'll put the past behind me, and in no time I'll be ready to face everything here."

She called Dr. Winters. He was pleased when she told him she was ready to move on. While he hadn't found anything promising that day, he said he'd keep looking on Sunday, and reminded her that Monday might bring new opportunities.

She felt more content when she woke up Sunday morning. The heavy dark feeling that had enveloped her for months seemed less oppressive. She felt better than she had since Martin had broken off their engagement, saying she wasn't any fun anymore. She wandered around the apartment, touching things and savoring her good memories, not just the pain. That afternoon she phoned her childhood friend, Becky Freemont and told her what she was doing. Becky was supportive, as she'd always been, and made her promise she'd keep in touch.

Monday afternoon, Dr. Winters called and told her he'd found a place in Saskatchewan that was looking for a ranch hand ASAP. He'd already phoned the number and gotten information about the job. It was at the Belanger Creek Ranch, three-quarters of an hour out of Maple Creek. The owner's accountant in Swift Current was handling the search for applicants. The owner didn't live at the ranch; he had a ranch manager on site and the new employee would work with him.

Dr. Winters was excited about the job. He hoped he hadn't overstepped his bounds, but he informed her that he'd already sent her resume from his office, along with his recommendation. Frank thanked him for his help, thinking it would be unlikely to find a job on the first try.

She was shocked when he called early Tuesday morning and told her that he'd gotten an email saying they wanted her to get there a soon as possible. Due to ill health, the person she was replacing had left suddenly, leaving Ollie Crampton, the 60-year-old manager, with the overwhelming task of calving out over 500 cows without help.

Frank was shocked at how quickly things had fallen into place. She went to see her doctor first. Then she met with her landlord and explained that although she would be away for a few months, she would continue to maintain the rent with automatic payments from her bank account. Then she packed her personal necessities and a few clothes in her duffle bag, put her guitar in its case and tucked her laptop in its carry case. By evening, the apartment was neat and tidy. She took a quick drive over to Dr. Winters' place and said goodbye. When she returned home, she put her duffle bag, laptop, guitar and camera by the door. She was ready to leave the next morning.

***

Frank Lamonte's fingers tapped restlessly on the steering wheel of her Toyota Tacoma. She glanced at her watch for the umpteenth time. Five minutes had passed. An accident involving a semi-truck, a pickup, and a small car, had closed the highway. She'd been held up in the line of traffic for three excruciating hours and her frustration was running deep.

There wasn't anything she could do, but wait. She checked her watch again and groaned. The owner would be expecting her at the ranch in half an hour. It wasn't an impressive way to start a new job.

She looked out across the fenced fields that stretched on either side of the highway. There wasn't a lot of snow, certainly not as much as there had been several hundred kilometers to the northwest, at Stettler. She wondered how much there would be at the ranch. It was situated close to the Cypress Hills in south-western Saskatchewan. The Cypress Hills actually straddled the southern Alberta and Saskatchewan borders.

During the past five days, everything had happened with numbing swiftness. Last Friday evening, when Dr. Winters had taken her into his office and told her she had to take a prolonged leave of absence, she had felt like her world had collapsed. She'd felt betrayed and angry. Now she was on her way to a new job at Belanger Creek Ranch. For the first time in months, she felt a sense of optimism.

The clearance lights of the semi-trailer in front of her lit up as the driver started the big rig. "Finally!" she said with exasperation and eased her truck ahead. It took more than half an hour before the lineup spread out and traffic was moving freely.

It was six-thirty in the evening when she drove into Maple Creek. Darkness had already settled over the land. She stopped to take out the email and study the directions to the ranch. They seemed pretty straightforward. *Turn south onto Highway 21 and follow the road until you come to the Belanger Creek Ranch sign on your left. Turn left into the driveway and follow it across the creek, past the corrals and barns, to the old ranch house.*

CHAPTER TWO

Colt Thompson set his coffee cup on the table and glanced at the clock on the wall... again. He was irritated. "Four hours late! I wonder if this guy's going to show at all. If punctuality is any indicator of his work ethic, he won't last long around here."

"It's a long drive. Maybe something happened on the road," Ollie Crampton said calmly.

"Hasn't he heard of a phone?"

"Can't tell you, Colt. I'm waiting, just like you are."

Colt looked at his watch again. "Well, I can't wait any longer. I'm two hours late already. Shauna Lee's going to kill me."

Ollie frowned. "Shauna Lee? Is she the hot date that's kept you itching in your pants all day?"

Colt grinned. "Not a hot *date*, Ollie. We're having dinner at eight, or at least we were supposed to."

"Are you gonna marry her?"

Colt scoffed. "You know the answer to that, Ollie." He stared at his friend and employee, defying him to judge him. "We're friends, and that's all either one of us is looking for. No romantic fantasies, no wedding bells, no promises we can't keep, no storybook ending crap. And I'm a damned quick learner; this way there's no worry about handing over half of everything I possess when we go our separate ways. For now, we enjoy each other's company; we're compatible in other ways. It works for us."

"You're too young to be so jaded, son."

Colt stood up. "Sounds like the pot calling the kettle black, old timer. I don't see a ball and chain attached to you."

"I'm not thirty-five either."

"You were at one time."

"Look, you young pup! My life was totally different from yours. You've got security, a business. I was a rolling stone until I landed here. I had no prospects, could hardly support myself. But I can tell you from experience; life is lonely without someone to share it with."

"I speak from experience, too. It can be a whole lot worse than lonely if you get tangled up with the wrong one. I had my heart ripped out and my life turned upside down once already. I won't be going back for another crack at it."

Ollie shook his head. "You're wasting your time with that woman. Other than the fringe benefits, you have nothing in common. She has no interest in the life you live. You love this ranch, and you've been a farmer all your life. That's definitely not where she's at."

Colt pushed his chair up to the table and jammed his hat on his head. As he stomped to the door, he spoke over his shoulder. "I'm not listening to another one of your lectures. I've made it clear every time you get into one of these spiels; I'm definitely not interested in putting my heart and soul on the chopping block again, so put a sock in it, old timer." He shrugged into his winter coat. "I'll call in the morning to see if that Lamonte character shows up. If not, I'll come back out to help you until we find someone else." He slammed the door when he went outside.

Ollie shook his head as he listened to Colt's diesel pickup roar out of the yard and down the driveway. He poured himself another cup of coffee and sat down at the table. He glanced at the clock again. "Okay, Frank Lamonte, where are you?" He yawned as he ran his hands along his jaw and up into his hair. "I hope you're as good as your references. I need some help here."

When the phone rang, he pushed back his chair and hurried to the office. The line was filled with static and breaking up, but he could make out a woman's voice. "Could I s... to... Thom...son?"

"He just left for Swift Current."

"Oh..." He could hear the frustration in her voice.

"He was late getting away. He'll be there in a few hours."

The connection wafted off into a hollow echo and Ollie replaced the receiver. He went back into the living room and sank down on the couch. He didn't need to check the cows for three-quarters of an hour. He'd just close his eyes for ten minutes or so.

Frank sighed as she shut off her phone. She'd lost service. *Damn! Thompson has already left. He probably thinks I'm a lost cause.*

She turned onto Highway 21 South and followed the road. Fifteen minutes later she met a pickup sliding around a curve. *What an Idiot!* Heart in her throat, Frank fought to hold the Tacoma onto the outside edge of the pavement. She lost the battle and the wheels sank into the snow and sucked her into its depth. She put it into reverse and tried to ease the truck back, but the wheels just spun. She turned the dial to engage the four-wheel drive, but the vehicle wouldn't budge. She leaned her head against the steering wheel. "Damn, damn, double damn," she cursed. "Can anything else go wrong?"

Colt Thompson handled the big pickup with ease. He'd driven the road so often, he knew it like the back of his hand and he'd barely noticed the smaller truck as he'd drifted through the curve. His mind was focused on the conversation he'd had with his ranch manager before he'd left. "Why doesn't he mind his own business?" he fumed. "He's right about Shauna Lee not wanting anything to do with the farm or a ranch, but it's not like I'm going to marry her. Why can't he get that through his thick head?" He was well out of the curve before the flash of brake lights caught his attention. "Shit, that guy must have gone off the road." He braked sharply, then backed up and jumped out.

A tall slender woman got out of the red pickup. He didn't get a good look at her, just a vague impression of a messy mass of auburn hair pulled untidily up on top of her head, but he definitely caught the tongue-lashing she threw at him. "Do you drive much, you idiot?" she yelled. "You hogged my side of the road when you barreled through here. You almost hit me!"

He bit back at her. "Do you drive much? This isn't the Trans

Canada. It's a country road. You're the one who panicked and pulled over so far that you got sucked into the bank. You're lucky I stopped." He looked the situation over, then stalked back to his truck and pulled out a short rope. "Look, I'm in a hurry. Get in your truck while I hook this to your bumper. When I give you a yell, put your truck in reverse and I'll pull you back onto the road."

Frank glared at his broad back while he hooked the tow rope between the two vehicles. When he walked to the open door of his truck, she jumped into hers. She had barely started it, when he yelled for her to shift into reverse. He eased forward, giving her vehicle a gentle pull. When she felt it move she hit the gas pedal and the Toyota flew backward. She braked hard, bringing it to a stop inches before she crashed into the bigger pickup.

He got out of the truck, cursing. "You almost hit my damned truck!" He glared at her in the dim glow of the taillights and shook his head. He was still mumbling while he unhooked both ends of the rope and threw it into the box of his pick-up. Then he turned toward her and brushed his hands together as if he was washing them of her. "I have no idea where you're headed, lady, but you're an accident waiting to happen. I'm just glad I won't be around for the next disaster." Then he jumped into his vehicle and sped away.

Frank was embarrassed. It had been a long day and she was tired. In hindsight, she realized she had panicked when she saw him careening around the curve, with the rear end of his truck drifting slightly to her side of the road. And then, she'd let his attitude unnerve her and she'd lost her cool. She felt like a fool; she'd known better than to hit the gas pedal so hard. Fortunately, she'd been able to stop before she slammed into his truck. She sighed and shifted the pickup into drive. "Well, thank God for small mercies. I'm sure I'll never see him again."

Half an hour later, the lights of her pickup shone on the sign she'd been looking for: *Belanger Creek Ranch.* She put on her signal light and turned left into the driveway. She drove across the creek and sighed with relief when she saw the lights that flooded a long line of corrals. She kept following the road until she drove past a barn and various outbuildings, and then pulled up in front of an older ranch house.

She yawned as she turned the key to shut off the motor, then sat for a moment, staring at the house. There was no sign of life, but a dim light shone inside and she noted a constant flicker of light that could be a TV playing. *This has to be it. Let's hope he's not so ticked about how late I am, that I'm fired before I start the job.*

She opened the truck door and slid out onto the packed snow. "Oh…it feels so good to stand up and stretch." She walked along the shoveled walkway, stepped up a couple of steps and then knocked on the door. No one came, so she knocked harder and waited.

She was getting cold. Finally, she tried the doorknob. It wasn't locked, so she opened the door and leaned inside. "Mr. Crampton, are you here?"

No answer. She stepped inside and yelled again, but there still was no answer.

Maybe he's out checking calves. I'll put on my work clothes and walk out to the corrals. I can give him a hand. Frank walked back to her pickup and opened the back door. She took out her insulated overalls and pulled them on over her jeans. Then she slipped into her warm jacket, grabbed her gloves and a toque and headed toward the corals.

Most of the cows were lying down and those with calves had them sleeping close by. A few were standing, calves latched onto a teat, tails flicking happily as they sucked. Frank was alert, watching for any animal that might decide to take a run at her. Cows were very protective of their young calves and anyone strange could be interpreted as a threat. She worked her way from the pen to pen and was puzzled when she didn't find Ollie Crampton there. *It looked like the TV was on. Maybe he fell asleep. I should have called him again.*

She wandered through the rest of the herd, making note of two new births. When she circled back through the pens, she noticed a young cow standing by itself, in the corner. The animal's back humped as it strained. Frank moved nearer and watched, thinking it must just be starting to go into labor. After a few moments, she realized that the membranes had broken, but there was no sign of feet. As she stepped closer, the animal moved away. Frank herded her against the windbreak that sheltered the corrals on the north side. The animal hunched and pushed again.

"Something's not right here," she said softly as she reached out to put a hand on the cow's hip. As soon as she got close, it moved away. "We need to check you out!"

Frank looked around, remembering that she had seen a chute for loading cattle into trucks when she'd come to the corrals. She walked back and discovered a handling system that was set up under a roof. She climbed over the corral and went to check it out. The cattle squeeze chute was modern and well looked after. She set the automatic headgate and opened the rear gate so the cow could walk in. Then she walked along a high, narrow alley until she came to a swinging gate. She swung it open and followed a wider runway that ran parallel to four handling pens. She continued along it until she reached the end, where she found a gate that swung into the corrals.

"This is good," she said softly to herself. "I can move her alongside the shelter and push her into this runway. She won't be hard to move until we get to the narrow alley that goes up to the cattle squeeze, but she may be so tired she won't put up much of a fight."

She opened the gate, then hurried across the corral and turned the cow around, moving her along the wall of the shelter until they reached the open gate into the walkway. As the cow walked through the open space, Frank closed the gate behind them. Frank encouraged the animal to keep moving, stopping occasionally to let her pause for a contraction. They moved slowly, and the animal finally made its way to the squeeze chute. The cow balked at stepping into it. Frank leaned against her back end and pushed until she moved forward.

The clang of the rear gate falling into place broke the silence of the night. Frank didn't see the figure that appeared by the sturdy corral fence that ran parallel to the handling facilities.

Ollie Crampton stared at the stranger in his corral. The person removed its coat. It pushed up its sleeves in preparation to push aside the cow's tail and reach in to help deliver a calf. Stunned, he walked back to the loading chute and flipped a switch, flooding the area with light.

"What the hell is going on here?" he yelled.

Frank was concentrating on what she was doing. "Is that you, Mr. Crampton? I knocked and then I opened the door and called…" She grunted as she pushed against the backside of the calf that the cow was trying to force into the birth canal. "Oh great," she groaned as the cow heaved with another contraction. "This calf is presenting in a breech position. I have to turn it. If I can't, I'll have to do a C-section."

This calf is presenting in a breech position? What kind of high falutin' talk is that? It's 'coming backward' in a rancher's language.

And she's talking about doing a C-section? He swallowed hard. *She! It's a woman? What the... Colt is going to go ballistic.* "Who the hell are you?" he demanded as he approached the cattle squeeze.

"I'm..your..new..ranch..hand," she stuttered, as she struggled to turn the calf."

She kept on working inside the cow, straining as she used her hand and arm to manipulate the calf. "This calf isn't that big. I'm sure I can turn it and save them both."

"What happened to Lamonte?"

Frank turned her head momentarily and glared at him. "Are you going to help me or not? This cow wants to lie down. Get in here and keep her on her feet so I can do this."

Ollie mumbled under his breath when he stepped forward to push against the cow's belly. She grunted, and straightened up. While he helped keep the cow on her feet, Ollie watched how intently the woman focused on what she was doing.

Suddenly she smiled. "That's it, baby! You're where you should be now. Let's get you started on your way." The cow pushed again, and this time tiny hooves peeked through the opening. "Thatta girl. Keep pushing; as soon as I can get a grip on that baby, I'll help you."

The cow gave another heave, and Frank grabbed the legs and held on. She worked gently with each contraction, pulling until the head and then the shoulders came out. She started a gentle continuous downward pull until the calf slipped to the ground.

Frank grabbed it by the back legs and lifted it up as high as she could, to facilitate the drainage of mucus and fluids. "Come on, little one. We have to get this stuff out of you so you can start breathing." She worked, her eyes filled with concern. "Come on baby, you can't give up now!"

She laid it on the ground, then picked up a straw, kneeled down and tickled the inside of its nostril. The calf's nose twitched. It sneezed. Mucus flew, and the animal's side heaved as it sucked in a breath. "Thank you," Frank whispered as she rubbed the calf's head.

The baby lay there, stretched out, hollow sided, but gulping shallow breaths of air. Frank stood up and looked at Ollie. "Do you have penicillin and boluses for infection? This was a pretty crude delivery, certainly not as sterile as it would have been in a clinic, but I didn't have much to work with."

Ollie nodded.

Frank looked at the cow. "She's not out of the woods yet. Ideally she should have had a C-section, but we weren't prepared for that and she didn't have time to waste." Frank sighed as she looked down at her bloody hands, arms and clothing. "Is there an electric water trough where I can wash the worst of this off?" Ollie pointed across the corral to an orange box.

She nodded when she turned and saw it. "I'll clean up a bit first, and then I'll finish up here. I'll give her a shot of penicillin when I'm done. I'll need a bottle with a nipple, too. I have to milk the colostrum and feed it to the calf."

Frank walked toward the electric livestock waterer, while Ollie went to the tack room to get the medicine and the nipple-bottle. When he came back, he could see the weariness in her face, but she wasn't trying to hurry things. She finished checking out the cow and then took the bottle and stripped as much milk as she could get from its teats. Then she coaxed the liquid down the calf's throat. When she finished, she turned to him. "We should put them in a pen by themselves. Could we use one of those along the alleyway over there?"

He nodded. "We can take them this way." He motioned to an alleyway to their left. There are gates on this end of those pens too. It's closer and it'll be easier."

When they were finished, the cow and calf were resting comfortably on fresh, clean bedding. Now time and keeping infection at bay would be the deciding factor for both of them.

Frank and Ollie walked back to the house. She grabbed her duffle bag out of her pickup, and once they were inside, Ollie showed her the bathroom. Fifteen minutes later, after she had showered, she came into the kitchen and sat down at the table. She wore a terry cloth robe and her hair was wrapped in a towel.

"Would you like a cup of coffee or something to eat?" Ollie asked.

"A drink of water would be great. What I really need is sleep. I've been up since four o'clock this morning. I'm sorry I was so late, but there was an accident on the highway, and I got hung up in the traffic for four hours, with no cell service." She yawned and rubbed her eyes. "It was frustrating, but I couldn't do anything about it. I was stuck there until the accident scene was cleared and traffic could move.

"And then, after I got onto Highway 21, I met some idiot who was driving like a bat out of hell and when he came into a curve, his truck drifted into my lane. It was one of those big diesel pickups and I panicked and got too far out on the shoulder. The snow pulled me in and I was stuck. Thank goodness he stopped and pulled me out, but he was so rude I wanted to plant the toe of my boot against his backside when he bent over to hook up the tow rope."

She brushed her hand across her eyes and yawned again. "I hope Mr. Thompson didn't leave because he'd given up on me. I tried to phone, but I lost service. I need a better phone."

Ollie handed her a glass of water. *He'd have sent her packing as soon as she introduced herself. What am I going to do?* He sat down and watched her drink it thirstily. *I'll deal with this tomorrow.*

When she set down the glass, he said, "I'll show you to the bedroom. You need to get some sleep."

Frank stooped to pick up her duffle bag where she'd left it by the bathroom door. Ollie showed her into a comfortable room that had a private bath. The bed looked like heaven. She set her bag on a chair and turned to look at him. "Thanks."

He looked at her with appreciation. "You did a good job out there tonight. Obviously you know what you're doing."

Her expression was weary. "Thanks. I've done it a few times before, but I cringe when I think about how unsanitary everything was. I hope she doesn't get an infection."

He nodded as he turned to close the door. "Get a good sleep. We'll talk in the morning."

Frank was awake by five o'clock. After a quick visit to the bathroom, she dressed in a clean pair of jeans and a warm sweater. The house was quiet, so she went to the entry and put on her coveralls and her work jacket. After she had stuffed her feet into her boots, she grabbed her gloves and slipped out the door.

When she arrived at the corral, she went directly to the cow and calf and was pleased to see the cow standing and the calf nursing. She opened the gate and walked into the pen. "Good morning, girls," she said softly. She looked at their eyes and was happy to note that they were bright and clear. Their noses were moist, which was a good sign. She let out a sigh of relief. "Nature is truly amazing. Give it half a chance and it'll heal and survive," she said softly.

Then she began to walk through the corrals, looking for new calves and any potential problems. She noted three new calves and was on her way back to the house when Ollie came down the path.

He looked startled. "What are you doing out here so early?"

She grinned. "Good morning to you, too, Mr. Crampton. As far as I know, that's what ranch hands do during calving season. They take their turn at checking the herd. Can you tell me you weren't up a couple of times since we went to bed last night?"

He smiled sheepishly. "Yeah, but that's my job."

"Well, since I came here to work, it's my job too."

He frowned. *How am I going to handle this? Who'd have guessed that Frank Lamonte was a woman? Certainly not Colt! I don't know how that slipped by on her resume', but he's not going to be happy.* He looked toward the corrals. "Did you check all the pens?"

"I did. I see there are three new ones since I was out here last night, but you probably know that."

He nodded.

"And my baby is up and doing well. The cow was standing and the calf was nursing when I went into the pen. Mom seems to have lots of milk. So far, so good; I'll give her penicillin for the next few days, to help fight infection."

"Well, since you've already done this shift, let's go have coffee."

When they went inside, Ollie set up the coffee maker and put two pieces of toast into the toaster. Frank asked if she could put cups and plates on the table and he told her where to get them. She was there at every turn, willing to help where she could and she didn't sit down to drink her cup of coffee until he did.

He looked at the woman across from him. *She's got a good attitude and she's a hard worker. Colt's going to blow a gasket when he finds out, but after seeing what she did last night, and finding her up and at it so early this morning, I'd be crazy to send her packing. Frank Lamonte is staying. Colt doesn't have to work with her anyway. I do."*

A heavy weight seemed to lift off his shoulders and he smiled at her. "Welcome to Belanger Creek Ranch, Frank Lamonte. I'll be honest, with that moniker I wasn't expecting a woman, but from what I've seen in the last twelve hours, I'm confident you can and will do the job."

Her dark brown eyes sparkled and she brushed back tendrils of auburn hair that glinted with fiery highlights. "Thank you. It feels good to be here. I've been in a slump and for the first time in months, I feel optimistic." She sipped her coffee and then frowned. "I never imagined my being a woman would raise an eyebrow. I thought we were past that in this day and age."

"It shouldn't, but the boss…well, he took a rough ride a few years ago, and he's pretty skittish."

She frowned. "Could this be a problem?"

"I'll take care of it. He's seldom out here anyway. Belanger Creek Ranch is a division of Thompson Holdings. They have a big grain farm near Swift Current and Colt looks after that end of the business."

"Well, thanks for taking care of things, Mr. Crampton. I've had more than enough drama in my life. I don't want anymore."

He leaned forward and looked into her eyes. "Let's get something straight right now. No one calls me *Mr.* anything. The name is Ollie."

She reached across the table to shake his hand. "Ollie." She smiled. "You're probably wondering if I have a nickname, but I was named for my grandpa and I wear it proudly. I've been called Frank all my life, and that's what I answer to."

He shook her hand. "Frank it is."

She got up and went to the toaster. She took out the slices that had popped up seconds before and put in two more. She looked at Ollie. "Butter?" When he nodded, she spread it thinly, then took the plate to the table and set it in front of him.

"I could get used to this," he said with a smile.

"You could, but don't take it for granted. We're a team."

"Right," he said with a chuckle. *I like this girl*, he thought.

At eight o'clock, just after he and Frank had finished breakfast, Ollie phoned Colt Thompson. "I thought I should let you know that Lamonte arrived about half an hour after you left. I'm impressed. We had a backward calf last night and Frank turned it and delivered it. Mom and calf are doing great this morning. This is going to work out fine."

"That's good," Colt replied. "Thank goodness he missed the ditsy city slicker I met on the road. She met me on a curve and panicked. She got out too far in the snow and ended up going into the bank and getting stuck. When I stopped to help her out, she lost her cool and blamed me for what happened. I have no idea where she was headed, but I'm certain she's either buried in another snow bank or maybe, she got lucky and managed to make it out of the country.

Either way, all I can say is good riddance! We don't need that kind hanging around."

Ollie almost choked. *Damned—that must have been Frank.*

CHAPTER THREE

The remainder of the calving season passed without serious problems and Frank and Ollie worked together like a well-fitting pair of gloves. March slipped into April, April slipped into May. One evening, Ollie and Frank were discussing plans for branding while they lingered over supper.

"Colt will come out to help," Ollie remarked as he toyed with his fork.

"I'll get to meet him then. I've been here for two and a half months and he's never come around. It seems weird."

Ollie shook his head. "It's not unusual. He pretty much leaves the ranch up to me. His accountant and bookkeeper in Swift Current handles payroll, and as you know, she deposits our paychecks directly into our bank accounts. Colt and I talk on the phone regularly, but unless I have a problem, there are times when he doesn't actually come out here for months.

"Right now he's seeding. It's been a late spring, so he's on a big push to get everything done. His heart is here on the ranch and he used to live here until his dad had a serious heart attack a year and a half ago. Then Colt had to go back to the farm. Bob Thompson has been warned to avoid stress, but he's always worrying about things and trying to stay in control. It's tough on Colt because it's a constant battle. At times, the old man resents him and gets pretty owly. And, of course, Bob wants to run the equipment, even though he's been warned not to push it and get overtired."

Frank nodded. "He sounds like my dad, but when he got hurt, the doctor laid it on the line. He told Dad that he had to sell the ranch. It was a tough thing to accept, but Dad had so much recovery ahead of him, that he knew he had to listen."

"Colt lives with his parents. I feel sorry for him because he's caught in the middle. He grew up on that farm. He's an only child and it's his birthright. Ideally, Bob and Serena would've moved into town and Colt would have hired a manager to run the farm. But, Bob went ballistic when Colt made that suggestion, so everything stays as it is."

"What a position to be caught in. I feel sorry for him." Frank picked up the dishes and took them to the sink. "When do you usually brand?"

"We'll get at it as soon as Colt finishes seeding. That should be any day now."

***

Colt drove to the edge of the field and parked the tractor. The last few acres had been seeded, and the air seeder was still attached to it. He yawned and glanced at his watch. It was one-thirty in the morning. He scowled as he looked at the truck parked on the approach. *That stubborn old man just won't give up*, he thought as he shut off the motor.

He groaned when he pushed open the cab door. He stood up and turned to place his foot on the ladder step, then began to ease himself down it. When his feet touched the ground, he stretched his back before he turned toward the pickup. Moonlight bathed the scene and he saw movement in the shadow of the cab. Before he reached the truck, the diesel engine sprang to life and the lights came on.

He opened the passenger door and shook his head as he looked at his dad. "You crazy old fart, what are you doing out here at this time of the night?"

Bob Thompson smiled. He was tired, but he felt like he was being useful. "I came to give you a lift home."

"I'd have driven the tractor in."

"I know what it's like keeping the hours you've been doing. You're tired. You can bring the tractor home tomorrow, or maybe you'll let me do it."

"Damn it, Dad; you know I can't do that. The best thing you can do is look after yourself and let me look after the farm."

Bob looked sad. "Have you any idea how it feels to be put out to pasture like a useless old horse that's waiting to die?"

Colt sighed. "You know that's not what's happening. You're supposed to take it easy and stay stress-free."

"Stress-free?" The older man put the truck in gear and eased it out onto the gravel road, heading toward home. "Give your head a shake, boy, there's nothing stress-free about watching everyone else do what I've done for years, what I still want to be doing."

Colt sat in silence as they made their way down the road. *I guess he's right. It has to be hell for him.* He stared out at the moonlight bathed fields. *But the doctor made it clear. Part of his heart muscle was damaged by the attack; we're lucky he's still alive. Sure they put stents in his arteries, but he's still short of breath when he exerts himself. And Mom... she watches him like a hawk. She'd kill me if I let him on the equipment.* He turned his gaze across the cab. "Does Mom know you're out here?"

Bob shrugged. "I hope not. She was asleep when I left the house."

Colt shook his head in exasperation. "Are you trying to give her a heart attack too?"

Bob swore under his breath when they pulled up in front of the house. Lights were on everywhere, and as soon as the tires crunched to a stop on the gravel, Serena Thompson came out the front door with her hands on her hips.

"Bob, what are you doing? It's after one o'clock."

"I know, Mom," Bob replied.

He always calls her Mom, Colt thought.

"It's no big deal. I couldn't sleep, so I drove out to pick up Colt."

She shook her head. "No. Big. Deal!" Anger and exasperation filled her voice. She turned around and went inside.

"I'm in shit now," Bob said ruefully.

"You have it coming, Dad."

Colt slept in the next morning. By the time he came downstairs, breakfast was over and the dishes were done. His mom was working in the backyard; his dad was sitting in the wicker lounge on the front deck.

Colt made himself a couple of pieces of toast and poured himself a cup of coffee, then went out and sat beside him. They shared casual conversation while Colt ate his toast and sipped his coffee, but he noticed his dad was quiet.

"Are you okay?" he asked as he looked at him more closely.

"Right as rain. I'm just a little tired, but I can't let your mom know that. She'd chain me up, padlock and throw away the keys."

"Why don't you catch a snooze? I'll give Ben Norland a call and if he's busy, I know Norm Walters will come by and drive me out to the tractor.

Bob scowled. "Judas Priest man, quit trying to baby me. I can drive you out to the tractor. I'm tired, not dead. Those two have been working the same shifts as you. They need a break too." He stood up. "Let's go."

"I'll put my dishes inside and let Mom know what we're doing."

"Just keep your mouth shut. We'll be back before she knows we're gone. No point in riling her up again. She's still mad about last night." He walked toward the pickup and got behind the wheel.

Colt took his dishes inside, then leaned out the back door and yelled to his mom, letting her know that they were leaving to bring the tractor home. When she nodded her head with resignation, he said, "We won't be long, I promise."

The two men rode in silence on the way to the field. Bob got out of the truck and watched Colt put the seeder in transport mode. He waited until Colt had pulled out onto the road, then he got into the pickup and followed him home.

He should have gone ahead, Colt mused. *The poor guy, I feel sorry for him. He's probably trying to make the drive last as long as he can.*

When they reached the farm, Bob parked in front of the house and went inside. Colt came in twenty minutes later after he parked the equipment by the machine shed and walked around it, kicking a tire or two and looking for any obvious problems.

He smiled at his mom when he closed the screen door behind him. "Well, that job's done for another year." He looked around. "Where is Dad?"

She frowned. "He said he was tired. He's asleep on the couch."

Colt frowned. "Already? Is he alright?"

"It makes me nervous when he feels so tired. Last time...."

"Don't go there, Mom. He was up late. I gave him heck, but I can see things from his point of view too. He's frustrated. He said he feels like an old horse that's been put out to pasture, waiting to die."

Serena huffed. "He just needs to change his attitude. We can still have a good life; it will just be different. I wish he'd agree to move into town and let you put a manager here, so you could go back to the ranch."

"Well, we both know what happened when I brought that subject up before. This isn't so bad for me Mom. I love the farm and I have my horses here, but it's true, if I had my druthers, I'd be at the ranch."

He looked at his watch. "Speaking of the ranch, I have to phone Ollie today and set up a date to start branding. We need to get that job out of the way. It'll be time to move them out to the lease soon."

Serena let Bob sleep through lunch. She and Colt sat on the wicker lounge where he and his father had sat a few hours earlier. They balanced the cold plate she'd made on their laps and chatted amiably while they ate. When they were finished, she took the dishes inside and Colt went to the shop and started the tractor. He took the air seeder out of transport mode and looked at every hose and coupling, making sure there was nothing that needed repairs before he put it in the large equipment shed, where it would stay until next spring. He was engrossed in his work and the hours slipped by.

It was late afternoon when Bob came up behind him and tapped him on the shoulder.

"Mom's got supper ready."

Colt looked at his watch. "Six thirty? Where did the day go?"

"Are you almost done here?"

"Yeah."

As they walked to the house, Colt noticed Bob seemed to be struggling to breathe. "You okay, Dad?"

"Don't start on me, Colt."

"You just seem short of breath."

"I'm always short of breath. It's nothing new."

After supper, Colt went to the office and phoned the ranch. He listened to Ollie rave about the new hand. It seemed like the guy was the best thing since sliced bread and Colt felt relieved. Colt made arrangements to go out to the ranch two days later to start branding.

Then he called Shauna Lee. "What does a guy have to do to get an invitation to your house for the night," he'd asked. His voice was low and sexy. He wasn't interested in marriage, but he had a healthy appetite for female company, and Shauna Lee had happily met those needs during the past four years. A smile played over his lips when he walked into the bedroom and laid his phone on his night table. He took a quick shower, put on clean clothes and shoved his phone in his jeans pocket as he went out the door. He smiled when he saw his parents sitting together on the wicker lounge on the front porch. *I guess they made up*, he thought.

"I'm going to Shauna Lee's place. I'll be back in the morning," he said over his shoulder, as he strode to his pickup.

Bob scowled. "That boy can't be my son."

Serena gave him a gentle poke in the arm. "I beg your pardon? You know darn well he is."

Bob chuckled as he shook his head. "Naw… I had good taste in women. His is deplorable. First he got tangled up with that damned Sharon. She was totally no good for him. Now he's hooked up with another woman, who has absolutely no interest in the things that are important to him."

Serena sighed. "Well, they've been seeing each other for a long time, so obviously they have something in common."

He snorted. "She's nothing but a convenient piece of tail."

"Bob! That's a disgusting thing to say."

"No, it's the honest thing to say."

Serena looked out across the field. "I always wanted to be a grandmother," she said thoughtfully. "Colt would be a wonderful father. He'd have made someone a great husband too, but he's so gun-shy now, I doubt if that will ever happen."

CHAPTER FOUR

Ollie was smiling when he came into the kitchen. "Good news! That was Colt. He'll be out here the day after tomorrow and we'll start branding."

"How long will it take to get the job done?"

His eyes twinkled. "Depends on how upset he is when he finds out who, or more accurately, *what* you are."

Frank looked dismayed. "I thought you'd dealt with that already."

"I made an executive decision and decided you were staying."

Frank chewed her lower lip. "I love it here. He…he wouldn't try to fire me…would he?" Indignation raised her voice. "That would be discrimination!"

"You have nothing to worry about. He's no fool. He'll know he can't fire you and once he sees you at work, it won't even cross his mind." He put his coffee cup in the dishwasher. "The three of us can easily do a hundred calves a day. There are shots to give the cows too, and hooves to trim on a few of them, as well as a few broken horns to lop off. But we'll do it easily in a week."

"And when will we truck them out to the pastures on the lease?"

"We usually move them on the May long weekend."

"I'm looking forward to staying out there."

He chuckled. "You sure you won't miss me?"

She laughed. "If I get too bushed I'll come back and visit, but I'm excited about riding every day. And, the travel trailer you're going to put out there will be a great place to live in."

"Yeah, I have to admit it beats some of the shacks I stayed in when I was a range rider before I came here."

The next morning they gathered the branding irons and placed a propane torch in a half-barrel to heat them. That afternoon they drove to Maple Creek to replenish the necessary supplies; a couple of new syringes, replacement needles, eight-way vaccine for the calves, and dehorning paste.

By evening, they were ready for the busy week ahead of them.

***

Colt didn't arrive home until mid-morning on Saturday. He spent the rest of the day checking over the sprayer, making sure that it was ready to go for the next round. He considered going out to the ranch that evening but decided to stay at the farm and leave early in the morning.

In the middle of the night, he was awakened by his mother's frantic cries. "Colt! Colt—."

He wasn't even completely aware of what he was doing when he shoved himself out of the bed. "What?" he hollered as he charged out of his room.

"Call 911," she screamed.

"What's going on? Is it Dad?"

She was sobbing. "Bob, just hang on. We'll get you to the hospital."

Colt burst into their bedroom, took one look at his dad and yelled, "Get him into his housecoat while I get dressed. We're heading for Swift Current right away." He raced back to his room and grabbed his phone to dial 911. While he pulled on his jeans, he made arrangements to meet the ambulance on the highway. He jerked on a T-shirt, then ran back to his parents' room and swept his dad up into his arms.

His mother was putting on her clothes when he turned and walked out. "Colt, be careful! He's too big for you to carry," she called as he moved out of sight. As often happens in times of trauma, Colt drew on the strength he didn't consciously know he possessed. He carried the big man down the stairs and outside to the truck without incident.

Serena scrambled behind him and opened the passenger door when Colt let Bob's feet touch the ground. "Okay, Dad, let's get you into the truck. We'll meet the ambulance on the way."

"Judas Priest..." the older man gasped, clutching his chest, his breathing ragged and shallow, his lips turning blue. "I'm going to puke," he gasped.

"It's okay, Dad." Colt held on to the older man, steadying him while he leaned forward and heaved. When his dad was finished, Colt reached back into the truck and grabbed a roll of paper towel that he kept there for cleaning windows, headlights, and dirty hands. Tearing off a piece, he gently wiped his father's mouth and said, "Grab the pail at the corner of the house, Mom. He might need it on the way!"

Later, he couldn't remember much of what had happened during that frantic space in time. Desperation had driven him. He had given no thought to speed and he'd driven with his four-way flashers on, bulleting down the highway until they met the ambulance a few miles from Swift Current. His dad had been transferred to the best medical care he could get at the moment, and his mother rode in the ambulance with him.

As the vehicle pulled away, with its red lights flashing and the siren wailing, Colt sat in his truck on the side of the road. Tears ran down his cheeks and his whole body shook. One thought ran through his mind: *Thank God I didn't go out to the ranch tonight*!

Once he collected himself, he pulled back onto the highway and pushed the pedal to the metal. He caught up with the ambulance just before it arrived at the hospital. He was at his mother's side when Bob was admitted to ER.

Three agonizing hours later, Bob's condition had stabilized and he was resting in the ICU. Serena was emotionally and physically exhausted: the doctor admitted her as well, for a much-needed rest.

Colt phoned Shauna Lee and asked if he could come to her place. He welcomed the comfort of her embrace when he drifted off to sleep.

At seven o'clock, he got up and phoned the hospital. Everyone was resting quietly, and the nurse in ICU told him that Bob would be sent by air ambulance to Regina as soon as a bed was available, but as long as he was resting comfortably, nothing would happen that day because it was Sunday.

Shauna Lee made coffee and a light breakfast. When they were finished eating, she reached out and touched Colt. "Are you okay?" Her eyes were full of concern and sympathy.

He ran his hand up over his cheeks, across his eyes and up into his hair. "That was too damned close. He's been feeling really tired the last few days, and I've noticed he's been short of breath. I asked him about it, but he always pushes our concerns aside. And he's always chomping at the bit, wanting to go to work. He brought the truck out to get me when I finished up the other night. It was one-thirty in the morning. I was pissed off with him, but you know, I understand how he feels in a way. He's been forced out of the only life he's known; he feels useless. I don't know how I'd handle that myself.

"We all rag on him. Mom constantly worries. I get on his case. I just wish he would accept that he can't do what he used to do and move to town. As long as he lives out there on the farm, he's going to fight for control because that's always been his role. Sometimes life just isn't fair."

Shauna Lee looked off into the distance. "No, it isn't. But people can make changes and they do survive."

He smiled at her. "I really appreciate you, Shauna Lee. It's comforting, knowing that we're on the same page. Everyone is after me to get married again."

She raised her eyebrow. "Everyone?"

"No... that's wrong. Not everyone; Ollie is, and I know Mom would like to see me settle down and bring a bunch of grandkids to her doorstep. I'm pretty sure Dad gets it though. After the disaster my first marriage created for all of us, I don't think he's anxious to go that route again."

"Well, you know where I stand, Colt. I'm definitely not interested in marriage or anything remotely like it. I care for you, but I've got no aspirations to take on the Thompson name. Too bad really," she said with a cheeky grin. "Since I'm your accountant and I know how well feathered your nest is. But it would take a lot more than money to catch me in yours or anybody else's web. My freedom is hard won and I'm never giving it up."

He studied her thoughtfully, taking in her striking blue eyes with those impossibly thick, long lashes, the soft curls of the blonde hair that just touched her shoulders and her petite body. He cleared his throat. "We've been hanging out for a long time now, but I just now realize how little I know about you."

"And that's how it's going to stay, my friend. I assure you I'm not an ax murderer or anything like that. You are safer than you could ever imagine. Just take me out to dinner once in a while, warm my bed now and then, and we're a perfect fit for each other. Oh yeah, and I appreciated the trip to Mexico. That was nice."

He yawned. "That was a change of pace, but I still prefer going out to the ranch."

She snorted. "You and that ranch!"

He grinned. "I know, it's not your bag, neither is the farm. It's a good thing we're both content to be friends with benefits." He straightened up. "Speaking of the ranch, I have to call Ollie." He glanced at his watch. "He was expecting me about an hour ago. We were supposed to brand calves this week, but that's out for me now. I have to be here for Mom and Dad.

"Fortunately, the new guy is really good. I'll tell Ollie to give the two Kowalski boys from Eastend a call. They're good workers and between the four of them, the job will get done. It's good to know I have a good crew."

***

Ollie came out of the office after he'd answered the phone. A seriousness Frank hadn't seen in him was reflected in his demeanor. "That was Colt. His dad had another heart attack last night. This is his second one; sounds like it was pretty bad. They're going to airlift him to Regina in the next couple of days. The first time they cleared his arteries and put in stents, but they knew there had been some damage to part of his heart muscle. Don't know what they'll do for him this time."

"There have been so many advancements in medicine now, Ollie. Maybe they'll give him a pacemaker. It's a successful option for many."

Ollie ran his hand through his salt and pepper colored hair. "Yeah, it's a tough situation though. Bob has always been a go-getter. You can tell a guy to cut out the stress, but I'll bet in his case, that almost creates more for him. That farm has been his life and it's literally killing him to have to sit back and take it easy.

"Anyway, Colt won't be coming out to help do the branding. He told me to call a couple of guys from Eastend. We've used them before. They're good workers if they're available."

Branding went smoothly and two weeks later Colt arranged for cattle liners to move the cattle to the lease pastures. He didn't come out to the ranch to help, and Ollie called for the Kowalski boys to help them sort and load the cows.

Frank and Ollie moved the travel trailer out to the corrals, where they set it up as her summer base. Frank fell into a comfortable routine of riding and checking different areas in rotation. The quiet and peacefulness, the beauty of the countryside, worked a magic she hadn't anticipated, soothing places in her soul that she hadn't even realized were hurting. Many evenings as she sat in the twilight, listening to the bark of a fox or the cry of a coyote in the stillness, she silently thanked Dr. Winters for forcing her away from the painful reminders in her environment at Stettler. Peace she hadn't known in years eased into her heart and she knew he'd been right in his decision.

One day in mid-June, she went back to the ranch to visit Ollie. She thumbed through the local paper and stopped to read an advertisement about the upcoming rodeo in Maple Creek.

Ollie saw her smile and stopped to look over her shoulder when he set a cup of coffee on the table beside the paper. "You like to go to rodeos?" he asked.

She put the paper down and lifted her cup. "I used to team rope with a neighbor boy. We mostly did it for fun, but I loved doing it. I've been to the Maple Creek rodeo several times in the past."

Ollie shook his head. "A team roper! You are full of surprises. You should take a couple of days and go."

She shrugged. "No. I need to go back to the trailer, ride my horse and herd my cows."

"You have to be careful. You'll become anti-social like I am, and you're too young for that."

"Antisocial pretty much fits my needs right now. Being out there is like drawing in a deep, cleansing breath every day. I had no idea how much I needed this. My old boss was way smarter than I was. He finally told me I had to take a leave of absence and get my act together. I was mad as hell at the time, but now I thank him every day. He told me I could come back once I got on top of things, but I love it here so much, I can't imagine ever going back."

"Well, I'm glad to hear that. You don't say much about yourself." He quirked his eyebrow as his pale blue eyes met hers. "What did you do? Run off and leave some guy broken-hearted?"

Her eyes clouded. She shook her head. "Not even close, Ollie.

My life has taken a few bumpy turns this past while. My Dad had a horse go over backward on him. He was experienced, and he should have been able to prevent what happened, but sometimes things just happen." She toyed with her cup. "I've learned that sometimes we just have to accept things that hurt; things that we don't like, but have no control over."

"I take it you were close to your dad?"

"I'm an only child, the son my father knew he'd never have." She met his gaze. "Hence the name Frank: I was named after his dad. He took me everywhere with him, I did everything with him. I never learned much about being a girl. I was one of the guys."

"One of the guys?" Ollie snorted. "I guess my eyes are deceivin' me." He drank from his mug and then asked, "Was your dad a rodeo hound?"

"Not really. Although he loved to go to the rodeos, he never got into competing. But he taught me to ride as soon as Mom would let him put me on a horse. Our neighbor, Wilson Roberts, was a roper. He and Dad were good friends, so his son, Clint, and I hung out together a lot.

"When we were about five years old, we started fooling around with a lariat, trying to lasso an old cow's head that Clint's dad had stuck on a bale for him to practice on. As we got older, we graduated to working off the horses. It took a few years, but eventually we made a good team. We would go to the local rodeos and some of the smaller team roping events in central Alberta. When we got into high school rodeo, we'd roped together for so long, it was just second nature.

"Dad always went with us. He kept a pretty close eye on me. As far as he was concerned, most of the cowboys were 'notch counters.' He didn't want his daughter to end up being just another notch on some guy's belt."

Ollie chuckled. "He was a smart man." He studied her face thoughtfully. "You've been here four months and you haven't taken any time off. You should take a break and go to the rodeo. The cows will be just fine for three days or so. It'll do you good to get back to civilization and who knows, you might run into some people that you roped with."

"I haven't competed for a few years now. I've been too busy studying and working."

"That's all the more reason for you to go. In fact, I expect you to be back here on Thursday night so you can head into the big show, Friday morning. There have been some big changes at the Maple Creek rodeo grounds. They expanded it, put in new bleachers and a racetrack a couple of years ago." He leaned back in his chair and gave her a crooked grin. "They run chuck wagons now, as well as horse racing. You can bet on your favorite piece of horse flesh, and I can tell you know your horses."

CHAPTER FIVE

While Colt Thompson waited for his horse trainer to show up, he crouched on his heels and leaned back against the wall, in the shade by the stable door. He was a good-looking man; not in the movie star handsome way, but in a satisfyingly strong one. The strength in his features didn't diminish a certain sensuality that women found appealing. Firm lines of humor creased the skin around the corners of his mouth and eyes. Beneath the brim of his Stetson, thick black hair tapered neatly to the collar of his crisp denim shirt. The set of his square chin suggested a stubborn streak.

As he scanned the crowd idly, a woman who was getting out of a red pickup in the parking area caught his eye. He knew too well that appearances were only skin-deep, but he could still appreciate a pretty face and a good body. She had both.

He watched with appreciation as she inhaled deeply, tilting her head back and sliding her hands under the heavy fall of her hair to lift it away from her neck. She slid her fingers into its glinting coppery length, letting it fan from her fingertips and float back around her shoulders as she extended her arms back and outward. *Not bad*, he thought.

Frank Lamonte arched her slender, long-legged body and

stretched to relieve the tension from the drive into town. *It's going to be another scorcher,* she reflected as she looked up at the cloudless Saskatchewan sky.

Squinting against the glare of the sun, she looked around, savoring the familiar scene. A soft smile curved her lips, and her expressive brown eyes began to sparkle with growing excitement. Her nose wrinkled as she sniffed, cataloging the smells that drifted in the air; dust, animal sweat, and the aroma of food from the concession stands. Her mind registered the sounds. The clanking steel gates, excited cattle bellowing, and horses whinnying blended with the human elements: talking, laughter, shouts, and curses. All those aspects blended, to create the traditional language of the rodeo.

"Maple Creek," she mused. "Even though it's several years since I've been here, little seems to have changed, except for the addition of the racetrack and the new grandstand." Her eyes swept the length of the wide oval that ran past the grandstand, and then stretched out to encircle a large area behind the arena and the holding pens. Briefly she let her glance linger on the pens. Just as briefly, she considered going over to have a look at the animals in them, then pushed the thought aside. "No point in it," she said to herself with a sigh. "That's part of the past."

She shielded her eyes with a slender hand as she looked in the direction of the stables. She turned and threaded her way through the maze of trucks and campers toward them.

Colt's green eyes followed her every movement from beneath the Stetson that shadowed his face. He'd give her a strong nine on a scale of one to ten, he decided as she came towards him. Surprisingly, she didn't seem to be conscious of her looks. At first glance, he couldn't detect any phony airs. In fact, she had a natural kind of grace—almost a sense of elegance, even dressed as she was in slim cut blue jeans, a western shirt, and serviceable western boots.

Reluctant admiration lurked in his eyes. *I wonder what it would feel like to run my fingers through that beautiful hair,* he mused to himself. Somewhere within, a warning sounded. Feelings that he had buried years ago and refused to acknowledge even now, stirred. He watched her hesitate and look around before she stepped through the door.

Pausing momentarily, she let her eyes adjust to the change of light and noted with appreciation the coolness of the building, in contrast to the heat outside. *Ahhh, that wonderful smell of horses,* she thought as she inhaled deeply, enjoying the scent. With a happy smile, she wandered from stall to stall. As far as she was concerned they were all beautiful, but her attention was drawn again and again to one particular animal.

"Well, Jetsetter's Lady, from Cantuar Stables," she murmured as she stopped to read the form stapled to the door of the stall. "You're impressive." She whistled softly as she studied the horse's pedigree. Straightening, she rested her hand on the stall door and eyed the horse with appreciation. "I'll bet you are dynamite on the track!" she exclaimed softly as she reached in and tried to coax the filly closer. The horse turned its fine head away, watching her cautiously out of the corner of its eye, its velvety nostrils flaring slightly.

"Oh ho, you're going to be coy, eh?" Frank quickly glanced over her shoulder to see if anyone was watching, then reached into her pocket for a sugar cube, and offered the sweet enticement to the horse. She hadn't paid attention to the cowboy by the door when she'd come in and wasn't aware that he moved quietly and swiftly now, crossing the distance from the door of the stable to the stall where she stood.

Colt's admiration had turned to suspicion, when she returned to the stall for the third time. When she glanced over her shoulder, while she reached into her pocket, that suspicion exploded. "What the hell are you up to?"

The warning note in the quiet voice sent chills rippling down her spine. Her heart stalled momentarily. She froze in position, leaning against the door with her arm outstretched. A firm hand fell on her shoulder. The muscle beneath its weight twitched involuntarily, as a dizzying surge of adrenaline shot through her body. Her breath shuddered out slowly as she looked out of the corner of her eye at the long calloused fingers that curved down toward her breast. Cautiously, she turned her head toward her captor. Her cheek brushed the hand that cupped her shoulder. The contact jolted her, and she jerked as if she'd been burned. The heavy lashes that shadowed her smooth cheeks flew up, lifting her startled dark eyes to meet a pair of compelling green ones that riveted her to the spot.

"Lady, I watched you come in here. This is the third time you've come back to this stall, and you looked damned guilty when you were fishing in your pocket for whatever you've got there. Let's see it," he demanded.

Shocked at first, she watched his hand slide down her arm. It was strong and work-hardened, the hand of a man who knew his strength. Now, as it captured her wrist, the touch was firm and authoritative. She tightened her fist and tried to wrench free. "Let me go," she demanded angrily.

"You'll only make it worse if you fight me. Now let's see what you've got in that hand." The words vibrated close to her ear, his lips so near that his warm breath fanned her cheek. She knew that if she turned her cheek ever so slightly, their skin would touch. His broad chest pressed against her back, pinning her to the door. She could feel the rippling muscles of his arm as it rested over hers, aligning with the hand that grasped her wrist. She hated being confined and she felt as if he enveloped her, imprisoning her. Panicked, she struggled to free herself.

He muttered a soft curse and whisked her away from the door, keeping her pinned against his hard chest. His steel grip pressed her against him as he squeezed her wrist, attempting to force her clenched fist open. Those strong fingers were hurting now. She willed herself not to cry out. Desperate, she lifted her foot and brought it down with all the strength she could muster, grinding the heel of her cowboy boot into the arch of his foot.

"You little hellcat!" The gasp that accompanied his words told her that she had made her mark. When his grip slackened momentarily, she took the advantage and sprang from the circle of his steely embrace.

Once out of his reach, she whirled to face him. He glared at her. His big hands rested on his hips, his feet were set slightly apart and firmly planted, emphasizing the strength of his thighs and the length of his legs. The way he stood told her that he intended to get what he wanted.

Her expression became defiant, her voice scornful. "If you had simply asked, instead of manhandling me, I would've shown it to you." She opened her clenched fist. "See?" Her voice raised several decibels. "It's a sugar cube." She glared at him. "Take it!" she shouted, as she threw it at him.

He flinched when it hit his cheek. She spun on her heel, intent on escaping before he could apprehend her again.

Two steps brought her to an abrupt halt. She became aware of the small crowd that had gathered to witness the skirmish. In an instant, she realized that she had let her emotions get uncharacteristically out of hand. A wave of embarrassment washed over her, sending a crimson flush sweeping up her throat and into her cheeks. With a gesture of false bravado, she lifted her chin and stared straight ahead, as she marched stiffly through the curious onlookers.

A hand came from behind and grabbed her arm. A male voice said, "Frank Lamonte! Is it really you?"

She wheeled toward him, her body language plainly defensive.

Hey! It's me... Jim."

She stared for a moment, trying to recall who he was. Suddenly she remembered. "Jim Greer." Relief flooded into her face. "I-I- Oh! It's good to see you!"

Colt Thompson watched from the stable door, as Jim put an arm around her and hugged her close. He sneered when he recognized the team roper. "She's another damned buckle bunny," he growled as he turned and went back inside.

Jim released Frank with a chuckle. Lifting an eyebrow, he looked at her questioningly. "What happened back there? Was that you yelling?"

The words tumbled out as she described the scene he had missed. "The horse didn't even get a whiff of the sugar cube," she concluded angrily.

"Frank, you're a vet. You should've known better," he chided. "You know that competition gets pretty stiff among some of these guys. Occasionally someone tries to slip a horse something to put it off stride for the race. It isn't any wonder he was suspicious."

She scuffed the dirt with the toe of her boot, staring at the ground. "I never thought about that," she admitted. "Maybe I overreacted a little bit." She darted a sheepish look at him.

Jim stopped and looked her over from head to toe. "You're still one hot babe, you know." He chuckled. "Even if your name is Frank."

"And I'm proud of it," she retorted.

"Yeah, yeah," he said, throwing an arm across her shoulders. "What brings you to Maple Creek? You haven't roped for years."

"It's been six years now. During those last years at vet school, things were just too intense. Since then, I've been busy working."

"Are you practicing here in Maple Creek?"

She looked away. "No, I'm working on a ranch just out of town.

"What one?" He frowned. "I didn't know there were any

ranches around here that would be big enough to merit having a vet on staff."

She shook her head. "I hired on as a ranch hand."

Jim stopped walking and stared at her, puzzled. "A ranch hand?" He took off his cowboy hat and ran a hand through his tousled hair. "What the hell is going on? This just doesn't make sense. You're a damn good vet, so why aren't you practicing?"

"I wanted a complete change." She kicked a pebble and sent it rolling in front of her. "I'd been under a lot of stress. I needed to get away." She sighed heavily. She wasn't going to bare her soul to a casual friend like Jim. "It's peaceful out there, and Ollie, the ranch manager, is a real dear."

Jim grunted. "He's probably trying to figure out how to get you into his bed."

"Not a chance. Ollie's old enough to be my dad and just as protective too."

Jim looked at her keenly. "Is this about that asshole you were tied to the hip with at vet school? What was his name? Martin Cole? Are you still with him?"

She shook her head.

"Thank God for that. He never was good enough for you." He turned and walked a bit farther. "So what are you doing at this ranch?"

"Right now I'm riding range. I'm staying out on the lease where they pasture the cattle for the summer."

He stared at her. "You mean you're out there roughing it in some range rider shack?"

She smiled "Hardly! The ranch has a thirty-foot travel trailer that the range rider lives in. Ollie pulled it out and we set it up near the corrals at the first water tank, when we moved the cattle onto the range. It has a shower and toilet, even a small microwave oven, as well as a good sized fridge and stove. It even has a built-in generator for electricity. I just have to flick a switch and it starts up or shuts off. I have all of the conveniences of home." She smiled at him. "So much for roughing it."

Jim suggested they go to the bleachers. "I competed last night, so I don't ride today. We could go to the grandstand, but I expect you'll like to get as close to the action as possible."

"The bleachers are great!" she assured him. She wanted a good view of the events. Twenty minutes later, the opening exercises started on schedule, with the Royal Canadian Mounted Police executing their dramatic, musical ride. The colorful display was followed by the introduction of dignitaries, judges, and queen contestants.

The familiar scene triggered happy memories from her past. Her heart sang with excitement. Her face was glowing when she turned to look at Jim. "I didn't realize how much I've missed all of this! It feels good to be in the flow of things again, even if it's just for the weekend. Have you ever noticed that it doesn't matter where you go, the smells and sounds and the atmosphere of the rodeo are always the same?"

Frank found the thought comforting. Like the hand of an old friend, it reached out to her from the past, reminding her of the happy times when she and Clint had team-roped at every event they could get to. Memories washed over her, resurrecting feelings of carefree happiness that had been a part of those days. She was filled with an invigorating sense of expectancy, embracing the possibility of finding the same feelings once again. Suddenly, she was glad that Ollie had insisted she come.

Jim introduced her to a few of his rodeo buddies. She didn't know any of them personally, but she enjoyed talking about the rodeo circuit and drinking a beer with them.

Colt Thompson made his way to the bleachers. Everyone who knew anything about the rodeo knew that was the best place to sit; right up close to the action. He was talking with a bull rider, when laughter erupted from a group in the far corner seats. A smile tugged at his lips, when he turned to see who they were. There was a time when he knew all the contestants, but he didn't anymore. His eyes found the group. There were five guys, whose faces he recognized as being team ropers, as well as a couple of bareback riders. His gaze sharpened when he saw the woman with them.

Frank Lamonte laughed when she reached for the phone that Kirby Wisehart held. "I can't believe that you have pictures of Clint Roberts. I knew he married a barrel racer from Texas and moved down there, but I haven't seen him since I left for vet school."

Kirby moved closer to her, showing her the pictures and explaining what each one was.

"Oh, look at this." She turned her face toward his. "Clint's still ripped and hard, and he's got a beautiful wife and three kids." The sun glinted on her hair, bringing out the fiery sparks as she slid her finger across the screen and brought up another picture. "Look at this—those kids are just too cute." She rested the phone in her lap and smiled into Kirby's eyes. "Please be sure to say hello to him for me."

Kirby nodded and she threw her arms around him and gave him a hug. Then she asked to see pictures of his wife and kids. He nodded and took the phone from her hand, flipping through the pictures until he found some of his family.

Kirby's dark head and Franks were close as they looked at them.

Frank smiled. "Your wife is gorgeous."

He nodded. "And look at these two kids of mine," he said with pride.

Frank looked at them and smiled. She reached out and touched his hand. "They are adorable."

From a distance, their innocent actions looked far too intimate to Colt Thompson and he was seething. *That little tramp*, he thought. *Kirby is a married man and look at how she's flirting with him.*

He kept an eye on her for the rest of the afternoon. He watched her laugh and talk with the group and his gut burned. *She's just like Sharon, he thought. Men are such suckers for a pretty face.*

After the afternoon events had finished, the announcer reminded the crowd that the horse races would start in forty-five minutes. The grandstand had to be cleared, and the tickets for the races could be purchased at the front windows. Frank and Jim left the bleachers with the rest of the crowd, crossing the grounds to the concession stands behind the grandstand. Jim had bought them each a hamburger and a cold drink before they joined the lineup at the grandstand, waiting for their turn at the ticket window.

Once they were inside the grandstand, Frank searched through the program, looking for Jetsetter's Lady. "Here she is!" she said excitedly, jabbing the program with her finger. "She runs in the fourth race. Let's see what they have to say about her." A frown creased her forehead. "Hmm. It's her maiden run, and they don't make any fancy predictions. But Jim, I know she can do it! I have a feeling about her. I'm going to run up and place a bet on her."

Jim gave her an amused look when she returned. "Hey, isn't the guy you had the run in with this morning? He's sitting up there a couple of rows behind us."

Frank twisted to look back. Her look collided with the same green eyes she had looked into earlier that day. They no longer shot fiery sparks; instead they studied her with contempt. *He doesn't like me*, she thought. She stared back, her dark eyes wide and startled, her lips slightly parted.

"Isn't that him?"

"Yes and he still looks like he's ticked off at me." She shrugged. *I can hardly believe he's still mad about a sugar cube.*

"The horses are loaded in the starting gates," Jim said. Almost immediately, they heard the sound of the electronic bell and the clank of metal as the front gates opened. The horses bolted onto the track, Frank stood up, straining to see where her favorite was in the running. "Go *Lady*! Go! Go! Go!" she yelled. As the horses entered the backstretch, she dashed up a couple of rows to stand on a seat to get a better view. *Lady* held third place until they rounded the last curve. Then Frank saw the jockey flick his whip, and the little black filly surged forward, maneuvering past second place, gaining steadily on the lead horse.

"Take her! Take her! Come on. You can do it. I know you can!" She was screaming, jumping up and down as the horse edged alongside the front-runner and held the pace neck and neck for a few strides. "Take her now, girl. You can do it!" The jockey flicked his whip lightly once more and Jetsetter's Lady edged ahead to win the race by a nose

"She did it! She did it! I knew she would," she cried, swinging to the man beside her. "Didn't I tell you?" In her excitement, she almost lost her balance on the edge seat.

Strong hands steadied her. Maybe it was his scent, or the feel of his big, strong hands on her forearms. Maybe it was the strange chemistry between them that sent her senses tingling, but suddenly she realized she wasn't standing beside Jim.

Her startled eyes flew open to meet hostile green slits just an eyelash from her own. She stiffened. His voice was harsh. "I'm not like the rest of the rodeo guys. I know all too well about the games you *buckle bunnies* play. Save your performance for someone else."

"Oh!" Her face flushed crimson. "I- I didn't realize…" she stammered, looking around in confusion. She pushed herself away, lost her balance and staggered backward to teeter on the edge of the seat. His hand shot out to steady her again, pulling her back against his solid chest. She jerked away. Face flaming, she wheeled and dashed down the steps to the safety of Jim.

An hour later, Frank had collected her winnings. Jim asked her to join him for supper, but she declined. She went to her truck and drove back to the ranch.

CHAPTER SIX

Ollie was sitting at the kitchen table, nursing a glass of Jack Daniels, when Frank arrived at the ranch.

"What're you doin' *here*? I told you to take the weekend off and you're back home the first day. You know how the old sayin' goes, all work and no play? I wasn't expectin' you until late Sunday night or even Monday."

Frank poured a cup of coffee and sat down. "One day of the bright lights was enough. I'm glad to be home again. It's peaceful here."

"Peaceful," he snorted, tipping his chair onto its back legs. "A young'un like you shouldn't be lookin' for peaceful. You should be out there in the thick of it, enjoyin' life. Why in tarnation did you come back tonight?" He scowled as he ran a hand over his neatly trimmed beard and let the chair rock forward to rest on four legs again. "The rodeo isn't over until Sunday evenin', is it?"

"No," she said with a sigh. The last thing she wanted to do right now was explain why she was home.

"Well?" he asked, puzzled.

She shrugged. "I enjoyed the rodeo events. And, I met a guy that I knew when I was younger. It reminded me of old times before I went to vet school."

"Vet school? You never mentioned that one before."

"Yeah, I'm a vet." She sighed. "But, that doesn't have anything to do with what happened at the rodeo. There was a guy there," she said wearily. "I don't know his name, but I seemed to run into him everywhere I went. I got the feeling that he'd taken a dislike to me, and then he... he called me a *buckle bunny*."

"A buckle bunny?" Ollie's chair grated on the floor. "What the hell...."

"It's a term some of the rodeo guys use to describe girls who hang around looking for...." She turned the cup nervously in her hands. "It certainly wasn't a compliment. The whole thing unnerved me. I just decided to come back here, where I'm comfortable."

Ollie leaned back and contemplated the swirl of smoke that spiraled up from his cigarette, while he remembered hearing Colt use that term. He looked away and said "He must have had a burr up his ass. Anyway, tell me what you liked about the day."

Her face brightened, her eyes suddenly sparkling. "I went to the stables and I saw this gorgeous little filly. I had a feeling about her, so I placed a bet on her. She didn't let me down. Talk about exciting! She was called Jetsetter's Lady." Her voice became stressed. "I think the guy who called me a buckle bunny owns her."

She didn't notice Ollie's reaction to her words; the barely perceptible start of surprise that he quickly hid as he drained his glass, the muscle that twitched in his cheek.

"I don't understand why he thought that," she continued. "But then, you never know what a man is thinking," she said bitterly. A strained smile brushed her lips. "I'm going to bed and I'll head back out to the lease in the morning."

Ollie pushed aside his empty glass. "Would you come back here on Tuesday night? I thought I'd take two or three days off. I need to do a few odds and ends in town and I'd like to look in on some of my old buddies. Besides that, I've got a date with the dentist on Wednesday."

She carried her cup to the sink, then turned back to face him. "I'll be here," she promised. "I'm glad to hear you're going to get away for a few days. I'll bet it's been a long time since you last took time off."

"Aw, this is my home. I like being here. If I get away once a year, that's good enough for me."

Frank spent all her time in the saddle during the next four days, enjoying the peace and quiet of the hours spent alone. She was relaxed and refreshed when she came back to the ranch as arranged on Tuesday evening. Wednesday morning, she smiled with affection as she watched the dust whirl behind the pickup when Ollie drove down the lane to the main road. It would do him good to get away. Still, she understood how he felt. Ollie loved the ranch and his work and everyday life seemed satisfying enough, that he didn't need an escape.

She turned toward the barn, humming as she went. It was going to be another hot day. The sky was a clear blue, and there wasn't a cloud in sight.

By the end of the day, it was hard to believe it had been sunny and clear in the morning. She had been busy and hadn't noticed the dark, threatening clouds that had formed during the late afternoon. By the time she finished the evening chores, they hung low over the ranch, their darkness shrouding the area oppressively. The air was still and warm and humid. Forked lightning riddled the black sky to the west, and the roll of thunder cannoned through the surrounding coulees.

The Thunder Breeding Hills, she mused as she fanned herself with her hat, appreciating the movement of air as it wafted across her face. Native people had called the Cypress Hills that, because they thought they were the home and breeding ground of the storms. She lifted her face to the sky. The night was going to be spectacular. It was a good thing she wasn't afraid of thunder and lightning, or being by herself.

When she stepped out of the tub an hour later, a loud clap of thunder shattered the night. Within seconds, rain sluiced down in a torrent. Frank dried off, wrapped a fresh towel sarong-fashion around her body, and then stepped back into the bedroom. Shaking her hair loose around her shoulders, she went to stand at the window. She smiled as she watched the welcome drops bounce on the cement walk below. Their pounding rhythm on the roof was almost exciting, and she was stirred by the sound of it as she ran her fingers through her heavy, damp hair. She turned to pick up the electric hair dryer and a styling brush and worked her hair until it floated around her shoulders like a soft, fragrant cloak. Fiery lights glinted off it like sparks borrowed from the lightning that pierced the evening sky.

After spraying herself lightly with her favorite perfume, she put on a two-piece, silk lounge set. The string straps of the camisole top kissed her shoulders, and heavier decorative flat lace flowers studded with sparkling rhinestones, made their way across the top of her cleavage. The pants were wide legged and flowing. The material caressed her body with loving intimacy, accentuating her lissome slenderness. The rich purple complemented her coloring and gave her skin a luminous glow.

She twirled away from the mirror and did a bouncy little dance step down the hall to the living room. She stopped to put one of her favorite CDs in the player and turned up the volume. She swayed with the beat as she sashayed into the kitchen. Foot tapping, she hummed along with the music while she made a salad. She took two pieces of chicken from the fridge, buttered a dinner roll, and then went back into the living room and set the plate on the coffee table by the couch.

She was about to sit down when one of her favorite pieces started to play. She hesitated as the music teased her, then she let herself go and began to dance with fluid, sensuous abandon. She discarded all her inhibitions and moved instinctively to a primitively erotic choreography, bending and swaying, stretching and sighing to the rhythm of the music. She wasn't aware of the heady picture she made with her fiery cloak of hair drifting and fanning around her, while her silky loungewear moved against her body like a lover's hands, caressing and molding here, floating lightly over her curves there, changing with her every movement. She was only aware of the beat that carried her to the last note. When the music finished, she sank on the couch and sighed with contentment.

She was lifting her hair off her neck when she sensed another presence in the room. She looked up, expecting to see Ollie. For a second, her mind didn't register what her eyes saw. Her heart suspended in mid-beat. She stiffened. A billion tiny shards of ice prickled under her skin, moving upward along her arms, slipping across her shoulder blades, raising the hair on the back of her neck. She shivered, and then sprang to her feet like a startled cat.

"You!" she gasped as her stalled heartbeat accelerated. "What are you doing here?" Startled fear registered on her face and in her voice, as she met the sardonic green eyes across the room. The cowboy didn't answer.

"Who are you?" she cried, bewildered. Anger flashed through her, interlacing with the fear. "Haven't you ever heard of knocking?"

"A lot of good it would've done. Do you really think you'd have heard a knock above that racket?" He was using that now-familiar, chilling, velvety tone of voice that barely masked the steel edge of anger. "What the hell are you doing here? You certainly aren't anything that Ollie would bring home. That only leaves the new fellow—Lamonte."

His voice was hard and cold, but his green eyes seared her. "Ollie swears that Lamonte is the best help he's ever had, but obviously he has one weakness. Damn! Why didn't you move on with the rodeo crowd? Good help is hard to come by, but even a good hand is trouble when he's constantly got his mind on a woman like you." He strode across the room to face her. "Why couldn't you leave a good man alone?"

Frank went hot with anger. Blood pounded in her ears, a muscle twitched in her jaw. Her eyes narrowed. Her hands clenched into tight fists, and she lifted her chin, ready to do battle. "I don't know who you are, but you are way out of line. I work here. I have a right to be here, which is more than I can say for you."

"You lying tramp!" His hand darted out to cup her chin with an iron grip, forcing her face up to his. "I happen to own this place. I know that you don't work here. And now *I'm* giving the orders. Pack your bags and I'll take you to Maple Creek. Then I'll know you're gone for certain."

As she stared at him, his words registered. Was it possible that this man owned Belanger Creek Ranch? The elusive Colt Thompson? Her large brown eyes slowly filled with tears that she sought to quell. One by one, they brimmed over and slipped down her cheeks.

"Don't try the tears on me," he warned harshly. "It isn't going to work." He scowled and turned away abruptly. "I don't understand why Ollie allowed this to happen. He knows the rules. I'm not running a whorehouse here." He swung back to face her; his expression stiff and wary. "Where the hell is Ollie?"

Confused and angry, she raked her fingers through her hair. "Ollie went to Swift Current for a few days. I don't expect him back until the weekend."

"What did he go to Swift Current for? He didn't mention it to me." She didn't answer. "Then where is Lamonte?" he demanded.

She yelled at him in exasperation. "*I am Frank Lamonte!*"

He froze. He seemed momentarily at a loss for words, then he exploded. "What kind of fool do you take me for? I know Ollie wouldn't hire a woman in the first place, but if he had, he would have told me."

"Why wouldn't he hire a woman?" she stormed. "I've worked with livestock all my life. I'm good at what I do. I keep my mind on the job, which is more than can be said for some of the men around here," she added bitterly. "If Ollie didn't tell you I was a woman, it was probably because he knew what a chauvinist you are." Angry spots of color flamed in her cheeks.

He stiffened at her words, his eyes narrowing to angry slits. This little termagant had some nerve, standing here in his house, calling him a chauvinist. His look pinioned her for breathless seconds.

"Let's just imagine, for a moment, that what you're telling me is true," he sneered icily. "If you are Frank Lamonte, why would you want a job in an out-of-the-way place like this? It doesn't make sense. And, remember, I saw you in action at the rodeo," he said with disgust. "Kirby Wisehart is a married man. He has a terrific wife and two beautiful little kids. And you two were canoodling like…like I would have expected from a buckle bunny. But not Kirby; I've never seen him step across the line until you were all over him."

Her mouth fell open. "Kirby Wisehart? He and I canoodling or whatever you call it? I wasn't all over him. Kirby knows a guy I use to team rope with and…"

"Team rope? You team rope?"

"I said I used to team rope with him. I haven't team roped for several years, and I haven't seen Clint Roberts since I went to university. He married a barrel racer in the US…"

He nodded. "I know that."

"Kirby was showing me pictures of Clint and his wife and kids on his phone."

"You flung your arms around him and hugged him. And then you two sat head to head…"

"You were *watching* us?" she asked in disbelief.

"It would have been hard for anyone to miss. Everyone could see you flirting with all those guys."

"I was not flirting with all those guys," she blazed. "You really are a judgmental, narrow-minded ass." By now she was yelling. "Jeez! You ask why I took a job in an out-of-the-way place like this. I wanted to get away from people like you. Until I went to the rodeo,

I managed to do that quite nicely." She slammed a cushion across the couch, stood up, and turned toward her bedroom. "I'll go and pack now, but I'm not leaving at this time of the day. I'll be on my way early in the morning. Then you can look after your ranch yourself, Mr. Thompson; at least, that is who I assume you are."

Colt paced through the kitchen and living room. Gradually his righteous anger gave way to uncertainty and frustration. "If she really is Frank Lamonte, Ollie's going to kill me for sending her packing. After the way he's been singing her praises, he might up and quit too. What the hell have I done?"

He poured himself a drink of rum and coke and sat down at the table. "Who'd name a woman like that Frank?" He stared unseeingly at the folded paper on the table. "Ollie never let on. How was I supposed to know?"

The more he thought about the situation, the more anxious he became. "I may have stuck my foot in my mouth. I can't afford to have everything fall apart on this end now. I've got my hands full with Mom and Dad and the farm." He stood up and put his glass in the sink. Then he walked down the hallway and knocked on her door.

She didn't answer immediately. Maybe she was asleep. He knocked a little harder.

"What do you want?" Her voice was surly.

"Would you come out? I... We need to talk."

"As far as I'm concerned, there's nothing left to say!"

"Look, I *need* to talk to you."

"I'm not interested in talking to you. All I want to do is get a good sleep so I can hit the road early."

"This doesn't have to take long. I could come in there."

"Don't you dare come in here! Just give me a moment to put something on, and I'll come out."

Put something on? His mind did cartwheels. *Is she naked?* he wondered.

She picked her old terrycloth robe off the back of the chair and pulled it over her pajamas, then opened the door, and blasted him. "This is bordering on harassment! What do you want?"

He was disconcerted. "No!... I'm not trying to harass you." He swallowed hard. "I... I've been thinking... I might have been a little hasty earlier." He stammered uncomfortably. "I... It seems... Well, I admit I jumped to the wrong conclusion when I saw you at the rodeo. I never suspected you were...who you are." He shifted uneasily. "Dammit!" he said defensively. "All I knew was that your name was Frank and that you were the best help Ollie's ever had. There was never any indication that you were a woman. Who calls their daughter Frank?"

"My parents did."

"I realize that now; but I still don't understand it. Anyway, can we talk about you *not* leaving? I mean...would you consider staying on?" He ran an agitated hand through his hair. "I screwed up here, and Ollie will probably quit too if you leave. All he does is rave about how great Frank Lamonte is. It would have been so much simpler if he'd told me who you were. I mean, what you were."

"It's your own fault that he didn't tell you. He obviously knew what your reaction would be."

He looked guilty. "You're right; he knew that without a doubt. But we need a good hand, and according to Ollie, that's what you are. You know the lay of the land and the routine here on the ranch. I admit that I was out of line and I'll apologize until the cows come home. Now that everything's out in the open, will you please consider staying? "

She stared at him wordlessly. Absently, she ran the back of her hand across her lips. *Darn! Why couldn't this phase of my life have stayed simple?* She sighed heavily. "I love it here. I don't really want to leave, but I won't work for someone with your attitude."

"I was inexcusably judgmental and I deserve that. But you work with Ollie, and as long as Ollie's satisfied, I'm not going to interfere. Can we shake hands on it and start over again?"

Frank's weary gaze searched his face, then shrugging her shoulders she turned and walked to the living room window. She watched the rain pelt down for a minute or two, then, with a sigh, turned to face him. "I'll stay because I like working with Ollie, but you have tossed some pretty insulting insinuations around. One thing has to be clear; I will not tolerate that sort of thing. If it happens again, I'll be gone, no matter what the circumstances."

"That's fair enough."

She wheeled around and glared at him. "What is wrong with you? Why would you jump to such a wild conclusion? You had no idea who I was." She made a move to walk past him.

He looked embarrassed, almost desperate, as he stood in her way so she couldn't flounce back to her room. "Look. I've been around the rodeo circuit for years and I've seen so much crap go on. When I saw you flirting with all those guys—"

"I was *not* flirting with them."

"I thought you were." Colt ran his hand through his hair. "Dammit, Kirby Wisehart has everything a man could ask for in life, but you're an attractive, sexy woman, and sometimes what starts out as a flirtation sticks like a burr in a guy's mind. They end up doing stupid things and it ruins marriages and destroys families. Now that you've explained what you two were doing… well, I realize I was wrong. I should have trusted Kirby, but I let my past experiences cloud my judgment." He shrugged his shoulders. "I'm sorry. I don't know what else to say, except that I hope you'll accept my apology."

She turned and moved across the room to another window. *What a way to end a perfectly enjoyable day,* she reflected. All her spontaneous happiness had fled. He had apologized, but she was tense and uneasy in his presence, and his unfounded accusations hurt. She walked over to the counter and plugged in the electric kettle. In an effort to cover the awkwardness of the moment she asked, "Would you like coffee or something to drink?" She wondered if he was planning to stay the night. He didn't usually, but maybe he wouldn't trust her here on her own.

"Sure," he said, hesitating. "Actually, I could use something to eat too. I expected to get one of Ollie's home cooked meals, so I didn't eat before I left."

Fury flooded through her. If he thought she was going to start waiting on him, he was crazy. "There's chicken in the fridge. You can grab a couple of dinner buns out of the breadbox. I made strawberry cheesecake this afternoon. You've got two legs and a heartbeat, and you're not hogtied. Help yourself."

His eyes narrowed as he studied her, biting back the retort that he knew would only create more problems. He hesitated momentarily, then, with a barely perceptible shrug of the shoulders, walked over to the fridge.

She bit back her anger and measured instant coffee into two cups. Bully for him. He was darn lucky she even offered to make instant coffee. She hoped he disliked it as much as she did.

When he had finished eating, he gave her a tentative smile. "Good cheesecake!" he said appreciatively. "That really hit the spot. I'm beginning to see why Ollie thinks you're such a great hand. It must be a welcome change for him to have someone around the place to cook."

Frank stiffened at his words. "Ollie's opinion of me is based *solely* on my ability to perform as a ranch hand; outside, doing all the things that any man would do. In some cases, I dare say, I do more than some men would. I seldom cook or clean; although, there are occasions when we share both jobs and make it a joint effort. I have not relieved Ollie of the cooking as you seem to imagine. A housekeeper would do that, and that hardly covers my job as a ranch hand, does it?" She picked up her cup, carried it to the sink, then turned and walked stiffly toward the door.

"Just a minute, I didn't mean it that way." He took three hurried steps to the door and blocked her escape. "Damn it! I was paying you a compliment. Ollie's no fool. You have to be a good ranch hand or he'd never be so impressed. But it must be nice to have you around the house, too."

She rounded on him angrily. "That isn't how it came across to me. It sounded to me like the old, 'a woman's place is in the kitchen' routine. Truthfully, I'm not a great cook. I spent most of my life working outside with my dad and I missed out on learning most of the finer domesticated things. But, I am very capable of doing what I was hired for." Her dark eyes flashed furiously.

"I seem to be a genius when it comes to finding ways to offend you," he said, looking at her in dismay.

"Maybe you should learn to think before you speak." She took another step forward and looked at him chillingly. "Excuse me. I'm going to bed."

His stare pierced her for a long moment before he stepped aside. "Good night, Fran."

Resentment flashed in her eyes. "My name is Frank."

"Damn it!" he protested. "Every Frank I know is a man. Whatever else you may be, there's certainly nothing masculine about you. I can't call you Frank. It just doesn't fit."

"Then you have a problem. Frank is my registered birth name, and it's what I answer to." She turned and she could feel his eyes on her, as she walked down the hall and into her room. She closed the door firmly and leaned against it with a sigh, shutting out his piercing gaze. She was exhausted. And no wonder! She had spent more emotional energy in the past few hours than she had in the entire past year.

Hours later, Frank snuggled into the warmth of her blankets and drifted dreamily. A muffled sound kept twigging at the edges of her consciousness, nagging at her until she surfaced enough to realize that it was the sound of rain drumming on the roof. She glanced at her watch. "Five thirty," she groaned. She would love to sleep in, but she knew she couldn't. Colt was still there, and it wouldn't be smart to add to his list of bad impressions. Forcing her reluctant body out of bed, she went into the bathroom that adjoined her room and had a quick shower. She toweled her hair dry, then combed it out, and braided it into one long plait. Returning to her room, she dressed in a pair of jeans and a crisp red and blue plaid shirt. Surveying herself in the mirror, she decided that she looked efficient.

She tidied the room and made the bed, before a quick glance at her watch told her it was already five minutes after six. She groaned. If she didn't get a move on, Colt would be up before she had shown her face.

As she had feared, Colt was already in the kitchen. She found him buried in the pages of the *Swift Current Sun* that he had brought with him. The aroma of freshly brewed coffee floated on the air, and she cursed herself for not having gotten up sooner.

"Good morning," she said cheerfully.

He lowered the paper and smiled. "Good morning. Why are you up so early? It's wet and miserable out there. You should've slept in."

"There's a fat chance of that happening! By now the inner time clock is set, and I automatically wake up." She poured herself a cup of coffee and looked out the window. "I can't believe it's still raining so hard."

"This is a real soaker. I'll have to check Belanger Creek and make sure the culvert isn't in danger. It washed out once before, and I don't want that to happen again." He folded the paper and asked her what she preferred for breakfast.

Half an hour later, when they sat down at the small kitchen table, awkwardness remained between them, despite the initial small talk they had exchanged earlier. Frank thought of the many times she and Ollie had shared a meal, chatting amicably throughout. But today, it didn't seem possible to maintain an easy dialog. She was too conscious of Colt's attitude toward her. More than that, while the feeling may have been missing the night before, in the light of the new day, she was disturbingly aware of his masculine attraction. *What a fool I am.*

After a couple of futile attempts to start a flow of conversation, she withdrew and ate her meal in silence. When she finished, she picked up her dishes and put them in the dishwasher. Without further comment, she went to the back entrance and put on her rain slicker and rubber boots. Picking up her gloves, she opened the door and stepped out into the pouring rain.

When she reached the barn, she entered by the small side door. Seething with frustration, she slammed the door behind her. "Why! Why! Why!" she cried to the darkened building. "Why did this have to happen when I was so happy here?"

Fifteen minutes later, Colt made his way to the corrals, where she was breaking a bale of hay for the yearling bulls. He stood back and observed her as she worked, noting the ease with which she handled the bales and the heavy buckets of ration. A smile tugged at his lips as he recalled her indignation the night before when she'd thought he was suggesting that Ollie appreciated her for her ability in the kitchen. She was a firebrand. Stepping closer, he asked, "What's left to do? You'll have to tell me. It's been so long since I've worked out here, that I have no idea what your routine is."

"Everything is finished. There isn't much to do for chores right now. I still have to feed the horses, and then I'm going to spend a bit of time with Jade. He must think I've deserted him. I worked with him every day before I went out to the lease."

They walked side by side to the barn. Automatically, Frank slid the heavy door open. She didn't notice his movement to help her or the wry grin that twisted his lips when she shut it with automatic ease.

Frank moved from stall to stall, talking gently to the horses as she went, and they answered her presence with welcoming nickers. She stopped to pet each one and talk to them like old friends. When she had given them individual attention, she fed hay and poured a measure of grain for each of them. She reached Cypress Jade's pen last and leaned against the door, watching in silence as the horse ate. When he stretched his nose and nuzzled her jacket, she laughed and reached into her shirt for a sugar lump.

Remembering their first meeting, Colt was unable to resist the temptation. He walked up behind her, and with laughter in his voice said, "What the hell are you up to? I've been..." The words faded when Frank started violently and spooked the horse.

"You stupid ass," she blurted angrily. She blushed, realizing what she had said. "I apologize for saying that, but I'd forgotten you were here. You startled me, sneaking up behind me that way. Poor Jade," she said, turning toward the horse. "Come here, boy. I didn't mean to scare you. Poor baby," she crooned.

The horse stood in the middle of the stall, crunching the sugar lump and eyeing her carefully. Frank moved to the door and opened it enough to ease through. She went to the animal and brushed her hand along its side. She moved easily to his head and slipped her fingers through the halter. Speaking softly, she wooed his confidence and soon had him at ease. She led him back to the grain trough, then reached outside the pen to collect a brush and curry comb that lay on a ledge. She then proceeded to groom the horse with loving care.

Colt observed them in silence. He had to admit, she did have a way with animals. When Frank finished her task, she stepped out of the stall and looked at Colt with sheepish surprise. "I'd forgotten you were still here."

"I seem to be pretty easy for you to forget. Obviously, I haven't made much of an impression on you. Or are you deliberately trying to put a dent in my ego?"

She snorted disdainfully. "Don't be ridiculous. Why would your ego matter to me? I assumed you knew the chores were done. You didn't need to stay."

"I did know that, but I enjoyed watching you work with the horses. Now, if you're finished, why don't we go in and have coffee. Do you realize that it's already after eleven o'clock?"

"Is it? When I start working with the horses, time gets away on me. Today, I didn't think it would matter."

"It doesn't matter. I was just pointing out that on such a miserable, rainy day you should take a coffee break."

"Let's make it lunch. I'm going to ride out to check the cattle in the back pasture this afternoon."

"In this rain?" Disbelief colored his voice.

"I'll stay dry with my slicker on."

Colt eyed her derisively as she went back into the tack room to put away the curry comb and brush. "It seems I'm going to get a full dose of the lady's sense of responsibility," he mumbled.

Frank made soup and sandwiches while Colt set the table and made a fresh pot of coffee. He ate the simple meal with relish, and when he was finished, he sat back and looked at her with a grin. "I know I shouldn't say it, because you'll be mad at me again, but I'm finding it harder than ever to believe that Ollie isn't somewhat influenced by your abilities in the kitchen. That hit the spot. I believe I saw some of that cheesecake left in the fridge. Can we have a piece?"

"Sure," she said, starting to rise.

"Just sit right there. I'll get it," he commanded, springing from his chair and going to the fridge. "Where are the strawberries?" he asked as he rummaged through the shelves.

"They're on the bottom shelf."

As they ate dessert, Frank's mind wandered to the horse at the rodeo. "Where is Jetsetter's Lady now?" she asked.

"She's with the trainer. In August, she'll race in Regina."

"She's a beautiful horse. I've seen her sire and he's outstanding. That's why I was so intrigued when I saw her at the rodeo...."

She flushed, realizing that she had brought the embarrassing episode to mind again. Flustered, she looked away as she picked up her plate. She rose to put it in the dishwasher and spoke over her shoulder. "I'm going to saddle up now. I shouldn't be in too late: probably around four o'clock."

"I'm coming with you," he said as he cleared his own dishes away.

"In this rain?" She echoed the words he had used earlier.

"Why not? I'll use Ollie's slicker and stay as dry as you do. Besides, I'm not made of sugar. I won't dissolve."

Frank was speechless. She hurried to the entrance and pulled on her rain gear. She slammed an old cowboy hat on to her head, let herself out of the house and marched to the barn. She'd been looking forward to getting away for a while. With Colt underfoot all this time, she felt like an elastic band stretched to the breaking point. She entered the barn through the small side door and then slammed it vehemently, venting some of her frustration.

CHAPTER SEVEN

Colt was leaving the house when he heard the resounding slam of the barn door. He frowned. There was nothing he'd like better than to stay inside where it was cozy and dry. She was the one who was determined to ride in this downpour, and it was pretty clear that she didn't want him to go along. While she might be one of those liberated females, he'd been raised by the traditional code. As much as she might hate it, he couldn't let her go by herself.

She'd almost finished saddling her horse when he reached the barn. Her irritation spiked when he stopped to watch. "You can use Ollie's Appaloosa. I'm just about ready to go." Her voice was as stiff as shoe leather. He noted the fact with amusement, reflecting that if she wasn't careful, it would squeak.

He turned and sauntered across the barn, ignoring the glare that she directed at him. "I didn't realize you were in such a hurry. There's plenty of time, we've got the whole afternoon." His amusement reflected in his voice, exasperating her even more.

She ran a hand across her face, suddenly conscious of the stress in her body. He was right. There was no reason to hurry. She closed her eyes and took a few deep breaths. *I need to put this situation in proper perspective.* She willed herself to release the tension. *Just calm down, relax, and act normal*, she admonished herself as she concentrated.

"Are you all right?"

She started, her eyes flying open. Embarrassed at having been caught off-guard, her temper flared once again. "Of course I am. Aren't you ready yet?" She glared at him and the unsaddled horse at his side.

"Sorry, I didn't mean to startle you, but you were standing there with your eyes closed and you were breathing so hard I thought maybe... well, I wondered if..." His words faltered as he met her unrelenting glare.

"I was not breathing hard. I was breathing deeply. There is a distinct difference."

"If you say so," he said. He shrugged and turned away. "I'll saddle up right away." He took a few steps, then looked back at her questioningly. "Are you sure you're feeling all right? You know, you don't have to ride today. Hell, I'll go by myself if it'll ease your mind about the cattle."

Shamed by the sincere concern in his voice, her face reflected embarrassment. "Really, I'm okay. The fresh air will do me good. I'll go outside and wait for you." She opened the heavy sliding door and led her horse through it. After swinging up into the saddle, she adjusted the yellow slicker so that her legs would be protected from the rain. While she was waiting, she considered the events of the past twenty-four hours. In all fairness, ever since Colt had found out who she was, he had made an effort to get along. If she weren't so emotional herself, most of the little things that upset her would've passed without a thought. From now on, she would try to meet him halfway. He'd been genuinely concerned for her well-being, and she hadn't deserved it.

She watched him lead the Appaloosa outside, then slide the barn door into place. With practiced ease, he swung up into the saddle, adjusted his slicker for maximum protection and reined his horse over to where she was waiting. "Are you feeling better?" he asked.

"Yes, I'm fine. I just needed a little fresh air."

"Does that sort of thing happen to you very often?"

"No. Really, it was nothing. I'm fine now and a good long ride will clear the cobwebs from my mind. Shall we go?" She turned her horse in the direction of the trail that led to the pasture.

Colt kneed his horse to catch up with hers. They fell into step and rode in silence. When they reached the first gate, she started to swing out of the saddle, but he stopped her with a tone of voice that left no room for argument. "I'll get that."

She waited while he opened the gate, then guided her horse through and waited for him. When he swung up into the saddle again, she urged her horse ahead slowly until he caught up, then nudged it into a fast walk.

She eyed the swollen waters of the Frenchman River as they licked at the bank running parallel with the trail. "It's amazing how much the river has come up since yesterday."

"Yes. In many ways, a slower rain is better. When it rains this hard, most of the water washes off the hills into the gullies and creeks, and floods down into the river. Which reminds me; don't let me forget to check the culvert on Belanger Creek when we get back. I should've done that this morning. The last thing we want is to have the road wash out."

Silence fell as they both indulged in their own thoughts.

Frank prayed the road would stay intact. Ollie would be back in the next couple of days, but if the culvert washed out, Colt wouldn't be able to leave until it was fixed. She threw a sideways glance at him. She didn't know if she could handle being around him that much longer. She already felt as though she could fly apart.

Colt rode easily, watching her out of the corner of his eye. She was a mystery. He couldn't really figure out who she was, but he was pretty certain she was not the kind of woman he'd pegged her to be at first. He was thoughtful as he looked at the rain-washed countryside, noticing how green everything was. He frowned. Why would a beautiful young woman like her come way out here to work? Was she running from something? Had she been hurt? He shook his head. Behind the strong front she projected, there seemed to be a vulnerability and a sadness about her. Maybe that was it. Maybe she was just as wary as he was. That could account for her defensiveness and that explosive anger. But how could a guy hurt a woman like her?

He gave himself a mental shake. *Watch out, Thompson, those thoughts will get you nowhere but into trouble. That woman can bring you nothing but grief. She doesn't look like Sharon in any way, shape or form—except that she's downright beautiful, but damn it all, whether you like it or not, she pushes all your buttons, just like Sharon did fourteen years ago.*

Irritated, he brushed the raindrops from the brim of his hat. *That was the real problem,* he thought. And it scared the hell out of him. Of all the women, he'd met since his disastrous relationship with his ex-wife had ended, not one had made him feel vulnerable.

So why now? He wondered. "W*hy does this firebrand with a man's name do it? Well, I've been burned once, and one thing's for certain,* he vowed. *I'm never falling into that trap again.*

They continued to travel the winding trail that followed the river. When they came to the gate that entered the pasture, Frank waited for Colt to dismount and open it. She waited for him to swing up into the saddle again before she spoke. "Maybe we should split up and ride to the opposite sides of the pasture. We could meet at the top end. What do you think?" she asked as she wiped a trickle of rain from her face.

"Sounds like a good plan. It'll cut down on time."

"Good, then I'll ride through the coulees to the north. You can go along the river and swing up at the east end, and we'll meet at the top."

"The ride through the coulees is the toughest part of the pasture," he said doubtfully. "It might not be a very pleasant one today."

"Mr. Thompson, I've been out in the rain before. I assure you, it's no problem." Irritation sharpened her voice.

"All right, Miss *Frank* Lamonte," he said testily. "It's neither here nor there to me. If that's your choice, I'll go the other way." He urged the Appaloosa onto the trail that followed along the river. "They say beauty is only skin-deep," he grumbled. "She's a prime example. Pretty face, but she's as prickly as a porcupine and as headstrong as a mule."

I've done it again, she thought with dismay. Why was she so touchy about everything he said and did? She was sure he only meant to be considerate rather than question her ability, and she'd jumped at him again; so much for her good intentions.

Turning her horse, she slackened the reins and nudged him forward, letting him thread his way up the steep incline that would take them north through the series of coulees, to the bench at the top end of the pasture. It was a more demanding ride, but she needed something to concentrate on, to free her mind of the emotional web she was caught in. The horse had been over this territory many times before, and with the wisdom of experience, it chose the easiest path.

The trees released a shower of water over her as she brushed by them, and the squish of the horse's hooves on the water-soaked ground could be heard as it picked its way through the coulees that broke onto a small bench covered with aspen, balsam, and cottonwood trees. Frank rode with practiced ease, and before long she lost herself in the familiar rhythm of the animal's movement. Tension drained from her body and mind.

Halfway up the trail, she found a small herd of cows and calves sheltering in an aspen bluff in a gentle draw. She counted them, then gave her horse free rein, and let it find its way up the final stretch of trail to the top bench. Riding across the open area, she reveled in the freedom she felt. Urging the animal into a gentle lope, she savored the motion and realized that she was completely relaxed. A good ride did the trick every time. Ahead, she could see Colt astride the Appaloosa, resting beneath the branches of a lone tree.

He noticed the change in her as she rode toward him. She was aglow, and a happy smile curved her lips. The tense defensiveness was gone, replaced with an air of contented relaxation. Resolving to make no personal comments that could make her temper flare, he kept the observations to himself. Instead, he asked how many cattle she had found.

She told him, then asked, "How about you?"

"Well, I found an injured bull. He's about halfway down in one of the coulees. He's been fighting. I hope he hasn't dislocated or broken his shoulder. We'll move him to the bottom corral, and then I'll bring the truck out, and haul him back to the ranch. We better get started. He's feeling pretty cantankerous, besides having one hell of a time getting around. Moving him is going to be a slow job."

Colt nudged his horse forward and led the way through the draws and coulees to the spot where he had found the bull. As they approached, the animal eyed them malevolently. Colt rode up beside him, and Frank automatically moved her mount into position on the opposite side.

The bull slung his gigantic head, snorting and blowing when Colt shouted at it, urging it to move. When it didn't budge, he rode his horse against its flank and crowded it, then prodded it with the toe of his boot. The animal turned toward the horse, lumbering in an ungainly fashion as it tried to favor the painful shoulder, putting as little weight as possible on the leg.

"Watch him!" Frank cried in warning. "He'll charge you." As

she spoke, the heavy animal lunged to bunt the Appaloosa's chest.

Colt whirled the horse away and turned to face the irritable bull. "Crazy old bastard, he's still riled up over the fighting, but that might work in our favor. I'll ride in front of him and as long as I don't let him get too close, he won't be able to get me when he tries to take my horse. It'll be slow, but if we take our time and have a little patience, it'll work."

"I think you're right. I'll bring up the rear. I can give him a nudge once in a while if he needs it, but be careful. He is a big animal and he's in a lot of pain. Right now, he's not really serious about getting you, he's just telling you to bug off and leave him alone. By the time we get to the bottom, he's going to be hurting a lot more, and he could really get mean."

"You're going to have to watch, too. If he takes a notion to, he'll lunge at your horse just as quickly."

"I know. I'll be careful."

The trek to the corral was a tedious game of cat and mouse with the injured animal. Colt and Frank both knew that they couldn't push too hard, or he would become stubborn and defensive. The whole effort could become a standoff, pitting the strength of the bull against the dexterity and skill of the horses and riders. As it was, he limped in the direction they wanted to go for a few yards, and then stood stubbornly still. A few times he dodged off course and tried to hide at the edge of a clump of willows. Then, they would have to outmaneuver him and coax him on the way again.

Frank flinched each time she saw the bull stumble or step into a depression in the ground, empathizing with him, knowing how much pain each unbalanced step would cause. She admired Colt's patience and understanding for the animal. She was pleased to note that his basic instincts for dealing with the bull were compatible with her own. In spite of their other differences, they worked together like a team that had been doing it for years. Anticipation of the movements of the animal and the needs of the other individual, in any particular situation, came automatically.

When the bull saw the corral, he gave up the fight and moved at a steady pace toward the open gate. Frank smiled compassionately. "It's almost as if he realizes now that we want to help him. Do you think you can get him into the chute? I'd like to examine that shoulder."

"He's sort of gotten over his miserable attitude now. It shouldn't be a big problem getting him in there." Together, they headed the animal toward the opening of the cattle chute. They gave him time to consider when he got balky, then patiently edged him forward again until they got him inside. Colt darted to the front to close the head gate around his thick neck, and Frank slammed the back gate down behind him.

She reached through the metal bars on the side and searched the swollen area with knowing hands. The animal snorted and blew, flinging his head from side to side, trying to escape the foreign touch, even though it was gentle. Frank bit her lip with concern, shaking her head as she thought.

"What do you think?" Colt asked.

"There's so much swelling, it's hard to be certain. I don't think it's broken or dislocated. I'd say the muscles have separated. He probably has torn ligaments. It's something like what could happen to a football player after taking a hard hit on a tackle. But he's heavy and those muscles are so strong. I don't know for sure what the chances of him ever working again are, but I'd say not good. We'll put him on an antibiotic to keep any infection down. DMSO should work on the swelling. Other than that, there's not a whole lot we can do. We'll just have to keep him quietly confined and let time take care of the rest."

"Damn." Disappointment was obvious on Colt's face when he turned away. "He's a good herd bull. I'd hate to lose him. We'd better head back to the ranch and get the truck. It's nearly six o'clock, time to do chores too."

They swung up into their saddles and rode out of the corral, galloping the horses toward home, leaving each gate open as they passed through so they wouldn't have to stop when they came back with the truck.

It was nine o'clock when they came to the house that evening. It had been a long day, and Frank was cold and tired. Weary, she stripped off her clothes and eased herself into a hot bath. She sighed gratefully as warmth crept back into her limbs. Eventually, she stirred herself to release her wet hair from its braid. Shaking it loose, she shampooed and rinsed it thoroughly, then stepped out of the tub, and dried herself.

When her skin was tingling with restored circulation from the massaging action of the towel, she stepped back into her room and slipped into a fleecy blue one-piece pajama. Its cozy warmth was just what she needed. She blew her hair dry and gave herself a light spray of perfume, then hurried to the kitchen.

Colt was there already. Her eyes slid over him as she entered the room. He had taken a shower, and the clean scent of his soap teased her nostrils. His hair curled damply over his ears and the velour robe he wore gaped open at the neck, revealing a soft mat of dark curls that splayed across his broad chest. The robe was cinched loosely at the waist, and now as he bent to search the lower shelves of the fridge, it fell open to reveal a portion of hairy, muscular leg. He was absorbed in his task, and totally unconscious of the masculine appeal that he exuded.

Suddenly, Frank was devastatingly aware of him. It hit her with the impact of a blow, leaving her weak-kneed and breathless. A molten response boiled in her belly. It splashed upward, making her breasts tingle and her nipples snap to rigid attention. It flooded down to fill her sensitive parts with a scorching heat that left her swollen and aching.

She couldn't control her thoughts. Surely he had something on under that robe. But if he did, she couldn't tell. All she could see were tantalizing expanses of muscled flesh sprinkled with a covering of dark hairs that looked soft and springy. She curled her fingers into her palms, fighting the desire to reach out and brush them. *What was wrong with her?*

She was still struggling with the unexpected maelstrom of emotion when he stood up and closed the fridge door. She turned away, desperately trying to smother the naked desire that raged inside, afraid that he would see it reflected on her face. Stalling for time, she walked to the sink and turned on the cold-water tap. She filled a glass and drank it slowly. As she set the glass on the counter, she asked, "Well, have you decided what we're going to eat?"

"No. I wish there was a fast-food joint at the end of the lane."

"If there was, I'd be too tired to go. Why don't I scramble some eggs? You can make the toast."

"That sounds like a practical solution." He took a loaf out of the bread box and cut a few slices. But his attention was not on the task. She could feel his eyes on her as she diced cheese and ham to add to the eggs. He laid the knife down and moved within an arm's reach, leaning a hip against the counter. Out of the corner of her eye, she could see that his arms were crossed loosely, covering his chest, but a short expanse of thigh and a bony knee poked out through the front of his robe. She shifted uneasily, raised her eyes, and found him looking at her intently.

"Fran, I've misjudged you and it's no wonder you're defensive around me. Can we call a truce and start over? Could we work at becoming more like friends, than adversaries?"

He'd apologized the night before. Now the admission that he had misjudged her caught her off guard. The request for friendship confused her even more. A soft flush stained her cheeks, and she fidgeted under his entreating gaze.

"We can try," she stammered, looking down at her slender hand as it gripped the knife. "I should apologize for being so touchy. I don't know what got into me." *Liar*, she chided herself silently. "The ride helped." Her eyes darted back to meet his. "I'll make an effort to not be so defensive from now on."

She swallowed hard and turned her attention to cracking eggs and beating them with a whisk. He didn't move, and she was intensely aware of his proximity. Her composure quickly deserted her, as she grew increasingly uneasy under his scrutiny. Finally, she had to look at him again. As she met those eyes that followed her every movement, her heart began to race.

With a sense of desperation, she searched for a way to break the overpowering awareness that was constricting her. "Ollie tells me you lived here at the ranch before your dad had a heart attack. Are you happy running the grain farm?"

He looked away as he turned to pick up two slices of bread and drop them into the toaster. "I'd prefer to be out here," he admitted. "Right now, that isn't an option. Dad won't ever be able to manage the farm again, but he still hopes that he will one day. Even after this last heart attack, he doesn't seem to get it. I have to keep an eye on him all the time. He has a pacemaker now and he's feeling better than he has for months, but he still can't take on the whole shit-load of stress.

"When he accepts that fact, we'll probably look at another alternative. We could hire a manager. If we did that now, Dad wouldn't stay out of it. He'd be looking over the guy's shoulder all the time; making sure things were done right. Even if he wasn't doing any physical work, the stress factor would be as big as it would be if he was running the operation himself. Basically, he trusts my judgment. So this way, I can more or less keep him out of things."

She poured the beaten eggs into the pan, and then added the ham and cheese and a handful of sliced mushrooms before she spoke. "My dad had to sell our small ranch too. A horse reared over backward on him. It made a real mess of him. Maybe we were lucky in some ways. Dad's doctor told him bluntly that he would have to sell the farm. He would never be able to do the heavy work again. Dad accepted his advice. It all worked out for the best. The land was sold and everything was gone in a couple of months."

"And it was as hard for you to let go of it as it was for your dad, right?"

"How did you know?" She was surprised by his perceptiveness. "The truth is, it was even harder for me. Dad was fifty-eight. He could look at the decision as early retirement. But that place had always been a haven for me. It was my roots. It represented stability, happiness, security... love. Whenever things got me down, I would go to the farm and ride my favorite trails or go to my secret spots. At the time, I was worried about how Dad would handle it. Now I realize it was a traumatic thing for me too, and I could hardly face losing something that had been such an integral part of my life."

"So your dad adjusted to the change without any problems?"

"Well, he had a lot of mending to do. When he was able to get around halfway decently, he and Mom went to Arizona for the winter. I came out here shortly after they left, so I haven't seen them since. From their letters, they sound happy. Dad's pursuing different ideas and seems to have a new lease on life."

"Did you have any brothers or sisters?"

"No, Mom couldn't have any more children. I became the boy Dad knew he could never have. From the time I was little, he took me everywhere with him. We were good buddies, and naturally I learned to do the things he did because I was with him so much."

"How do you get along with your mom?"

"Super! Mom's a sweetie. We're a close family." She turned to take two plates from the cupboard, spooned the scrambled eggs onto each one, and set them on the table. Colt poured coffee and brought the plate of toast. They sat down and began to eat in a surprisingly comfortable silence. Talking had eased the tension for Frank, and she was finally able to relax in his presence.

Colt ate hungrily, finishing before her. He leaned back in his chair and nursed a cup of coffee in his big hands. "Last night you said you hadn't been team roping since you went to university."

"That's true. Did you go to university or college?"

"I took agriculture at the University of Saskatchewan in Saskatoon. After I graduated, I worked at a feedlot near Swift Current for a year. Then Dad and I bought this ranch. We combined it with the grain farm at the home place and formed a partnership. The course material was an excellent background for management of our operation. Anyway—tell me about you. What did you study?"

She toyed with the few bites of eggs left on her plate. Then she looked up at him and met his inquiring gaze. "I went to U. of S. too. I took veterinary medicine."

"You're a vet? Well...I guess that fits. That's why you knew what to look for when you checked the bull. But what are you doing here? You could get a job almost anywhere and make a lot more money than you can working as a ranch hand. As far as that goes, you could set up a practice right in this area. Working as here seems to be a waste of your training. Don't you like vet work?"

"I love it." She chewed her bottom lip while she played with her fork. "I..." She shrugged her shoulders and looked up at him. "I'd been through a difficult time, personally. I needed to get away from everything and do something that wasn't so intense. This has been excellent therapy for me. Ollie seemed to sense my need for privacy, and he hasn't asked questions. I didn't tell him that I was a vet until after the rodeo. I hadn't intended to, even then. It just slipped out. I mentioned that I'd gone to vet school with Jim Greer. He's one of the guys I ran into at the rodeo."

"An old boyfriend?"

"No! He isn't my type." She frowned. "You still haven't explained why you thought I was some tramp," she blurted. "I don't dress like one. The last thing I'd want to do is look or act like one. Why did you think that about me?"

A look of regret flashed across his features. "Fran, I'm sorry about that. I don't know what to say, except that maybe I was just doing it in self-defense."

He insisted on calling her Fran and it irritated her. "Self-defense," she snorted. "That's ridiculous."

"No, it's not as ridiculous as you might think." He looked at her, searching her face as if looking for an answer. "There was... actually there still is... something about you that is so familiar, so reminiscent of a part of my past. Maybe not even that. There was almost a sense of déjà vu. My life hasn't always gone smoothly.

There was a period when I completely lost control of things, and now everything in me resists getting into that situation again. We all make judgments based on our past experiences. You hit a raw nerve and it scared me. In fact, if I'm honest, it still does," he concluded as he finished his coffee. Gathering his dishes, he stood up and went to put them in the dishwasher. Then he began to tidy around the stove, putting things away and washing out the frying pan she had used.

Subject closed, she thought resentfully as she watched him. He had piqued her curiosity. She couldn't help but wonder what had happened in his past and how on earth he could associate her with it. Whatever it was, it hadn't been a happy experience.

By the time she picked up her dishes and put them in the dishwasher, he had finished with the cleanup. "It's been a long day," he said. "Sleep in tomorrow morning. You've earned it."

Frank lifted a hand to her mouth and caught a yawn. "It has been a long day. If it is still raining in the morning, I may take you up on that." Suddenly she became alert. "Oh! We didn't check on the culvert."

"Damn it! I forgot about that. I'll do it now."

"Can you do anything about it in the dark?"

"I won't bother unless it looks like there will be a problem before morning."

"Give me a minute, and I'll slip into a pair of jeans and go with you."

"You don't have to," he protested.

"I want to. If something needs to be done, the two of us should be able to deal with it better than one person on their own. It'll just take a minute, and I'll be ready. You have to change too," she reminded him. "Unless, you're planning to go out there dressed like Tarzan, in his nothings."

A silly grin spread across his face. "I guess I do."

Fifteen minutes later, they were at the creek. When they searched the area with a flashlight, they could see that a tree had floated downstream and splayed itself across the mouth of the large culvert. A collection of finer debris had wedged against it, creating a dam. The creek was swirling furiously up onto the road.

"By morning, we would have been in serious trouble. This is going to be one hell of a job," Colt said with frustration. "If we can get that tree out we'll have it made." He frowned. "It'll be nearly impossible to do that by hand. We'll need to put the bucket on the tractor and bring it out here. Then we'll try to hook a chain to the log and attach the other end of it to the bucket. I'll raise it, and hopefully, that will dislodge the tree and pull it out of there."

Frank nodded. "Let's go."

They drove back to the barnyard. Colt got into the tractor and started it. Frank guided him into position so that arms of the front-end loader lined up with the bucket attachment. Then she dropped the sturdy pins into place and secured it, before Colt raised it off the ground and headed the tractor down the road. Frank followed in his truck.

When they arrived at the creek, Colt stopped and jumped out of the cab. He reached into the bucket and pulled out a length of tow chain that had a grab hook on the each end. Standing precariously on the edge of the road above the culvert, they managed to snag one hook through the crotch of a sturdy branch. Then Colt attached the other end of the chain to the bucket. He ran to get into the tractor and worked the hydraulic lever to lift the bucket.

The chain tightened and gradually, the tree started to move. Frank stood close to the culvert, watching and guiding Colt with hand motions. When the dammed up water began to suck under, she knew they were making progress.

Frank smiled when she turned, looking up to where he sat in the cab, motioning for him to keep lifting.

The tree came free. The debris and water roared through the culvert. In that instant, the road crumbled beneath Frank's feet and she scrambled to avoid falling into the rushing water. She flung herself backward and landed awkwardly, with one leg twisted underneath her, taking the weight of her body. A sharp pain shot through her ankle and up the calf of her leg.

Colt climbed out of the tractor's cab as quickly as he could. When he reached the ground, he found her sprawled in the mud. "Fran! Did I hit you? Are you all right?"

Her face was white and strained, but she shook her head. "No, you didn't hit me. The ground gave away underneath me. I'll be all right." She pushed his hand away as he reached to help her. She sat up and tried to hoist herself to her feet. Wincing, she slumped back.

Colt hunkered beside her. "You're not alright. You can't walk on that foot," he said decisively. Without another word, he slipped an arm around her shoulders and slid the other one under her knees. "Put your arm around my neck," he ordered.

She stiffened with protest. "Just support me and I'll walk to the truck with you. I'll drive to the house. You can get rid of the tree and bring the tractor back to the barn."

"You are *not* driving. After I get you into the truck, I'll move the tractor away from the creek and park it. Quit wasting time and put your arm around my neck." He leaned back and looked into her face. "Damn it, I'm just going to carry you to the truck."

Hesitantly, she did as she was told. To her dismay, her heart began to beat a wild tattoo that she was certain he would be able to hear. Cradled in his arms, she couldn't help but notice the strength in his body and how secure his arms made her feel. *Secure, but not safe*, she reminded herself. She was not safe with this man. He was very dangerous to her peace of mind.

CHAPTER EIGHT

"You can put me down now."

She pushed away from him as the screen door banged shut behind them, but he ignored her protest and carried her up the four steps to the main floor.

"Colt, my boots are muddy and so are yours."

He hesitated momentarily, deciding which way to go, then stepped toward the living room.

"You can't take me in there. My clothes are covered with mud. I'll get everything dirty!"

He sat her down on a chair. "Who's worried? Once the mud dries, it'll vacuum up. If it doesn't, a little soap and water will take care of it. Right now, the important thing is to get you comfortable and take a look at that foot. Here, let me take your rain jacket and give me that crazy hat."

He removed both items and tossed them in a pile on the floor. Next, he pulled the boot from her uninjured foot, then, squatting down beside her, carefully worked the other one free. When the boot finally slid off, he looked up to find her eyes glistening with tears.

"I should've insisted that you stay at the house and this wouldn't have happened." He drew her head against his broad chest and held it there momentarily, comforting her as he might a child. One big hand cradled the back of her head; the other soothingly brushed over her shoulders and back. He drew back, gently. "Let me have a look at that foot."

He probed with gentle fingers, and she winced when he moved her toes experimentally. "Sorry," he said softly, continuing to explore until he was satisfied. "I know it hurts like hell, but I don't think it's anything serious. Nothing seems to be broken. Give it a few days' rest, and it should be as good as new. Do you hurt anywhere else?"

"The muscle at the back of my leg hurts. It feels tight, like there's a knot in it."

"Well." He hesitated. "Those jeans will have to come off. The legs are too narrow. They'll never roll up." He reached for the button at her waist.

She shrank from his touch. "Just take me to my room. I'll undress myself," she murmured hurriedly.

"All right...." He drew back. "But you're being unnecessarily modest." He gave her a rakish grin. "If you're worried that I might try to take advantage of you, I promise I won't."

"I'm not worried about that," she interrupted.

He smiled as he watched her, willing her to look at him. When she refused, he stooped to sweep her up in his arms again. He carried her down the hall, nudged the door of her room open with the toe of his boot, and strode to the bed. After he put her down, he framed her chin with his fingers and tilted her face up so she would look at him. "You sure you can do this by yourself?"

Color flooded her cheeks. "Of course I can." She was surprised at the steadiness of her voice; it felt inconsistent with the rest of her. Her legs felt like they had turned to jelly; her hands trembled; her mind was in a whirl. Their eyes met and held. Frank's lips parted, an unconscious invitation, as she sat staring up at him, mesmerized. The air filled with tension. For a moment, she wasn't conscious of anything else, not even the pain in her foot.

A muscle twitched in Colt's jaw and he withdrew his hand. Reluctantly, he tore his eyes from hers, turned on his heel, and left the room.

Stunned by the supercharged awareness that had flowed between them, Frank dropped her face into her hands and pushed her fingers into her thick hair. She squeezed her eyes shut, denying reality.

Damn, damn, double damned! What is wrong with me? This shouldn't be happening...but it is! She groaned. *Why couldn't he have been sixty-five, fat, bald, and happily married with a dozen kids? Please God; make Ollie come home tomorrow*, she pleaded silently. *Then he'll leave before I make a complete fool of myself.* She lifted her head and looked at the door. *If I don't get a move on, he'll come back, and I'll still be sitting here, mooning over him.*

She stood up and unbuttoned her jeans. When she had slid them down onto her hips, she realized just how awkward shedding the slim-fitting garment, and protecting her sore foot at the same time, would be.

When Colt returned, he found her trying to brace herself against the bed while she tugged at the wet, clinging material. He stood in the doorway, with a bag of frozen peas balanced in his hand. A smile flitted across his face as he moved into the room. "Let me give you a hand," he said huskily as he laid the peas on the night table by the bed.

"No! I can do it myself."

He laid a silencing finger across her lips and bent down to grasp the stubborn material. He tried to ignore the milky texture of her skin and the scrap of scarlet silk and lace that showed when he wiggled the wet denim over the curve of her hips and slid it down the length of her slender legs. Gently, he eased the jeans over her injured foot and tossed them aside on the floor.

Frank's face was as scarlet as her bikini panties. Trembling, she sank down on the bed and scrambled to pull the quilt over her exposed limbs.

But Colt didn't notice her discomfort; he was cursing his biological responses and struggled with his own problem. He fought the urge to tug at his zipper. He knew it wouldn't help, and it would draw unwanted attention to his dilemma.

Not only was the situation uncomfortable; it was damned embarrassing. What should he do? He couldn't face her, looking like a stud that had gotten the scent of a mare in heat. He had to make some excuse to get out of there. There was an extra pillow on the bed, but he was grasping at straws. He hurried out the door, speaking over his shoulder as he went. "Lie back and I'll get another pillow to elevate your foot,"

A flood of relief washed over Frank. *If I don't get this*

foolishness under control, he's going to realize what is happening and he'll be convinced that I am the tramp he accused me of being in the first place.

In the other room, Colt was giving himself a stern dressing down. When he was convinced he had psyched his biological responses into dormancy, he returned to the room with a purposeful, detached air.

"All right, let's get that foot elevated. I'll massage your leg to ease the spasm in the muscle. We'll use the bag of peas as an ice pack for your ankle. Lie back and I'll put this pillow under your foot." Raising her leg, he supported her foot so that it was elevated, then allowed his hand to slide from her ankle up to the calf of her leg.

In spite of her resolve, Frank tensed at his touch. But gradually she relaxed while he worked the muscles.

"That's better," he said.

She tried to stay calm, but she was acutely aware him. A wild excitement flared, threatening to spiral out of control, and she struggled to overcome the trembling that engulfed her.

He watched her questioningly. "Does that feel any better?"

"A- actually I- it does," she stammered. "You... have a good touch. Thank you." She tried to smile.

"You're trembling. Are you cold?"

"A... little," she lied. *Please, let him think that's what's wrong.*

"I'll make you a hot drink." He adjusted the position of her leg on the pillow and drew the quilt over her before he left the room.

She cursed her own stupidity while she listened to the sounds of his movements in the kitchen. It was humiliating to be so out of control. She didn't understand why it kept happening, but her biological responses seemed to defy reason when he came near. She scarcely knew this man, and she wasn't sure that she even liked what she did know about him. The whole situation was a crazy, mixed-up mess.

She was still considering her predicament when he returned with a steaming cup that gave off the aroma of spicy, sweetened rum.

"This is guaranteed to warm you up," he promised. He sat on the edge of the bed and slipped an arm around her shoulders, helping her to sit up. He put the cup in her hand and urged her to drink it.

What had she done to deserve this? He was killing her with kindness. If only he wouldn't be so considerate. The hot liquid scalded her throat and warmed her stomach, but a completely different kind of heat raced through her veins, setting her body on fire. Blood pounded in her ears, keeping precise rhythm with the thudding of her heart. An uncontrolled trembling surged through her, increasing until she could barely hold the cup.

"Fran, what's wrong?" He took it from her and set it on the night table. He drew her into his arms and cradled her close, his hand stroking with a steady rhythm along her back. "Just relax," he crooned in a soothing voice.

She shut out every thought and concentrated on the movement of his hands. The warmth of his body seeped into hers and gradually the trembling ceased. Several minutes later, he pulled away and looked into her eyes. The naked desire he saw there made him inhale sharply.

Colt's masculine instincts thundered to the surface. Answering desire leaped in his eyes. They stared at each other, startled by their mutual hunger. Then he lowered his lips to hers and claimed them with a kiss that became a passionate pillage. Somewhere in the distance, Frank's reason told her that she couldn't let this happen, but her emotions betrayed her. Her arms crept around his neck, pulling him closer as she instinctively arched toward him.

His hands played over her body, searching, caressing, and teasing. Beneath her cotton shirt, he felt her nipples harden as his fingers touched her. Impatiently he fumbled with the buttons, and then his eager hands pushed the shirt open and back over her creamy shoulders. She had no bra on.

He groaned as his eyes fell on the unfettered breasts that strained in response to his caresses. Unerringly his mouth sought one swollen mound, sucking it, nipping it gently with his teeth. His tongue swirled around the rosy tip, tantalizing it, setting loose another wave of fire that coursed through her veins like molten liquid. His lips trailed along her breasts to find the other swollen tip. One arm held her close to him while his free hand moved up and down her body, exploring her slender curves and secret places.

His fingers trailed up the inside of her thigh, searching until he was gently probing the center of her desire. She responded with a soft cry. He let his lips burn a fiery trail upward until they possessively claimed hers. His tongue traced her lips, probing the sweetness of her mouth, drawing from her sensations she had never known before. She responded mindlessly.

She frantically reached to help him take off his shirt. Her hand moved over his body, caressing, searching, until his hand grasped it and guided her to the hardness straining against his jeans. She touched him hesitantly, and then hearing his groan of pleasure, gently ran her fingers up and down his length. A tremor shook his body, and he arched against her, seeking the ultimate heights. His hand grasped hers again, holding it against him, forcing his hardness into it.

The last vestiges of reason pricked his conscious thought. "I know this doesn't make any sense," he said thickly, as he feathered moist kisses across her lips. His breath was raspy as he moved against her. "Your body is telling me that you want the same things I do, but I have to hear you say the words first."

Reason screamed No, No, No, but she was far beyond reason and her all-consuming desire overruled. "I do." The words were a hoarse whisper; her breathing was as ragged as his as she reached for his belt buckle, fumbling to undo it.

He rolled away and pushed off the bed. His urgent hands did the job for her. Jeans and underwear skimmed down his legs, and he kicked them into a crumpled pile on the floor. He sank down beside her and held her against him. His lips covered hers once more, as he urgently turned her and moved on top of her. She opened herself with passionate eagerness, inviting him in.

They both gasped with pleasure as he plunged. After the first wild, joyous, seeking strokes, he caught himself. He stopped, buried deeply in her secret place, savoring the heated moistness. He began to probe her gently, stoking their mutual need, slowly at first, then with increasing tempo until they were drowning in an ocean of sensation.

A tidal wave of release started deep within her, sending forth violent ripples that spiraled outward, creating successive waves of sensation that carried her to a crest. So intense was her release that she didn't realize he had made the same ascent, until he fell against her, drained and satiated. Trailing soft, moist kisses on her cheek, he whispered the enchanting words of a lover, telling her of her beauty, of his satisfaction, and of his desire.

The next morning, Frank awoke slowly, savoring the feeling of warmth that surrounded her. Gradually, she became aware of a warm weight that lay across her. The events of the night washed into her consciousness and with them the realization that Colt was still in her bed—his lean, hard body molded to her back and a strong arm around her waist, pinning her against him.

She lay still, remembering their lovemaking and wondering at the desire he had stirred in her. In all the times, that she had been with Martin, she had never experienced such raw, overwhelming passion, such completion or such satisfaction. In spite of his initial urgency, Colt had controlled himself and taken time to please her. He had banished forever any doubts that she was capable of normal sexual responses.

Her mind drifted in a filmy cloud, recalling the ecstasy they had shared. Gradually, the cloud dissipated and a lifetime of personal values rose to confront her. She squeezed her eyes shut as if to close off her thoughts, but they reached out from behind her consciousness anyway. She'd never been one for casual affairs or sex without some sort of a commitment. Yet, the previous night she'd lost herself completely to a man she hardly knew.

The thought disturbed her. She tensed to swing herself out of bed, but as she moved, Colt's hand came to rest on her arm, restraining her. Turning to look at him, she met solemn green eyes. Mirrored in them were emotions that hadn't been there the night before when he had been caught up in the heat of passion. Now they reflected uncertainty, doubt, almost a look of apprehension. "Fran, I..."

Now, he's worried, she thought angrily. She pulled away and stood up, grabbing the quilt as she moved, wrapping it around herself to cover her nakedness.

"Don't worry, Colt. We were two consenting adults. I regret that I didn't have enough willpower to stop before everything got out of hand, but it's too late for that now. Whether you believe me or not, I don't make a habit of doing this sort of thing. The truth is, this was a definite exception to the rule, but I'm not naïve enough to imagine that one night in the sack gives me any claim on you. The fact is, I don't want you or any other man." Bitterness edged her voice.

"Fran, that's *not* what's on my mind. Last night, I didn't think about protection. I guess I didn't think, period. But now, I'm wondering... will everything be alright? You won't get pregnant, will you?"

The thought hadn't occurred to Frank and it shocked her. The very last thing she needed was to get pregnant. It was pretty obvious she still couldn't look after herself, let alone a child. Quickly she searched her mind, and after a few confused mental calculations decided there probably wouldn't be a problem.

"No... I mean, it should be all right," she stammered. He was sitting up on the bed, devoid of any covers, watching her anxiously. In spite of herself, Frank's heartbeat quickened when she looked at him, her eyes darkened as they met his and held.

"Fran, about what happened last night. I can't say I regret it. I'll admit, it wasn't very responsible of me to give in to whatever this crazy thing is that draws me to you, but what we shared was beautiful. It was for me anyway, and I believe it was for you, too. Don't spoil it by flogging yourself with guilt. It happened. Accept that. You are a wonderful, warm, and passionate woman. I believe you don't make a habit of doing this. And Fran, I want you to know that while I'm no monk, I don't make a practice of falling into bed with just anyone on a moment's notice either."

He ran a hand through his hair and looked at her as though he was willing her to understand. "The truth is, I've been attracted to you since I first saw you that day at the rodeo. I watched you get out of your truck. You stretched, and I noticed those long legs and your terrific body. Then you lifted that beautiful hair off your neck. You ran your hands through it, and it floated around your shoulders. I wondered what it would be like to run *my* hands through it.

"I was crouched down resting against the wall of the stable and I watched you weave through the trucks on your way there. I felt things I hadn't felt in a long time. You walked right past me and went inside. I got up and watched you move along the pens, looking at the horses. You kept going back to mine, and I felt ridiculously pleased...until you looked as suspicious as hell when you looked around to see if anyone was watching while you took something out of your pocket. Then I felt like a fool. I imagined the worst, and I got mad. I jumped you over it, and you fought back. When you left, I saw you meet up with that team roper. He was hugging you, kissing your cheek, and I decided that you were a buckle bunny."

Frank shook her head in denial.

Colt closed his eyes momentarily, and then continued. "I couldn't seem to help myself that day. My eyes searched for you everywhere I went. I was furious when I saw you with Kirby Wisehart. When I looked back on it now, I was jealous... but I never would have admitted it. It was easier to think you were a tramp; then I could justify the anger I felt when I saw you two sitting so close, smiling into each other's eyes, laughing and touching. You and a married man, a happily married man...."

Frank started to protest, but he waved it away.

"I didn't want to think about you, but these past weeks I've did it more often than I liked. I remembered how it felt to have my arms around you, how it felt to touch you, even the smell of your perfume. I was convinced you had moved on with the rodeo crowd, and I was relieved. Finding you here the other night shocked me: but more than that, it scared the hell out of me. That's why I was so damned mad. I knew that you could be a threat to my peace of mind. I never wanted to feel this compelling desire again. This overwhelming need... I don't want to now, but, God help me, I do."

He ran his hand over his face and sighed deeply. "I've been down the rocky road of romance once already, Fran. Love and marriage... it'll never happen again for me. Deep down, I have a feeling that this attraction could go a lot deeper than just wanting to hit the sack with you. But I'll never give it a chance," he said fiercely.

He got up and walked to the window. "If we'd met before, maybe something could have happened between us. Now I'm only sure of one thing. I'll never take the risk of loving again. If it doesn't work out, it's too painful. I'm not sure I would survive that experience again."

"That's alright with me, Colt. I'm not looking for love and marriage either, and we agree on another thing; this can never happen again. Let's just close the door on what happened last night and lock the memories away."

Turning, she walked to the door of the bathroom. As she went in and closed it, she realized that her foot only hurt slightly. *It couldn't have been as bad as it seemed last night. His lovemaking wasn't that magical.* But when she looked in the mirror, she had to blink furiously to dispel the tears that threatened to overflow. How easy it was to say they'd lock the memories away. She hoped she could. Damn him! Why did he have to come along, just when her life was starting to get back in order? She hoped he would go home soon. She had to overcome the attraction she felt, but she didn't know how. He was so virile... and so impossible to ignore.

The smell of fresh coffee filled the kitchen, and Colt was at the stove, cooking bacon and eggs. He looked up as she came in, commenting casually that she was responsible for setting the table—

as if nothing had happened between them that was any different than usual.

I guess that's my cue, she thought as she took the plates and cutlery from the cupboard.

"How's your foot this morning?" he asked when they sat down to eat. "It seems to be a lot better than it was last night."

"I'm amazed, but it is."

"That's good. You'd better stay in the house today. If you give it a rest, it should be a hundred percent in a few days. I'll do the chores and after that I'll go check the culvert and bring the tractor in."

Her first reaction was to protest, but soon she realized he was right. It would be easy to slip on the wet grass or twist her foot in the mud. Besides, if she went outside, it would throw her into constant contact with him, whereas if she stayed in the house, it would give her ravaged emotions a chance to relax and calm down.

"You're right. I can do some baking."

"Apple pie for supper?" he asked hopefully.

Frank sat back in her chair and looked at him. "Now the truth comes out," she jeered. "I was beginning to think you might not be such a bad guy, after all. All that solicitous concern about my foot, and now I see it was really a bid for apple pie. A case of self-serving interest if I ever saw one," she said, amusement filling her voice.

The amusement grew as she watched his face fill with consternation. He was afraid he had offended her again. When he started to protest, she cut him short. "You'd better get out of here while you're still ahead." Her smile and a twinkle in her eye softened the effect of her words.

He looked at her with uncertainty, and then shrugged his shoulders as he turned away. "What else can I say?" When he reached the door, he turned with a grin on his face. "Except, that apple pie is my favorite." Then he was gone.

When Colt came in later, she had several kinds of cookies spread out to cool.

"It smells like a bakery in here. The lady lied when she told me she wasn't a good cook." He grinned and reached to take a cookie. Then he hesitated. "Is it all right?" His look was warm and friendly.

"Help yourself. It's after eleven, a little late for a coffee break, but a little early for lunch. What do you want?"

He moved close to her. "What do I want?" he asked softly.

There was no way she could miss the implication in his voice or the caress in his eyes.

Her heart leaped in her breast. Damn him, what was he trying to do? They had agreed; she thought he wanted to forget what had happened. He was confusing her, tearing her between logic and desire. His eyes and his voice were weakening her defenses. The conflict showed in her face.

His eyes lingered on her hungrily. For a moment, she thought he was going to reach out to her. Then his expression changed subtly. It was as if he had drawn a shutter across the screen of his emotion, and although there was reluctance in his action, he turned away and walked to the window.

"I'll have a glass of milk and a few cookies." He threw the words over his shoulder.

She was simultaneously relieved and disappointed. The tension flowed from her, but it left her body aching, crying out silently. She wanted the feel of his muscled strength against her, the feel of his hands on her skin, knowing they would bring her stunningly alive. She was trembling. "That's not much for lunch. Will it be enough to satisfy you?"

He turned to face her. His hunger was unguarded now, and it had nothing to do with food. "You know it won't. *You* are only the thing that will satisfy me, and that would satisfy *both* of us."

Frank turned a rosy pink. "Colt, we agreed...,"

"I know; I'm not playing by the stupid rules. I haven't been able to keep my mind off you all morning, and since I've come back inside, I have to fight to keep my hands off you. I don't want to lock away the memory of what happened between us. I want to make more memories. I want to take you back to bed and find out if making love to you is really as wonderful as I thought it was last night. This morning, I imagined I could play it cool and act like nothing unusual happened. But clearly it did for me, and I think it did for you, too. "

Frank remained silent, but he saw the anguish in her eyes. She turned away, and when she spoke, her words ignored his passionate outburst. "Why don't you pour a glass of milk and help yourself to some cookies. The noon news will be on pretty soon. You can go to the living room and watch it."

She busied herself, filling the cookie jar. She heard him take a glass from the cupboard, then go to the refrigerator and fill it with milk. He came to stand beside her at the counter and took some cookies from the jar. Her skin prickled. It was tormenting to be so near him, so vibrantly aware of him. Her body flooded with tension.

I can't give in to these feelings, she thought desperately. Yet somewhere in the back of her mind, she wondered if they shouldn't take what they could.

CHAPTER NINE

She was standing at the window, staring absently at the rain, when Colt came back into the kitchen. He walked up behind her, placed his hands on her shoulders, and turned her to face him.

"Fran, I can't concentrate on the news. I can't ignore how I feel. I can't think about anything, except how much I want you." His voice was tense and husky with desire. "We're adults, and we both need the same thing. Why don't we accept what's between us and take the stolen moments? Ollie should be back tomorrow. Then I'll leave, and we won't be thrown together like this anymore. Eventually, this attraction will burn itself out."

She brushed the back of her hand across her face. "I know we're both adults, and neither one of us have obligations to anyone else. I guess there's no reason why we shouldn't be with each other, just for the sake of enjoying. It's just that I was raised to believe that there should be a commitment with intimacy. I've never done this before, and yet last night I felt better in your arms that I can ever remember feeling. I didn't think about the future or the past. I just felt and it was good."

"Then don't think now," he urged, pulling her into his embrace. "Just stay here in my arms and feel." Cradling her against him, he swayed gently, his big hands moving in caressing patterns along her back. Anticipation made his voice husky and the ache in his groin uncomfortable. He leaned back and looked into her eyes; there he saw desire mixed with uncertainty.

He hesitated briefly and then crushed her to him again. "Maybe it's a crazy idea. To be honest, I'm damned scared. Common sense tells me not to get involved. I sat in the rain this morning and thought about all of this." He sighed deeply as his eyes roamed over her face. "I was tempted to say, 'To hell with caution, go for it,' but the more I thought about it..." He shook his head. "I'm getting along fine with my life the way it is. Why should I risk changing it?"

She agreed. "And I'm just getting over heartache. Why should I run the risk of it happening again? I'm tempted by the idea of being with you, just to experience the wild excitement, the passion, the wonderfulness that happened last night. But if we play with fire, we run the risk of getting burned. And part of me wonders what will happen if we light a flame that we can't extinguish."

He looked at her for a long moment, weighing her words and recognizing the truth in them. But the urgent need that had sparked in his body refused to be denied. It burned in his eyes, and when he bent to touch his mouth to hers, it burned there too. His tongue licked at her lips like a flickering flame at first, then gained strength, spreading its heat until they both were drawn into a spiraling vortex that seemed to come from the very core of their beings. Like lava from an active volcano, it traced through their veins, setting them aflame, consuming them as it flowed.

Frank dissolved against him. A groan rumbled through Colt's chest when he swept her up in his arms and carried her down the hall to her room. They raced through a fog of desire as they helped each other remove their clothing.

She arched her body into his as he pushed her back onto the bed and lowered himself over her. He ravaged her lips and then trailed a burning path of kisses down her neck to a hardened nipple. Grasping it gently, he nipped teasingly, and then sucked playfully. He drew from the innermost recesses of her being, feelings so intense she felt she would explode.

While his lips continued to inflict their special kind of torment, his hands caressed her, working a magic of their own. His fingers trailed downward, feathering across her stomach until they rested teasingly in the patch of downy softness that guarded the entrance to her aching womanhood.

She tensed, waiting in anticipation as they probed the warm entrance. With a gasp, she pushed against them, inviting their gentle invasion. At that moment, the responses of her frantically aroused senses all seemed to focus in an explosive summons at that one point, begging for release.

"Colt," she begged. "Please...." Her hips thrust forward to meet his, and she felt him, hard, and pulsing, against her soft belly. She arched away, giving herself room to brush her fingers over his hip and move across to just below his belly button. She followed a tantalizing path to the head of his swollen manhood. He held his breath as she touched the velvety tip, stroking with a gentle touch.

He could stand no more. With a groan, he pushed her onto her back, rolling with the movement until his weight pinned her beneath him. He shifted his body and moved above her. Slowly, gently, he accepted her invitation, resisting her feverish thrusts, which would have pushed him directly to their ultimate goal. He reveled in the fact that he could bring her so much pleasure, and he guided her surely, with deliberate slowness to the precipice of her fulfillment. Instinctively, he sensed when to make those final penetrating strokes, taking them both over the edge and floating down into an enfolding cloud of satisfaction.

They lay for a long moment, their bodies molded together. Then Colt rolled onto his side, pulling her with him. He caressed her face, observing the soft flush that blossomed there. Her eyes were bemused; her lips soft and full. "You're beautiful," he murmured. "There's only one thing I would change."

Her eyes widened with question as she watched him sit up in the middle of the bed. "It's nothing that I can't remedy right now," he assured her with a smile as he took her hand and pulled her up toward him.

She entwined her arms around his neck and pulled herself closer until her legs slipped around his hips. Their lips met briefly as his hands slid to her shoulders, reaching for her braid. With fumbling fingers, he stripped the elastic from the tip and loosened her hair from its confines. His hands moved through it, shaking it loose into a wavy curtain that floated around her shoulders, spilling over onto him. "Now you're perfect."

She felt him grow hard again. Deep within, a pulsation in her body responded. She pressed herself against him with rhythmic movements. Their lips met in heated response and she melted into him. He leaned forward, lowering her to the mattress beneath them, and then gently pulled back. He worshiped her with his eyes while she continued to arch her body against his. "You are such a beautiful, sexy woman. I wonder if I could ever get enough of you." The words were a hoarse whisper. He lowered himself to her once more, and she welcomed him again, lifting her hips to accept him.

She gasped with pleasure as he filled her, lifting her to the brink of ecstasy, then dropping back to let her coast down, before carrying her up once again, over and over, until at last there was no returning. Her whole body convulsed with the intensity of her release. After the first cry had torn from her lips, she lost all conscious thought in a storm of sensation. The completeness of her pleasure intensified his.

Frank drifted in a happy vacuum, untroubled by thoughts, simply satisfied. Time had no meaning, and she had no idea how long they had lain together before he rolled over, pulling her into his arms as he turned. Satiated and exhausted, they drifted into the deep dreamless sleep that comes when all tensions are banished.

When she awoke, she lay quietly, savoring the cocoon of warmth that she floated in. She was cradled loosely in Colt's arms, her face snuggled against his chest, and her body molded against the length of his, their legs entwined. She could hear the steady rhythm of his heart as it beat beneath her ear, and she was awash with the musky scent of his body.

His arms tightened around her with a gentle squeeze as he dropped a soft kiss on her forehead. With his other arm, he groped for the quilt they had pushed aside in their urgency. Finding it, he drew it over them, providing a sense of private intimacy as his hand caressed her body beneath its softness. They lay together, enjoying the closeness, sharing the gentle web of seduction that surrounded them.

Eventually, Colt stirred and looked at his watch. "Sweetheart," he said softly, nipping playfully at her ear. "It's four-thirty: time for me to do chores." He cuddled her, dropping moist little kisses over her face and nipping playfully at her bottom lip before he disentangled himself and rolled out of bed. His eyes caressed her face as he pulled on his clothes, tucking his shirt into his jeans and zipping them closed. "This wantonness of yours could be the ruination of a good man." He grinned as he dodged the pillow that she flung at him and then threw himself on top of her. "But what a beautiful way to go," he said with a chuckle.

Frank was playing her guitar when Colt came in from doing the evening chores. He quietly removed his coat and boots, and then stood listening to her soft, lilting voice as she sang an old song that had been a favorite of his father for years. As the last note fell from her lips, he walked up the steps and into the living room where she was sitting.

"That's an old favorite of my dad. You'd have him eating out of your hand if he heard you sing it. Where did you learn the words?"

"It was a favorite of my dad. Ollie likes it, too. He asks me to sing it every time I pick up the guitar. Are you ready to eat now?" she asked as she put her guitar in its case. "I just have to broil the steaks. I can do that while you wash up."

"Right on." He whistled the tune as he walked down the hall to his room. Frank went into the kitchen and put the steaks that she had marinated earlier under the broiler. Everything else was ready, and the aroma of hot apple pie wafted in the air.

While she waited for Colt, she poured wine for each of them, then took hers, and went to stand by the window. When he returned, he picked up his glass and came to stand beside her. "Mmm, you smell nice." He turned her toward him. "I noticed the smell of your perfume the first day we met. What is it?"

"*Fantasque.*"

"That's pretty close to fantastic, just like you look." His eyes roamed over her face, moving down to her throat, coming to rest on her loungewear. "That's the sexy thing you had on the other night when I got here, isn't it? The color is perfect on you. But you should've left your hair loose." He reached for the elastic that secured her braid.

"Don't," she protested, pulling it away. "There isn't time for that. The steaks will be ready any second now."

"Why don't you take your hair out of that braid and brush it loose. Please? I'll look after the steaks."

She wrinkled her nose at him and turned toward her room. "I'm not sure why I give into you like this. It's not like me, but you did say please."

She was brushing her hair into a rippling cascade when his reflection appeared in the mirror. He leaned against the door frame, wine glass in hand, watching the movement of her hand as it guided the brush. His eyes were filled with smoldering desire. He crossed the room to her side. She laid down the brush and their eyes met in the mirror.

"It's beautiful. I hope you never cut it short. I love it, just like this." He stroked the softness.

She moved into his arms when he reached for her, and her lips returned his kiss when he sought them. When he lifted his head, she leaned against him with a sigh.

Do we know what we're doing, Colt? We're acting and talking like people who are falling in love, like people who have a future. I wonder if we realize how far we've gone. She sighed again. What had he said earlier? Don't think, just feel—for now. Well, then she wouldn't think about it. She would just enjoy the feeling for now. Intuitively, she knew she'd have plenty of time to think after he was gone. She leaned back into his arms and looked up at him. "We better go and eat or everything will be ruined."

They ate in companionable silence. After Colt had finished his second piece of pie, he leaned back in his chair with a contented smile on his face. "That was delicious. I'm finding it harder than ever to believe that Ollie's glowing praise for you isn't as much for your expertise in the kitchen as anything else. You're great at your job outside, but who could resist having a good cook with a beautiful face to share their meals with every day? Not even Ollie, I'll bet."

Frank scrunched her napkin and threw it at him. "It's your turn to do the dishes. Ollie always does them when I cook."

At his request, she played the guitar while he did the dishes. At first, she strummed aimlessly and then began to sing as she swung into a medley of old-fashioned love songs. When she finished, Colt came to lean against the doorframe and watched her pick a few bars of a light melody before he spoke. "What was he like, Fran?"

She looked at him blankly. "Who?"

"The guy that hurt you: I know it's none of my business, but I can't help but wonder what happened." He moved to sit in a deep, comfortable chair across from her. "I assume you were engaged... or even married. Were you? Married, I mean?"

She looked at him startled. "No, we weren't married."

He sighed with what felt like relief. "You offer a man so much, with your natural warmth, intelligence, and passion. I find it hard to understand how he could have let you go."

His words surprised her. Her eyes slid away from him to the big window, where she absently watched the leaves of a nearby tree dancing in the evening light. A multitude of thoughts skittered through her mind before she pulled them together and realized, with a sense of surprise, that she wondered if she had ever actually loved Martin.

She strummed the guitar softly before she raised her eyes to meet Colt's again. "His name was Martin Cole." She hadn't discussed what happened between Martin and herself with anyone, except Becky. Now, she was surprised at how easy it was to tell Colt the whole story.

After she had finished speaking, she stared blindly at her hand as it rested on the guitar. "It was partly my fault too," she admitted. "I wasn't able to be completely honest with myself at the time, but I took too much for granted. A few months earlier, my life had seemed so perfect. Suddenly, my neatly packaged world was falling apart." She shrugged. "Maybe I was more insecure and frightened than broken hearted. Sometimes I wonder now if what we had wasn't just habit. But even if it was, I still can't help feeling betrayed. Can you understand that?"

"Yes." He hoisted himself out of the chair and walked over to stare out the window. "Yes, I can. That's pretty much how I felt. Betrayed."

Frank waited for him to continue, but he seemed lost in thought.

"What happened to your marriage, Colt?" She was reluctant to ask, but it wasn't idle curiosity that prompted the question. If he was surprised that she had been dumped, she was equally surprised that his marriage had fallen apart. To her, marriage was a commitment, not just a promise. She had seen glimpses of a tender, compassionate, sensitive man, behind the hard, chauvinistic exterior. She was pretty certain the man on the surface was an acquired defense and she wondered why he felt he needed it.

She could see the tension in his body. He turned to face her, and she sensed his reluctance to answer. "I guess you have as much right to ask me that as I did you. I don't like to talk about it. Ollie and I haven't even discussed it, but he was here, so he knows what happened."

"How long has it been since you went your separate ways?"

"Eight years." He walked over to the chair again and lowered himself into it. "We were still wet behind the ears when we got married. She was nineteen. I was twenty-two. It lasted four years, and then I grew up fast." He grimaced, then leaned his head against the back of the chair, and looked up at the ceiling. "I used to hang around with the rodeo crowd. I bulldogged steers when I was in high school. During my last year at university, a bunch of us went across the border, to Billings, Montana. That's where I met Sharon. I fell for her like a ton of bricks." He sighed and sat up to look at Frank.

"I think she loved me too in the beginning; at least, as much as she was capable of loving anyone other than herself. The first two years were like a fantasy. She was a barrel racer, and wherever she raced, I went with her. Our life was one big rodeo party."

He sighed heavily. "But it couldn't go on like that. I had responsibilities. Finally, Dad got fed up with me not carrying my share of the load. He made it plain that I couldn't expect to be gone rodeoing all the time if I wanted to be part of the business." He shrugged. "I knew he was right. So, I started to stay home and attend to business. Sharon was furious at Dad, and she pouted when she was with me. I wasn't happy about letting her go alone, but I wasn't worried. I'd put her on such a pedestal, it never crossed my mind that she would be unfaithful."

He drummed his fingers on the arm of the chair. "I bought her a new horse that she wanted. To be honest, it was probably more of a peace offering, than anything. The horse was a winner, and she did well with it. The better she performed, the more she was gone. Rumors started getting back to me. A hint here, a little dig there."

He hesitated, remembering. "At first, I ignored them, but gradually I began to notice a subtle difference in her attitude. I was scared as hell, and I blamed myself. I made a point of going with her more often, in spite of Dad's objections. I thought we could recapture the old magic if we were together." He stopped speaking, his expression revealing the painfulness of his thoughts.

"Colt, you don't have to tell me. It's none of my business. I shouldn't have asked you."

He continued speaking. "One afternoon, she slipped away. I had a knot as big as a football in my gut, but I followed through on a hunch. I caught her in bed with a bull rider who'd been traveling the same rodeo circuit." A muscle jerked in his jaw. "I had never been a violent man, but I beat him within an inch of his life. Then, she and I had it out and I brought her back to the ranch. For a while, it looked like she was going to put an honest effort into making things work. She knew I wanted to start a family. She didn't protest."

He sighed. "About three and a half months later, she wasn't around when I came home for supper. I checked all the usual places and couldn't find her. No one had seen her."

He shoved himself out of the chair and walked over to stare out the window again. "I knew she hadn't been feeling up to par. She'd been to the doctor, but when I questioned her, she told me it was a routine check-up and that everything was fine. She threw in a little line about needing to take vitamins, so she wouldn't be so tired. I had no reason to doubt her. When I couldn't find her that night, I got worried. I phoned the doctor to see if she'd been to see him."

He turned to face Frank again. His face was tight, his eyes hard. "He wasn't very friendly when I called, but when he realized that I had no idea what was going on, he was shocked. He told me she was pregnant. She'd told him I didn't want a kid." She could see his jaw clench as he shook his head in disbelief. "Apparently, he offered to talk to me, but she told him that I wouldn't even discuss it. She told him that my family hated her, and I wouldn't stand up to them and support her. She said that our marriage was on the rocks and we were considering divorce. She had been so distraught, that he had reluctantly been persuaded it would be in her best interest to have an abortion. He had arranged for her to have it in Regina because she wanted to avoid gossip."

He snorted mirthlessly. "I was stunned. The lies were bad enough, but I couldn't believe that she would destroy our child when she knew how much I would want it. It was as much a part of me as it was her. I should've had some say in what happened." He shook his head, still disbelieving. "I drove to Regina like a madman. I was determined to stop her, but I was too late. She'd had the abortion that afternoon."

He smashed a fist into the open palm of his other hand. Remembering brought back the hurt. It was like living the helplessness, the anguish, and the anger, all over again.

"I despised her after that. If I had known she was pregnant and didn't want the child, Mom and Dad would have helped me make it financially worth her while to take time out of her selfish existence to bring that precious life into the world. Mom would have been happy to help look after the baby, and I would have gladly taken full legal custody. But she didn't give us that option." His voice was harsh. "I filed for divorce the next day. She got herself a damned good lawyer and took me to the cleaners, without the inconvenience of being pregnant for nine months.

"After the dust settled, I realized she had planned to divorce me, even before I caught her with the bull rider. She just wanted to figure out how big a settlement she could expect before she did it. She counted on getting a chunk of Thompson Holdings, but she couldn't touch it and that was a big disappointment for her. Even so, she took our house and contents, her new pickup, the fancy horse trailer and her horses; basically all of our joint assets, except my old pickup and my clothes. I had to pay off the mortgage on the house and the money owing on her top-of-the-line pickup and the horse trailer before she would sign the papers. She went for a cash settlement too.

I could have fought her, but I just wanted to get it over with. Dad co-signed for me to borrow money against Thompson Holdings, and I paid her out. Thompson Holdings has done well. Financially, I'm personally starting to see daylight. I've worked hard and spent little on anything, except paying off the debt she left me with. If this is a good year, I'll finally come out on top." His voice was taut with controlled anger and pain.

He looked away and turned toward the window again. Silence expanded, filling the room uncomfortably. Frank stared at his back, sick at heart for him. She longed to be able to put her arms around him, to comfort him, to assure him that all women were not like his ex-wife, but she knew she couldn't. The timing wasn't right. All his old wounds had been exposed again. The pain was as fresh as when it happened.

When he spoke again, his voice was dull. "I've never wanted to get involved since. I'm not saying I don't take women out or that I'm celibate, but it doesn't mean anything to me. I'll never love anyone that way again. It made me too vulnerable. I was an emotional wreck for a long time afterward. The anger and the pain festered inside me. Every time I saw a little kid, it would start all over again. Every time I thought about what she'd done, I wanted to kill her. That's what she had done to our baby."

Talking about it had taken its toll. All the pain and anger that he had bottled inside for the past eight years had resurfaced. It had boiled over and spewed out, leaving him tired and drained. His shoulders slumped wearily as he continued to stare out the window.

Frank was startled when after what seemed endless minutes, he spoke again. His voice had a defiant note to it. "I have been seeing a woman in Swift Current for the past four years. Her name is Shauna

Lee Holt." He turned to face her. "There's no love involved. We're both mature enough to realize it is an illusion. We're good friends and that's enough. Neither one of us will end up expecting more than the other is prepared to give. If I ever get married again, I'll marry her."

He didn't look at Frank when he walked past her to the kitchen. He'd surprised himself when he blurted out his relationship with Shauna Lee. He didn't plan to marry her, but the idea served to warn Fran away, to make it plain that there would never be anything between them, in spite of what they had shared during the past twenty-four hours. Reviewing his relationship with Sharon had reaffirmed his resolve to stay clear of any emotional involvement, with Fran or anyone else. The pain had twisted like a knife in his gut once again.

The revelation jolted Frank. The thought of Colt with someone else was disturbing. She fingered the guitar absently. Suddenly, she felt cold and isolated from the situation. The companionable closeness that she and Colt had shared earlier was gone. She had sensed his withdrawal as he talked.

She put her guitar away, and then hesitated, not knowing exactly what to do. Colt was still in the kitchen. She wished she could offer him comfort, but she didn't know how to approach him. It might be best if she left him alone, but she didn't feel right about slipping off to bed without saying goodnight or something. Absently, she walked to the kitchen door. He was sitting at the table with a cup of coffee cradled in his hands.

"Colt?" Uncertainty reflected in her voice.

He looked up. His face was tired and empty of expression.

Suddenly she wanted to cry. "Colt... I... I don't know what to say." She lifted her arms to him in appeal, then let them drop, and shrugged her shoulders. "I'm sorry I asked. I can understand that it hurt you to talk about the past. I-I hope that, eventually, you'll be able to let the hurt go."

His face didn't change.

"We aren't all like Sharon," she whispered.

Later she lay in the darkness, unable to drift into the oblivion of sleep that would have been so welcome. Instead, she found herself listening for Colt's footsteps in the hall. They didn't come.

CHAPTER TEN

"Colt, what are you doing here? And, why are you sitting here in the dark? Where's Frank?" Ollie's voice boomed in the stillness, jolting Frank from the troubled slumber she had finally drifted into.

Ollie was back! She swung herself out of bed and slipped on her terrycloth robe. Knotting the tie firmly, she left her room and padded down the hall. She squinted against the brightness of the light that flooded the living room. "Ollie!" she cried. "It's good to hear your voice again, but you haven't been gone very long…you weren't supposed to be back until tomorrow night."

"It doesn't take much of that kind of craziness, to be enough for me. Just makes me appreciate life on the ranch all the more. How did things go here? Wasn't that some rain?"

"It was unbelievable. Do you want a cup of coffee?"

"Sounds good." He gave her an affectionate grin as he took off his cowboy hat and dropped it, along with his leather gloves, on the coffee table. Then he sat down on the couch and turned his attention to Colt.

The two discussed the events of the past three days while Frank made coffee and put out a plate of cookies. Colt's look was impersonal when she handed him his. Impersonal and disinterested, and Frank felt for a moment that she might have fantasized about the hours she spent in his arms and the passionate possession he had taken of her body.

Suddenly she felt alone and empty. She tried to focus her attention on what Ollie and Colt were saying, but a disturbing thought kept probing her mind, never quite surfacing. It wasn't until she was in bed again that she knew what it was.

She was very close to falling in love with him. The realization was a shock. She hardly knew him. It was too sudden. Besides, that she didn't want to love him. And to top it off, he had made it very clear that he would never fall in love with her, in fact, he had told her that he would probably marry someone else. She angrily brushed away the tears that slipped silently down her cheeks.

Colt left early the next morning. His manner remained as cool and distant as it had after Ollie's arrival the previous night. He didn't ignore her; he simply treated her like he would any other hired hand. There was no soft warmth in his glance; no tender smile to acknowledge what had happened between them. It was as if he had wiped it out of his mind.

She silently upbraided herself. What more could she expect? He'd told her that kind of relationship was meaningless to him. *But it wasn't for me,* her heart cried. *That's because I didn't stick to the rules.* Emptiness filled her, as she stood at the door and watched his truck speed down the lane.

Ollie detected sadness in her eyes as he watched her.

"Well, what do you think of the boss?" he asked, as he poured himself a cup of coffee. "I guess you know by now that I never got around to tellin' him about you. That you were a woman, I mean. I expect that may have been a bit tricky. What was his reaction?"

"To be blunt, he was mad as hell. Finding me here was like waving a red flag in front of a mad bull. But you know there's more to it than that, Ollie." The words were laced with accusation. "You must have realized he was the guy who called me a buckle bunny when I told you he owned Jetsetter's Lady."

Ollie flushed under her hurt look. "Yeah, I did. I didn't say anythin' because I thought you might pack up and leave. I reckoned I could make it work out in time. I wasn't sure how I'd do it, but I didn't expect him to come out here while I was gone. That sort of blew my chances."

"At first he refused to believe I was Frank Lamonte. He said you would never have hired a woman, and if you had, you would've told him. He remembered seeing me at the rodeo. I couldn't believe the ridiculous things he accused me of doing that day. He was convinced that I was a flirt and a…a husband stealer. I was livid and told him what an ass I thought he was.

"He decided that I'd hooked up with the new ranch hand, and told me to pack my bags and leave. By then I'd had it with his attitude. I said I'd leave in the morning and went to bed. I guess, he began to rethink the situation. He knocked on my bedroom door and said he wanted to talk. I told him there was nothing else to say, but he insisted. When I came out of the bedroom, I accused him of harassment. He almost fell over himself to deny that."

Ollie grinned, as he imagined the scene.

"He apologized for the way he acted earlier and asked me to consider staying. I was furious with him, but I like it here. Finally I said I would, because of you, but I made it clear that I wouldn't put up with his chauvinist attitude. He promised nothing like that would happen again.

"Then, he asked if he could have something to eat. That really ticked me off and I was rude. I told him he had a heart beat and two legs, and he wasn't hogtied. He could help himself."

Ollie burst out laughing. "What did he do?"

"If looks could kill, I'd be dead. He just glared at me. I knew he wanted to lay into at me, but he didn't. He went to the fridge and found something to eat." She smirked. "I was gracious enough to make him a cup of my favorite instant coffee. Yuck!"

Ollie roared with laughter. "He hates that stuff!"

"I do too." Frank grinned. "It was vindictive of me, but while I was making it, I was hoping that he disliked it as much as I did.

"Things were still pretty touchy the next day until we found the lame bull. By the time we got it in, we had relaxed enough to be civil."

Ollie shook his head. "I'm sorry Colt put you through all that. It was my fault because I didn't handle the situation right. I should have stepped up and told him the facts a long time ago, instead of pussyfootin' around him. I admit I was a little worried when I got here last night. You were in bed already and he was sitting out here in the dark. I wondered what was going on."

"I just felt like going to bed early." *That's not a lie, Ollie. It's just a bit short on the truth.* She turned away. "I'm going back to the lease this morning."

Ollie noticed the shadows under her eyes. When he watched her walk to her room, he sensed that things had not gone as smoothly as Frank had led him to believe.

She shut the door behind her and stood for a long moment, looking at the bed where she and Colt had lain in each other's arms less than twenty-four hours earlier. She closed her eyes, remembering the feel of his lips, his arms around her, and the scent of his body. She shivered as she recalled the heights his lovemaking had taken her to. Now he was gone, and she knew she had to try to lock those sweet memories away and smother that little flame that had flared, unbidden, in her heart.

***

July passed quickly. The days were warm, and the pastures grew lush and green. Wildflowers flourished in abundance, and Frank reveled in the beauty of it. She spent long hours in the saddle, riding across the hundreds of acres of lease land, watching the animals grow fat and sleek.

Life struck a leisurely pace. She often sat at a high point and looked over the rolling terrain that unfolded around her, imagining what it must've been like when the white man had first come there. She could visualize grass three feet tall, waving in the breeze, and see the herds of buffalo grazing in the open areas. She would imagine what it was like to see a bull train plodding slowly across the hills, the oxen yoked in pairs to brightly painted wagons. She could almost hear the bull whackers swearing loudly while they pushed the animals to keep moving. She had borrowed a book from Ollie that gave a detailed view of the area's past, and she grew to love the hills. Her imagination flourished on their stormy history.

In the evenings, she would read or play the guitar. If she had a need for company, she'd visit with the tourists who came to enjoy the beauty of the park. She often drove the short distance to Fort Walsh and toured the visitor information center, studying the large display of historical photos, sketches, and artifacts that brought the region's history to life. Whatever she did, it was done with one purpose in mind—to keep any thoughts of Colt at bay.

The first week in August was cool and rainy, an abrupt change from the warm weather she had become accustomed to. The rain brought back a flood of memories related to the time she had spent with Colt. Even though she struggled to push them away, they kept surfacing. In many ways, it seemed so long ago, but still an aching loneliness settled over her, subduing her usual cheerful outlook on life. She decided she'd been alone too long. A trip to the ranch and a visit with Ollie would cheer her up.

Ollie was surprised to see her. "What brings you back from the cows? Not that I'm not happy to see you. It's kind of nice to have someone else around to talk to once in a while."

"My thoughts exactly," she said with a smile. "It must be this dull weather that's getting me down. I've been feeling blue, so I decided to come back and let you cheer me up. Even the cows won't want me around pretty soon."

"Well, come in and we'll have a cup of coffee. I took some of your cookies out of the freezer this morning; must've known you were coming."

"I'll settle for a glass of milk, Ollie. I've had a touch of the flu lately. Coffee doesn't seem to agree with me. Besides, milk and cookies have always been a favorite of mine."

They chatted amicably for half an hour, then Frank decided to go to the barn and spend some time with Cypress Jade. As she stood up to go, she asked Ollie how the bull was.

"He's still lame."

She frowned thoughtfully. "I doubt if he'll ever be a sound breeder again. I'll have a look at him after I've seen the horses."

When she entered the barn, she went directly to the young stallion. The horse nickered a soft welcome and nuzzled her playfully. When she entered the stall and started to work with him, her melancholy feelings shifted and she lost herself in the enjoyment of seeing him respond.

She didn't notice when the barn door opened awhile later, or see the tall figure that stepped inside. When Colt spoke, it startled her, and she jumped like a spooked horse. The sound of his voice sent her heart into a stampede, and she was glad she had the excuse of calming the animal before she had to respond to him. When she had regained her composure, she turned to face him with a cool poise that belied the state of her emotions.

"Ollie didn't say he was expecting you today."

"I decided to drive out at the last minute. Mom and Dad came with me. Ollie said you were going to look at the bull. Have you seen him yet?"

"No." She nodded at the horse. "As usual, I lost track of time once I got started with this. I'll have a look at him now." She tried to fight the tight band squeezing her heart. Colt seemed distant, showing no sign of emotion. *Frank Lamonte, you're foolish to even look for anything more*, she chided herself silently. *You're the one who isn't living up to your end of the bargain.*

"That's why I came out."

With a jolt, she realized that he had been talking to her. "What did you say? I'm sorry, I was thinking about something else," she admitted, cursing inwardly when she felt herself blush. "Did you say that was why you came out now?"

"Yes." His eyes lingered on the color in her cheeks, and then settled on her mouth as she touched her tongue to her lips, running it nervously along them. A muscle in his jaw began to twitch, and he looked up to meet her strained expression.

Afraid of what would show in her eyes, she turned abruptly and walked to the big door that opened into the corrals. She slid it open partway, stepped outside, and led the way to the pen where the bull was kept. She observed the injured animal for a few moments, and then swung herself up and over the corral rails for a closer examination. Concentrating on the unfortunate animal helped to ease the tension, and when she turned to speak to Colt, it was with relative ease.

"I doubt that he'll ever recover completely. He hasn't made much progress since we brought him in. I think you'll have to replace him."

"I've been thinking the same thing. I may as well ship him." He turned away. "Are you coming in now? Ollie was making lunch when I left the house."

"I might as well." They walked in silence, going in the back door to slip off their boots and raincoats. She looked up at him with surprise when he took her jacket and hung it up. A look of softness had lurked in his eyes as he took it, but when he turned back, the familiar coolness was firmly in place.

You're grasping at straws; she scolded herself silently when he stepped back, to let her precede him up the stairs and into the kitchen. Ollie was at the stove stirring a pot of stew. A tall, slender gray-haired woman stood at the counter cutting bread, and a muscular man, who looked much like Colt, sat on a chair by the table.

Frank gave them both a warm smile when Ollie introduced her.

"Bob and Serena, this is Frank Lamonte, and I can tell you, she is the best hand I've ever worked with. Frank, these fine folks are Colt's parents." Frank stepped toward Colt's mother and extended her hand. "I'm pleased to meet you," she said, meeting the older woman's look. She knew that she was being appraised and felt acceptance in the smile that was returned. Then she turned toward his father and offered her hand.

"It's nice to meet you too. It isn't hard to tell that you and Colt are father and son."

"And I can easily believe that Ollie thinks you're the most delightful ranch hand he has ever worked with. But I wonder what a pretty young woman like you is doing out here. I'm surprised someone hasn't snapped you up by now. I don't understand today's generation." He shook his head. "Young fools. They don't know a good thing when they see it. I'll tell you this much. If I was twenty years younger, and Mother didn't keep such a tight rein on me, I'd be out here, giving them all a run for their money."

Serena Thompson laughed as she gave her husband's ear a gentle tweak. "Dream on—if you were twenty years younger, you would already be married to me and I'd have to keep an even tighter rein on you. Now, I think lunch is ready, isn't it, Ollie?"

Colt had little to say while they ate, even though the rest enjoyed a steady round of pleasant conversation. Occasionally, Frank felt him watching her, but whenever their eyes met, she found only a carefully masked expression.

Later that afternoon, Ollie asked her to play the guitar and sing for them. She didn't see Colt's eyes linger on her face, unguarded for a moment, as he remembered the last time he had heard her sing. She did notice when he slipped out of the room and went outside. She didn't see him walk briskly, almost angrily, through the lightly falling rain, as he struggled to shut down the feelings he had successfully kept at bay until he'd heard her sing again. At the sound of her voice, all his pent-up desire had threatened to overwhelm him. He knew he had to fight the feeling if he was going to keep up that barrier of indifference and preserve his peace of mind.

Frank chatted with his parents until late afternoon when a quick glance at her watch reminded her that it was time to go home. "It's been delightful meeting you folks. I was feeling blue when I got here this morning. This has been the tonic I needed. Now I think I'd better get on the road."

"I hope we'll see you again on the long weekend," Serena Thompson said with a warm smile. "'Colt's birthday is on August twenty-ninth. We always celebrate it with a barbecue at the farm on the September long weekend. Colt's friends and some of the older folks, like Bob and me, get together. Everyone at the ranch is included. We look forward to seeing you then."

"That sounds like fun." She turned to Ollie. "Thanks again. I knew I could count on you to cheer me up."

"Anytime, girl: I've missed having you around."

Colt was coming up the walkway when she stepped out the door. "You're leaving?" he asked.

"Yes. I don't want to get home too late. It's rained all day and the road across the Gap could be a slick."

Colt frowned. "Why don't you spend the night and go in the morning?"

"I'd rather go back now. I need to feed my horse." She smiled as she moved past him. Colt followed and watched her get into the truck. He denied the urge to ask her to stay. When she waved cheerfully, he lifted his hand in response.

He tried to fight the tight feeling that settled in his gut as he watched her drive away. He was tormented by the fact that he didn't want her to go. Instead, he wanted to hold her in his arms, to taste her lips, to feel the slender length of her pliable body against his. "Damn it all," he cursed, viciously kicking at pebbles that lay on the cement. "How did I ever get into this mess?"

The next morning, Frank wondered what had awakened her. Sleepily, she peered at her watch. It was only *five-thirty*. She listened closely. There it was again. Someone was at the door. But who would be there at that time of the day?

She slipped out of bed and went to the window to cautiously peek through the curtain. "Colt!" Apprehension showed on her face when she unlocked the door and flung it open. "Is something wrong?"

"No." He looked at her with surprise. "I decided to come out to check the cattle with you. I haven't been out all summer." As he spoke, his eyes strayed from her face; down to the pale yellow cotton nightgown she wore, stopping at the point where her nipples were protruding rigidly in response to the cool morning air. She saw his eyes darken, and she hugged herself defensively.

"Oh... you didn't say anything-- about coming out yesterday," she stammered, thrown off-balance by the desire she had seen in his look. "Give me a few minutes to get dressed. Will you feed the horses?"

His eyes moved over the arms that shielded her breasts, up to her shoulders, and then to her lips. A muscle twitched in his jaw and he swallowed hard. "Sure thing," he mumbled as he abruptly turned away and walked toward the corral.

Frank was shaken by what she had seen in his eyes. She fought the wild feeling that flowed into her belly, and then oozed down her legs, leaving her weak and trembling. *Don't go there,* she warned herself, closing her eyes and taking a deep breath as she shut the door.

She was rescuing the coffee pot that began to perk madly, when Colt came back. With a smile, she turned and asked him if he wanted some.

He took off his hat and slid behind the table. "Who could resist that aroma?" When he spoke, he avoided meeting her look. Frank poured a cup for him and pushed it over to him, then poured one for her. When she turned to put the pot back on the stove, she was swamped with nausea. Setting it down carefully, she gripped the countertop and took several deep breaths.

"Fran, are you all right?" Concern sharpened Colt's voice.

"I must have a touch of the flu. I've been feeling a bit queasy the last couple of days." Biting her lip, she blinked back the shimmer of tears that filled her eyes.

"Are you sure you're okay?"

"I'm fine. As I said, I've been feeling a little queasy, but it'll go away." The feeling returned, nagging at her, as she fried bacon and eggs. She handed Colt his plate and sat down to sip her coffee.

"Aren't you going to eat?"

"I'll pass on it, this morning. The last couple of days I've felt better if I left food alone. To be honest, even the coffee doesn't seem to be agreeing with me right now," she admitted with a wavering smile.

"Are you sure you feel like riding?" he persisted.

"I told you, I'll be fine," she said impatiently.

With a sigh of resignation, Colt reached for his hat and plunked it on his head before he pushed out from behind the table. He went to saddle the horses while he waited for her.

Once they were on the trail, Frank felt better. She wasn't surprised; riding always worked as therapy for her. They rode steadily during the morning hours, covering a lot of the range area, and giving Colt a good indication of how well the cattle were doing.

It was past lunch when Colt took a trail that led them out of the grazing area. When she looked at him questioningly, he grinned. "I want to show you something special." Half an hour later, they started down a steep slope and broke through the trees onto the shore of a tranquil lake. "This is it," he said softly. "I don't know if they'll be here this year, but a pair of trumpeter swans usually nest here. They're considered a treasured find. A few years ago, they were nearly extinct. Careful management has increased their numbers, but they are still rare. We'll sit here and have our lunch. We may get a glimpse of them and the young ones if they made it back again."

Frank swung out of the saddle and lifted the pack off the back of her horse. Colt took the thermos from his, and they walked over to sit on a huge flat rock. They ate while exchanging casual and companionable conversation and scanned the lake for a sign of the trumpeters. Colt spotted them first, skimming ghostlike along the opposite shore. He quickly put his cup down and grabbed her arm.

"There they are. Across on the opposite shore," he whispered. "See them?"

Frank shielded her eyes. "No," she whispered back.

"Here, lean this way, and I'll show you." He pulled her across his lap and raised a muscled arm alongside her cheek. "Look where I'm pointing. They're floating in the reflection of the trees along the shore."

She searched the water, but his proximity was disturbing, and she found it hard to concentrate. "I must be blind. I still can't see them."

He lowered his cheek until it was level with hers. "Right over there."

There were five of them, gliding smoothly in the shadows. "I see them now," she whispered. "They're beautiful."

"I come here every year, just to see if they made it back one more time."

"I can see why." She smiled tremulously, fighting the urge to lean back against his chest. Her position was precarious, and she fought to maintain her balance without collapsing on him. It was hard on her nerves, as well as her muscles.

Colt started to draw away, then inhaled sharply, and stopped. Frank turned her head slightly and their eyes met. He groaned softly. "Fran... I vowed I wasn't going to touch you." He closed his eyes, savoring her closeness. She could feel the tension in his body. He trembled as he held her and with a quick burst of urgency, he smothered his face in her hair. "I've tried so damned hard not to let you get under my skin." The he clenched his jaw with determination and pushed her gently, but firmly away.

Frank straightened and tugged at her blouse, then ran her hands over her hair, fighting for self-control. Her eyes strayed to the crotch of his jeans. She could see the bulging evidence of his arousal.

Her need had become as physical as his. Every nerve had been stimulated to screaming awareness. Their messages all focused at one point in her body, and the tensions had heightened to an uncomfortable ache that she couldn't ignore.

She knew one feathery touch would be all it would take to make him drop that stubborn barrier. If she reached out and touched him, all the tension could be eased and all the self-inflicted misery ended. It was tempting. But what would the consequences be? She knew it would be one more thing to bind him to her emotionally. Cold showers didn't douse unrequited love the way they did unrelieved sex. Deciding the situation was best left as it was; she determinedly gathered the remains of their lunch and walked toward the horses. They didn't speak when they swung up into their saddles and rode back in the direction they had come.

They spent the rest of the day checking cattle, covering a different area of the range, and it was late when they got back to the trailer. Frank made a quick meal, and after persuading Colt to stay the night and drive back the next morning, she helped to make his bed.

While Colt pried off his cowboy boots, she dodged into the washroom, slipped off her clothes, and put on the cotton nightgown she'd worn that morning. Colt was still fully clothed and stretched out on the hide-a-bed when she stepped out of the tiny room. She yawned sleepily as she edged past his bed and said a weary good night. After sliding the pocket door shut, she drew back her sheets and slipped between them. She was exhausted and within seconds, she was lost in the oblivion of sleep.

Colt wasn't so lucky. Sleep eluded him for what seemed like hours, as he lay listening to the rhythm of her breathing. His active imagination would not let go of the image of her body molded against his. Even though he was exhausted, his body responded uncomfortably.

When Frank awoke the following morning, he was gone. She got up and put on a pot of coffee, then pulled the blankets from his bed, and folded it back up. As she worked, she became increasingly nauseous.

"I hope I get over this pretty soon." She sat on the edge of the bed and tried to regain her composure. Then it deserted her completely. She could no longer ignore the problem. She made a mad dash to the bathroom and was copiously ill.

CHAPTER ELEVEN

"If I didn't know better, I'd think I was pregnant." Once the words were uttered, they seemed to echo in the room, filling her mind with horror. She froze, staring at the reflection of her white face and watering eyes. *I hope I know better.* A sick knot lodged in the pit of her stomach. *No. I can't be.*

Frank denied the possibility, but as she thought back over the past weeks, she was shocked to realize that it was possible. She reached for the calendar that hung on the wall and turned it back to June. *That's over two months ago*, she thought dazedly. "It can't be true!" she cried in despair, slamming the incriminating calendar down on the small counter. "Damn it! How could I have let this happen?"

During the next ten days, her thoughts constantly dwelled on the probability that she was carrying Colt's child. She considered the pros and cons of the situation, and as far as she was concerned, the negative overwhelmed any positive aspects, ten to one.

Each night, she lay in the darkness; her body tense, a tight knot of anguish burning her stomach while tears of uncertainty and frustration coursed down her cheeks. Every morning came with another bout of nausea. With each bout came a renewed sense of despair.

By the tenth day, she realized, with a sense of shock, that she was slipping backward into the same pit of fear and despair that she had been floundering in before she came to the ranch months earlier. But this time, she recognized what was happening and understood the danger. She knew she had to come to grips with the situation.

It would be different if Colt wanted to be with her. But at this time, she wasn't certain that she was strong enough to handle the changes brought on by pregnancy, without emotional support. There had been too many upheavals in her life during the past months. She could only see one alternative, and it filled her with anguish.

A week later, Frank drove to the ranch. Ollie was surprised to see her.

"What do I owe the pleasure of this unexpected visit to?" he asked, his keen eyes taking in the dark shadows under her eyes.

"I want to take a few days off to visit my friend in Calgary. I'll only be gone four days at the most, and I've checked all the cattle this week. Everything is looking good."

"There's no problem with you taking time off, but are you okay? You are looking kind of under the weather."

She smirked. "You sound like my dad. I'm fine."

"I swear you've lost more weight."

"Ollie, give it up. I've had a virus or stomach flu. It's nothing to worry about."

"When do you plan to leave?"

"Today."

"You're getting away kinda' late. That's a pretty long drive."

She smiled. "Yes, Dad. I know how far it is, and I'll be just fine."

"Then get on your way. Check in with me when you come back. Maybe this trip will help you feel better."

He frowned as he watched her red pickup move down the driveway and turn onto the main road. "She can't have the flu this long. Something else is going on."

At the beginning of the week, Frank had driven to Loch Levan and phoned Becky Freemont. She told Becky about her dilemma and made arrangements to stay with her. Becky had given her a doctor's name and phone number, and Frank had made an appointment for the following Tuesday morning. She was thankful she had not canceled her Alberta medical insurance. She would need it now.

She sighed with relief when she arrived in Calgary several hours later. She was tense and tired and a persistent knot was lodged in her chest. When she parked in the Freeman's driveway and got out of the pickup, Becky flew out the door to meet her.

"It's good to see you." Becky threw her arms around her, hugging her close. "You look exhausted. Come in and I'll make something to drink. You can put your feet up and we'll have a nice, long chat."

"That sounds like heaven. I was beginning to feel like I'd never get here." Frank smiled crookedly, biting her lip, to fight back the unhappy tears that threatened to overflow as their eyes met. Becky's face filled with concern, when she saw the stress and unhappiness that Frank was trying to hide. Silently she stood back and reached to clasp her childhood friend's cold hand in her own. The act of compassion broke the dam that Frank had carefully built. A flood of tears coursed down her cheeks, and she covered her face with her free hand as she tried to control her muffled sobs.

Becky enfolded Frank in her arms again. "Cry, Frank. Just let it all out. Then, if you want to, we'll talk about it. I wish I could help, but you are the only one who can decide what is best for you. You also know that I'll be there to support you, no matter what you choose to do."

Frank nodded. "When I first decided to do this I felt relieved, but now I'm torn. I know Colt would do everything he could to stop me if he knew what I am planning to do. His first wife had an abortion and he despises her. He'd undoubtedly choose to marry me if he knew I was pregnant with his child, but I couldn't live with knowing that he did it out of responsibility, rather than love. I'm in love with him, and he's made it clear that he will never allow himself to fall in love again."

She shook her head miserably. Her voice was filled with pain and uncertainty. "Under these circumstances, I honestly don't think I can deal with pregnancy and everything else right now. I feel almost as desperate as I did before I left Stettler and that scares me.

"This is awful." Her voice had risen to an unhappy wail, and she impatiently brushed the torrent of tears from her cheeks. "I thought I'd done all the crying I could do, earlier. But seeing you and knowing I don't have to keep it all to myself any longer is a relief. You'll never know how much I appreciate you." She squeezed Becky's hand and her voice broke, strangled by the intensity of her emotion. "Thank you for always being there for me."

A tear trickled down Becky's cheek. "You know, I'm happy to be there." She squeezed Frank's hand again. "Let's go inside and get you settled in."

"Russ is going to think I only come to see you when I'm in trouble." Frank glanced at Becky apologetically as she sniffed into a Kleenex.

"Don't be silly, there is no need to ever feel that way. As it is, he had to go to Edmonton last night, and I don't expect him back until Thursday night. By then, you'll be much more at ease because you'll know what you're doing.

They spent the evening talking about everything, except Frank's pregnancy. Becky discreetly left it up to her to reintroduce the subject, and Frank chose to avoid the painful topic. As she relaxed, exhaustion overcame her, and she decided to go to bed early.

"Frank...," Becky hesitated. She was uncertain how to approach the subject, but her honesty, combined with the bond of love she shared with her dear friend, made it imperative that she bring it up even though Frank had chosen to avoid it. "I understand how you feel right now, but are you sure that this is the best decision for the long term? Please don't misunderstand me," she pleaded. "I'm not condemning you, but there are so many unknowns. I don't mean the medical and physical aspects; I mean the emotional effects. I want you to be very certain that this is actually the best choice, because once you do it, there is no going back."

Frank closed her eyes. "Becky, this would never be my choice if things were different." The words ended in a strangled cry. "I'm afraid of the consequences, either way."

"Hon, you say Colt doesn't love you, but you think he would marry you if he knew you were pregnant. When a man says he that will never *allow* himself to fall in love, what he's really saying is that he's been hurt and he's trying to protect himself. What if he already has feelings for you and he's doing everything he can to fight them? What if this baby is the tipping point that would make him acknowledge his love for you?"

"Since we were together he has completely shut me out. He's so cold and remote it hurts." Frank began to sob. "If we got married because I was pregnant, I'd never be certain that he loved me and I don't think I could live with that."

"Don't cry, sweetheart. I didn't mean to upset you. You've had such a traumatic year already; you certainly didn't need this on top of everything else. It's just that …" Her voice trailed off. "Well, it's a good thing that you're going to see a doctor. You may need time to think after you talk to him. Don't rush into anything. Everything will work out for the best, in the long run. Have a good sleep."

Frank undressed and slid between the cool cotton sheets. She lay staring into the darkness through tear-washed eyes, thinking about the step she was planning to take the next day. Her fingers brushed the tears from her cheeks as they spilled over in a steady stream. *It's the best choice for me right now*, she thought, trying to shake the feeling of despair that threatened to overwhelm her.

The next morning, she checked in with the receptionist at the doctor's office, giving her the needed medical service number and answering routine questions before she went to sit in the waiting area. She felt exhausted.

She closed her eyes and drifted drowsily. Suddenly the stark reality of what she was contemplating hit her. She became instantly alert, her heart pounding crazily. *What am I doing?"* She started to tremble. *How did I ever think I could go through with this? It's against all my principles. How could I even have considered it? This baby is a part of me. I can't destroy it. It's a part of Colt too, and it may be the only connection I'll ever have with him.* Tears streamed down her cheeks, as she grabbed her purse and ran from the room. The receptionist called to her when she ran out the door, but she ignored the summons. When she was safely in her pickup, she laced her hands together at the top of the steering wheel. She leaned her forehead against them and wept until all the tension and tears were gone. Then she started the vehicle and slowly drove back to Becky's place. When she walked in the door, Becky took one look at her ravaged face and her eyes filled with tears.

"Frank, what happened?"

"I couldn't go through with it. I just couldn't do it," she said numbly. "I didn't see the doctor. I don't know how I'm going to deal with all this, but I realize now, that this wasn't the answer."

Becky crossed the room and hugged Frank when she burst into another storm of tears. Later, after the tears were spent, Becky made them both a cup of tea. "I think you made the wisest choice for you, Frank. Knowing you, I was afraid that ultimately you would find it hard to live with the other option. It won't be easy, but you have a good career. Supporting a child won't be a financial problem. And you'll love it to pieces. I'm sure you'll never regret this decision."

Frank spent the next day visiting with Becky. She left early the following morning and drove back to the ranch. It was suppertime when she arrived and Ollie insisted she stay the night. She was tired and she accepted without protest.

She caught Ollie looking at her curiously.

"What?" she asked.

"What *what*?" he shot back.

"Why are you looking at me that way?"

He sighed. "I'm concerned. You've got that haunted look that you had when you first came here, and I know it ain't normal, 'cause I watched you blossom afterward. So what is goin' on with you? You said you had the flu, but that shouldn't last so long."

She shook her head and gave him a weak smile. "You're acting like my dad again, Ollie."

"Well, if I had a daughter I'd be proud if she was you. Somethin' is not right. Is this somethin' to do with Colt?"

Frank flushed. "Now you really are off base. What could my feeling punky possibly have to do with Colt?"

"I don't know. I've just been wrackin' my brain. It just seems that after he came out here that first time, you haven't been the same. I've been thinkin' that maybe I need to have a talk with him and give him a kick in the arse or something."

Frank burst into genuine laughter. She got up and hugged the older man. "Thank you for caring, but there is no reason to kick Colt's arse. And I'm not a fragile little flower that needs to be pampered. You are looking for something that isn't there. I'm fine."

"Okay. But I'll be happier when I see some meat on your bones and those beautiful eyes sparklin' again."

When she left the next morning, Ollie reminded her about the barbecue at the ranch on the long weekend.

"I'll be here," she assured him.

The following Sunday morning, Frank awoke as the autumn sun filtered through the curtains, bathing the trailer with a golden glow. She luxuriated in the peace of the moment. The trip to Calgary had been exhausting. She was thankful to be back. But the peace lasted for only a moment, before the languorous cloak of sleep evaporated like morning fog, and tension flooded through her once again.

"Well, baby, today your daddy learns about you. I wonder what he'll think of our birthday surprise." She sighed heavily. She showered and applied a light touch of makeup before she slipped into a brown pair of jeans and a matching tank top. Then she brushed her hair until it fell around her shoulders in a shimmering coppery curtain. When she was finished, she tried to imagine what she would look like in six months when her abdomen was distended with Colt's child. She let her hands fall to the flatness of her stomach and roam imaginatively around the bulge she knew would be there. With a sigh, she turned away, wondering again what Colt's reaction would be when she told him.

She drove slowly along the dirt road that led to the Cypress Hills Provincial Park. When she crossed the park boundary, she glanced at her watch and realized that she had an hour to kill before she was supposed to arrive at the ranch. On impulse, she decided to climb Bald Butte. When she reached the top, she looked to the west, over the rolling hills of "The Gap," from which she had just come. On the horizon, she could see the escarpment of the West Block, where her trailer was located. She always marveled at the beauty of the view, but today it was spectacular. The brilliant hues of autumn had stolen over it in the few days she'd been gone. The change had begun gradually before she left, but now it was there in full force—a mosaic of red, oranges, gold, and brown mixed in perfect harmony with the green of the conifers that were blotched at random throughout the hills. She smiled with pleasure, savoring once again the beauty of her favorite season.

She returned to the pickup and drove on to Lookout Point. A breeze lifted her hair gently when she stepped out to look at the panoramic view of the prairies to the north. The varying muted shades of gold and brown, accented by the brilliant splashes of copper and vermillion, blended together to cloak them with a colorful tapestry that contrasted sharply with the green of the coniferous forest that grew abundantly in the moist, northern face of the hills. The azure sky sparkled in the autumn sun.

In the distance, she could see the settlement of Maple Creek, and beyond that, the Great Sand Hills rose on the horizon. She had grown to love this country, with all its unexpected contrasts. It was going to be hard to leave it behind, but she knew it was inevitable that she would before long. A tightness grew in her chest as she stared at the vista before her, and tears misted her eyes when she turned back to the pickup.

The tightness lingered as she drove toward Loch Levan. Several tourists and locals were lounging on the beach or sitting in the picnic area, enjoying the sun. No one was swimming, but she noticed a canoe out on the lake as well as a couple of paddleboats, and a few fishermen were trying their luck. Then she continued on to the ranch.

She thought about Colt while she drove, wondering when she would have the opportunity to talk to him. "How do you tell a man that you're going to have his child?" she whispered. "I hope he doesn't think I'm trying to trap him. Telling him today may be bad timing, but I can't wait much longer."

When she drove up to the ranch house, she turned off the motor, then closed her eyes and leaned back against the seat. Breathing deeply, she willed herself to relax, consciously trying to fight the tension building within. *All of this is getting pretty hard to handle,* she reflected with an unhappy sigh.

She sat up when Ollie came out to greet her. She smiled at him when he appeared at her door. She reached for her sweater and overnight bag and got out to follow him to his truck. He had opened the passenger door for her when she reached his side. "Mornin', girl," he said cheerfully. "How are you this beautiful fall day?"

"Fine. It is a beautiful day, isn't it?" she responded gaily, shrugging aside the feelings of apprehension. They shared easy conversation while they traveled through the rolling countryside that flattened into prairie as they neared Maple Creek. By the time they reached the main highway and turned east toward Swift Current, Frank had buried her tension and anxieties beneath a light-hearted facade that she was convinced would even fool the discerning Ollie.

They traveled for a couple of hours before Ollie turned north onto a gravel road, posted with the sign "Cantuar 12 km." He guided the truck along the smoothly graded road for a short distance, and then turned right. Frank observed with wide-eyed interest, when they traveled on a long driveway which was flanked on either side by a row of maple trees that fluttered their leaves in the afternoon sun.

She could see several rows of large metal grain bins and a long machine shed that protected a complete line of modern farm equipment. There was an assortment of other outbuildings too. Off to the right there stood an older two-story house, complete with veranda. The yard was beautifully landscaped and tended. Everything had a neat and orderly appearance.

Ollie parked the truck, and then turned to look at her with a grin. Pride was reflected in his face. "Pretty impressive, isn't it? I've watched it grow through the years. Bob is a darn good farmer, and Colt has the same basic instincts. I just hope he eventually chooses a wife who will understand his dreams and support him...." His voice trailed off.

Frank had the feeling he wanted to say more but was hesitant to do so. He heaved a heavy sigh and turned to her. "You'll want to see the stables. They've got a great setup."

"I didn't realize how big Thompson Holdings is. Colt has a tremendous responsibility."

"He does. He consults with Bob on a lot of things, but he doesn't want to put him under too much stress, so Colt makes all the major decisions. What he needs is someone who cares about the business and is willing to work with him. That was one of the problems in his marriage to Sharon," he said, looking at Frank. "She was his wife," he explained.

Frank nodded. "He told me about her." Ollie's surprise was obvious, and when he looked at her with an expression she couldn't read, she wished she hadn't said anything. She shifted uneasily and then looked away as she brushed an imaginary hair off her face. "He mentioned it once when we were talking," she said defensively.

"I'm glad. I'm just surprised that he did, because he doesn't talk about her. I'm glad to know that he felt comfortable enough to talk to you. He hasn't done that since the divorce." He frowned as he ran a hand over his beard. "I'd like to see that boy find real happiness. But there I go, talking too much again."

He turned to Frank and smiled affectionately. "Well, girl, you ready to go beard the lion in his den?"

"Wh- What?" she stammered.

"I know you're nervous about this whole thing. I've seen it in your eyes ever since you got back. You don't need to worry. Just relax and enjoy yourself."

"You're too perceptive for my peace of mind, Ollie. But you're right, I am nervous," she said and sighed. "Let's go and get this over with."

People were scattered around the yard. A small group was standing in front of the storage shed, and Frank could see others lounging on the neatly trimmed grass, under the trees that had been planted years before, as a windbreak between the house and the machine area. Another group was gathered around the barbecue pit.

"Bob's over there," Ollie said, motioning toward the smoking pit. "Let's say hello to him."

Bob gave them a hearty welcome, and then introduced Frank to a group of women who were close to her age. The majority of them were wives of neighboring farmers and ranchers and the mothers of small children. Her attention wandered as she let her eyes flick through the growing crowd in search of Colt. He was nowhere to be seen. She tried to push away a rising sense of apprehension as she turned her attention back to the group she was with. It bounded out of proportion when she caught their last words of conversation.

"Shauna Lee said they are engaged, but she wasn't flashing a ring. Still, they've been seeing each other for years. You never know."

"She's nice enough," someone else added. "But she certainly has no interest in farming or ranching and that's Colt's life. He loves kids, but she's made it clear that she doesn't want a family. Personally, I think he's making a mistake."

"Give the woman a break," someone else defended her. "She's had a rough go of it. I've heard that her dad took off when she was almost thirteen. It practically ruined her mother, and if you ask me, Shauna Lee was starved for love and attention. Rumor has it that she got married or lived with some guy when she was really young. I don't know what happened there, but he didn't stick around." The woman shook her head. "It was sheer determination that got her into business and made her as successful as she is today. Her attitude isn't too surprising. Everyone who has ever been close to her has let her down. She's probably afraid to get really involved with anyone for fear it will happen again."

Frank's nerves screamed. She reached blindly toward a toddler that was standing in front of her, seeking anything to focus her attention on until she could get her staggering senses under control. The little girl grasped her hand, and Frank drew her towards her. The child jabbered in a form of baby talk. Frank didn't even try to decipher it while her mind swirled dizzily around the words she had just heard.

She didn't have a ring. She clung to the thought desperately. Blinking back tears, she buried her face against the child's tummy, bringing a laughing response from her as her little hands reached for Frank's hair.

Frank smiled widely as she disengaged them. She glanced beyond the child and her heart lurched. She looked across the crowd and directly into Colt's eyes. The expression on his face was soft, but it held a hint of sadness. Frank smiled hesitatingly and he smiled briefly in answer and then turned to the petite blonde who was at his side. She was, probably, Shauna Lee Holt.

Trembling overtook Frank. She stood up unsteadily and directed the child to its mother. Turning away from the crowd, she walked blindly in the direction Ollie had indicated the stables were. A tight, cold lump formed where her heart used to be, its iciness spreading downward into her stomach as she fought a nauseating feeling of despair and anxiety. She shivered in spite of the warmth of the sun.

"I have to stop this," she told herself. "No matter what happens, one thing I can keep is my pride. No one will ever know how I feel. If he really is engaged to her, I won't tell him about the baby."

Frank dashed the back of her hand angrily across her face as if to dispel the tears that threatened to spill over. Ahead, she could see the stables and the horse runs. She walked toward them purposefully, gathering her shattered emotions into a tight ball, as she went. When she entered the stable, she pushed away every other thought and concentrated on the horses. She wandered past the stalls and went out to watch the animals in the runs. It wasn't until she heard footsteps behind her that she realized she'd been there for some time. Heart in her throat, she wheeled, afraid, yet hopeful that it might be Colt. She sighed when she saw Ollie standing there.

"I thought I might find you here. You were gone so long, I figured I should check on you. Are you alright?"

"Ollie, what's with you?" she protested. "I swear you're starting to fuss even more than my dad would. What would be wrong with me? I wanted to see the horses. You know me, I forgot about the time."

"They're gettin' ready to eat, so we should be headin' back." Ollie shuffled nervously as he ran a hand through his hair and down across his beard. He turned slowly to face her. "Rumor has it that Colt and Shauna Lee Holt are engaged," he said abruptly. She could see the concern in his eyes as he watched her for her reaction.

She turned and started to walk back toward the crowd. "I heard something like that earlier," she said, thankful for the calmness in her voice.

"She isn't wearin' a ring. Maybe it's just speculation."

"Maybe, but Colt did tell me that if he ever got married, it would be to her. Possibly, he has decided it's the right time to make that move." The cold numbness was creeping back into her body. She prayed that Ollie wouldn't see the inner misery she was fighting.

He stopped abruptly. "He told you that? The crazy fool, he doesn't love her. I don't understand him when it comes to women."

"Ollie, he's a grown man. There isn't anything you can do about it if he has gotten engaged to her. In fact, it isn't anyone else's business."

Ollie shoved his hands into his pockets. "Damn it! I know you're right. I just hate to see him make another mistake like that."

The food was excellent; spirits, wine, and beer were plentiful. When darkness fell, everyone was in a party mood. A boisterous crowd danced to live music on the cement floor of the shop, which had been vacated and prepared for the evening entertainment. Frank was swept into the flow and found herself constantly dancing.

She was catching her breath after doing a dizzying version of the polka, when the spokesman for the band announced that he had a special request. "You all know Ollie Crampton, from Thompson's ranch down south in the hills. Well, tonight he has a special request. He wants the best ranch hand he has ever worked with to come up here and sing his favorite song. Frank Lamonte," he called out. "Would you come up here? By the way folks, Ollie says that Frank is the prettiest little *girl* you ever laid eyes on. Let's give her a hand."

Ollie, how could you do this to me, she agonized, looking around, desperately seeking an escape.

"You wouldn't let Ollie down, would you?" She inhaled sharply. The words were spoken gently from just behind her shoulder. Her pulse quickened at the touch of Colt's fingers as they closed around her elbow. He steered her toward the raised platform, and she went unresistingly, moving in a daze. She took the hand extended by the announcer when he reached to help her step up. He threw a few teasing remarks her way, and Frank found herself answering with a light banter that she couldn't recall later. When he handed her his guitar, she drew up a tall stool that stood nearby and sat on it. She sought Ollie out with her eyes and dedicated the song to him, adding teasingly, "I promise I will get you for this, Boss."

The audience listened in silence as she sang an old love song that most had all but forgotten, and many had never heard before. A loud round of applause followed, and when she was about to put down the guitar, the crowd called for an encore. She strummed a few bars and then softly began to sing a song that had been popular several years earlier. Her clear, sweet voice carried on the evening air, ringing with a poignant note that she was unaware of. The lyrics told a story of unsought desire, of trying not to love but being unable to resist. They pleaded that the two people involved belonged together, sharing life and keeping each other satisfied.

Colt's eyes drew her like a magnet. The rest of the crowd vanished, and they became the only two people in the building. She sang to him, the words a cry that expressed the feelings of her own heart. She had come to know him and she had learned to love him. What would she do if she couldn't share her life with him?

He stared back, motionless, except for the muscle that twitched in his jaw and the pulse that jumped in the hollow of his throat. He shifted uneasily as she finished the song, then turned and quickly threaded his way through the crowd and out of the building.

CHAPTER TWELVE

It was some time before Colt returned. Frank watched Shauna Lee join him, noticing the flash of impatience that crossed his features before his expression softened, and he slipped his arm around her shoulder.

Frank's pain seemed physical as if a dull knife had been plunged into her chest, twisting, turning and tearing. *Lamonte, get a hold of yourself,* she chided herself. *Don't let this awful dying feeling show.*

At midnight, Colt and Shauna Lee moved toward the band platform. When the music stopped, Colt took the microphone, thanked everyone for coming, and reminded them that there was still plenty of food. He drew Shauna Lee to his side. "I have a very special announcement to make. Shauna Lee and I have decided to get married early next year. The ring had to be sized, so she isn't wearing it yet, but we wanted to share the news with you tonight."

Frank stared at them. A vice-like pain squeezed her heart, radiating out until it washed over her whole body, leaving a sense of numb detachment in its wake.

The air was filled with whistles and applause as the band swung into a waltz. Colt and Shauna Lee led the dance and gradually other couples joined them. Frank allowed herself to be drawn onto the floor. She moved mechanically, her mind an empty void as she stared past her partner's shoulder. She comprehended little; until her eyes met Colt's when they passed on the dance floor. The contact was electrical, jolting her back to life. The sanctuary of numbness vanished, but the pain remained.

Frank turned abruptly and fled to the exit. She pressed her hand over her mouth when she stepped out into the darkness and felt her way along the side of the building. When she reached the end of it, she sagged against the wall and wrapped her arms around herself. Her breath came in deep, ragged sobs as she struggled to maintain the little composure she still had, grateful that she'd told him nothing about the baby. She rocked back and forth, hugging herself in an effort to soothe the pain. Gradually, the sobs subsided, and she gathered her self-control and sat quietly in the darkness.

She had no idea how long she'd been there when the side door swung open and people began to drift outside. She pushed herself away from the wall. Ollie would be looking for her, and she couldn't let him find her there. He read her too well. Crossing over a short expanse of grass to the road, she turned back toward the crowd. When she moved into the light, he appeared at her side.

"Time we hit the road, don't you think?"

Frank looked at him with blank astonishment. "I thought you were going to spend the night here?"

"Naw. I'd just as soon go home tonight unless you want to stay."

Relief flooded through her. "No... No, that's fine with me. I'm ready anytime you are, but we should say goodbye to Bob and Serena first. And congratulations are in order for Colt and Shauna Lee too."

"They're goin' to be so busy they won't even notice if we skip that formality." Frank followed him as he threaded his way through the crowd, shaking hands and saying goodbye as he looked for the older Thompsons. She spotted them first. "Ollie, they're over there with Colt and Shauna Lee."

Ollie hesitated, and then turned to her. "Heck, there's a real mob of folks around there talkin' to them. Maybe we should just forget about it, tonight. We can thank them the next time we see them. They'll understand."

"I'd rather do it now."

Ollie observed her pale face closely, then mumbling words she couldn't hear, turned, and led the way through the crowd.

Bob took her hands in his and she thanked him for a pleasant evening. "The pleasure was all ours. But what's this about you leaving for home tonight?" He frowned as he turned to Ollie. "You know, we always have a room in the house for you. There's a bed for Frank too," he said, drawing her into the circle of his arm.

"Not this time, Bob. With the announcement of the engagement, this party will go on until dawn. I have to be back in the morning anyway."

"Well, it's up to you, but I think its insanity. Frank looks like she's ready to drop. Have you been sick?" His hand slid down to her ribs, probing them gently. "You're skin and bones!"

Frank squirmed away from his touch, laughing lightly. "You're imagining things, Bob. I agree with Ollie. I'd just as soon go home now."

"What's this about you going home tonight?" The hair on the back of her neck prickled, as Colt's voice interrupted. She raised darkly shadowed eyes to his face, and her lips parted as she started to speak, when Ollie quickly interceded.

"We were just goin' to offer our congratulations, and then we're goin' to be on our way."

"What's your big hurry? You always spend the night, Ollie. Driving all the way back to the ranch at this hour doesn't make any sense."

Colt observed Frank with concern. "You look exhausted."

Ollie looked at her, noting the strained expression around her eyes. "Frank can curl up in the truck and get some shut eye. I'll do the drivin'."

"He's right." She extended her hand to Colt. "Congratulations. I hope you'll be very happy." Her attention shifted to the woman standing silently at his side. In that brief moment, as she smiled at her and offered her best wishes, a multitude of thoughts and impressions raced through her mind. Part of her disliked this woman. Because of her, Frank had to accept the fact that she would never have a meaningful relationship with Colt. The child she was carrying would never know its father. But another part of her reached out in compassion. It seemed that circumstances had brought an overwhelming amount of pain into the other woman's life already. She sincerely hoped that marriage to Colt would bring some happiness, even though he'd sworn that they weren't in love.

She struggled to keep the cold sense of emptiness that was creeping around the edges of her consciousness at bay. She knew she didn't dare give way to the emotions that were storming within her. There would be time enough for that later, when she was alone. Until then, she would have to be strong.

She stayed at the ranch that night and left for the lease early the next morning. Ollie protested when she declined having breakfast.

"You have to eat, girl! You are way too thin."

She had brushed his concern aside and insisted on leaving. It was noon when she arrived at the trailer. She went to the corral to feed her horses, and then went inside. Her head felt fuzzy and she was tired, so she decided to lie down and have a nap. Although she was exhausted, sleep did not come immediately. She lay contemplating the drained, lethargic feeling that clung to her, realizing that it was the result of emotional stress. Scenes from the previous night flashed across her mind, and she squeezed her eyes tightly against the tears that trickled down her cheeks. She had to accept it now. Colt would never be a part of her life.

"Damn!" She dashed the dampness from her cheeks as she sat up and swung her legs over the edge of the bed. There was determination in her voice when she addressed the four walls that surrounded her. "We don't need Colt Thompson. We can make it on our own. Baby, I promise you, we are going to be fine."

We! The word reverberated in her mind. Suddenly she realized that she wasn't alone anymore. She ran her hand over her tummy. She already had someone to love, someone who needed her and would love her in return. Why had it taken so long for her to see that?

Like a ray of sunshine creeping into a darkened prison cell, a new sense of purpose stirred inside her. The dark cloud lifted and a brightness that rivaled the sun flooded her with warmth. Her life took on a sense of meaning that had been missing for months, and suddenly she felt as light as air. Tears filled her eyes. They were tears of joy and expectation.

She pulled on a pair of jeans and a comfortable sweater, then took a banana from the bowl on the counter, and went outside. She stood for a few minutes, soaking up the warmth of the afternoon sun, marveling at the new expectancy that colored her thoughts.

Her horse whinnied from the corral, and at that moment, she decided to saddle up. For the first time in weeks, the ride was not an exercise for therapy. Her excitement was high. Her mind danced with plans and ideas and dreams that centered on the baby.

When the sun began to settle in the western sky, she directed her mount along the path across the grazing land to intersect the main road. When they reached that point, she turned the horse in the direction of the trailer and let it move at a leisurely pace.

They had traveled for several minutes before she detected the surging sound of a motor in the distance. It grew louder, and within seconds, the peace of the afternoon shattered as two motorcycles crested the hill in front of her. Wincing at the intrusion, Frank reined her horse to the side of the road and let them roar by. She had already reined the horse back onto the road when she realized that they were coming back.

"Just like little boys out spinning their wheels," she muttered with disgust. She pulled her horse over to let them pass once again and was startled when they pulled up beside her and stopped.

"Well, well," drawled the larger and grubbier one of the pair. "You look kind of lonesome riding out here by yourself. Are you lost? Or maybe you're just looking for some company?"

"You're wrong on all counts," she said stiffly. "I work out here. I'm neither lost nor lonely, and I'm not looking for company."

"Well, we are." He stared as his eyes roamed suggestively over her body. "And, you look like good company. It might be fun to get to know you better."

"Yeah," his partner snickered. "You live in that traveling pad back up the road?"

A desperate need for self-preservation and a determined measure of self-control came to the rescue, giving her the inner strength to hide the fear that flooded through her. She assumed a haughty look that was pure bravado. "As a matter of fact, I do . . . with my husband."

"Oh? We kinda figured you'd been living there alone."

"I have been most of the time, but Colt's coming out tonight and he'll be staying until we get the cattle rounded up," she lied. "In fact, he's probably waiting there for me now. He'll be wondering where I am."

"Wasn't anybody there when we came by."

"Well, I'm expecting him for supper, so he won't be long." With that, she dug her heels into her mount and urged him to a gallop, shuddering at the lecherous laughter that followed her.

"We'll check on you again."

A sick feeling of fear followed her home and stayed with her all evening. She knew the majority of bikers were decent, hardworking people, but some of them were known to be crude and ruthless, and the behavior of those two told her they fit in the latter category. She feared she would be at their mercy if they decided to harass her. She shuddered, remembering the bigger man's filth, his scraggly beard, his stained dirty teeth, and nausea threatened, as she recalled the lecherous way he looked at her.

She locked the door carefully and checked each window before she went to bed. But sleep eluded her until the early hours of the morning. Several times she drifted into a light slumber, only to start awake, heart pounding, listening for the dreaded sound of a motorcycle.

She was up earlier than usual, in spite of the lateness of the hour when she had finally fallen asleep. She was dressed, in the saddle, and on the trail within minutes. The sense of uneasiness that hung over her did not leave until she was out of sight of the trailer.

By noon, she was exhausted. She wrapped her arms around her knees and sat on a grassy knoll, watching her horse while it grazed a few feet away from her. "This is crazy," she whispered, "and it's not good for the baby. My nerves are stretched to the limit, and I'm so tired. I could go to sleep right here." She sighed wearily. "This biker thing is unnerving," she admitted. "But what can I actually do? They haven't done anything, other than make a few suggestive remarks. They probably did it out of a perverted sense of humor."

It was getting dark when she rode up to the trailer that evening. She stopped on the trail, cautiously checking to see if she had unwelcome visitors, before riding into the clearing. After taking care of her horses' needs, she went inside and carefully locked the door behind her.

She took a quick shower, then slipped into a cotton nightgown, and blew her hair dry. After that, she made a light meal and ate it in silence. Normally, she would've turned the radio on, but she didn't now because of the nagging fear that she wouldn't be able to hear if anyone drove up.

It wasn't until she was washing dishes that she decided she was letting fear rule her life and it had to stop. She refused to be intimidated. If it came down to the worst scenario, she had the gun Colt had left her to use for predators. She could threaten them with it.

With deliberation, she turned on the radio and got into bed. Within moments, she dropped into an exhausted sleep, only to be jolted awake half an hour later by the sound of someone pounding on the door. She laid rigid, heart hammering against her ribs, and fear suffocating her. The pounding persisted, and she grew deathly cold. A sickening knot grew in her stomach, and she began to shake.

"Fran! Open the door. It's me-- Colt." Relief flooded through her with dizzying suddenness. He rattled the doorknob, and she heard him grumbling. "Why doesn't she answer? The horses are in the corral and her pickup's here. She has to be in there."

She rolled out of bed and stumbled to the door. Trembling fingers fumbled as she hurried to undo the lock. Colt's face was lined with concern when he flung it open. His eyes searched her face, taking in the startling whiteness. He noticed that her lips trembled when she spoke his name, and he could see her body shaking. She stepped back to let him in and reached out to steady herself on the counter.

"Fran, what's wrong? Are you sick? You're shaking and you're as pale as a ghost. You've gotten so damned thin. You look like a gust of wind could blow you away. What's going on?"

"N-nothing," she stammered. "I fell asleep, and I didn't hear you drive up. I wasn't expecting you, and I...you startled me."

He looked at her keenly, his eyes searching her face, and then moving down over her shoulders, stopping on the thinness of her arms, and then slipping lower to the soft roundness of her breasts.

Frank hugged her arms around herself protectively, shielding her body from his gaze. "What are you doing here?" she asked, moving to the bathroom door to take her old terry cloth robe from the hook on the inside. She turned her back to him as she shrugged her arms into it and wrapped it around her.

Colt didn't answer. He was trying to subdue the tumult of the emotions that seeing her had unleashed. Those moments of anxiety for her well-being had snapped his rigid self-control. Now he was overwhelmed by a desire to take her in his arms, to feel the warmth and softness that he knew he would find and taste the sweetness and the passion he knew he could bring to her lips. His longing became an agony, and when she turned to look at him, she saw it mirrored in his eyes.

They stared at each other for a long, breathless second. Then in an effort to break the electrical tension that gripped them, Frank turned away and made a pot of coffee. "What brings you here at this time of the night?" she asked again.

Colt sank down on the upholstered bench behind the table. *Why had he come?* He had told himself that he wanted to see how the cattle were doing, but that was only an excuse. He winced. He was a fool. He had thought that being engaged to Shauna Lee would give him immunity, but he was no safer now than before. It wasn't Fran that he had to be afraid of—it was him. And here he was, tormenting himself again.

"Colt," her voice, sharp with concern now, pierced his thoughts. "Is something wrong? I asked you twice why you were here, and you haven't answered me."

He shook his head as if to clear it. "Sorry, I guess I'm tired. We had a heavy rain and we won't be able to harvest for a couple of days, so I decided to drive out and see how the grass is holding up. It's time to consider when we'll move the cattle back to the ranch."

"I saw most of them today. Everything is okay. Are you planning to stay overnight and ride with me tomorrow?"

"Would you find it inconvenient if I did?" He sensed her tension.

She turned and looked at him. "Of course not; you've slept on the hide-a-bed before. And the cattle are yours. You should know how they're doing." She took a cup from the cupboard, filled it with coffee, and set it on the table in front of him. She picked up a magazine that she'd been looking at earlier and sat down at the end of the table. Nervously, she thumbed through it, feigning an interest she didn't have while she tried to hide her awareness of him.

Colt watched out of the corner of his eye as he sipped his coffee. A grim smile ghosted across his lips. He was getting the message loud and clear. She wanted him to keep his distance. Not that he didn't intend to, he assured himself silently. He owed Shauna Lee loyalty in his actions, even if he couldn't give it in his heart. Besides, he knew that he'd be in trouble if he didn't keep a lid on the attraction he had for Fran. He got up and took his cup to the sink. Frank watched silently as he washed it and put it away. When he finished, he turned toward her and their eyes met. She could see the pulse beat at his throat and noticed the twitch in his jaw.

Damn him, she thought angrily. *Why did he come here? He is engaged to Shauna Lee. What does he expect from me? Why doesn't he stay away now like he did for most of the summer?* She tossed the magazine on the counter and stood up. "I'll make up your bed now. Then we should go to sleep. You seem tired, and I know I certainly am."

Wordlessly, Colt took the cushions off the hide-a-bed and rolled out the mattress. Frank took bedding and an extra pillow from one of the closets and they worked quickly to make the bed. When they were finished, she checked the door to be sure it was locked, and slipped past him, and went to her own bedroom. "Morning comes early," she said, her hand ready to close the sliding door between them.

"Good night, Fran," he said softly. "Sorry, I woke you up. Sleep in, and I'll make breakfast in the morning."

Just what I need; she turned away, avoiding his eyes. "Not for me, Colt. I never eat breakfast anymore."

"But you should. You're far too thin."

"Don't you know that thin is in?" she responded with irritation. "Anyway, no thanks: I don't want breakfast. Good night now. I'll see you in the morning." After she had shrugged off her robe, she reached up to shut off the light, then slipped between the sheets.

She could hear Colt's muffled movements in the tiny bathroom. When he came out and took off his shirt, the soft pop of each snap button was as erotic as a feathery kiss. Her vivid imagination brought to mind an image of his broad chest with the mat of dark curls that nestled on it.

Seconds later he unzipped his jeans, and the normally imperceptible sound of the metal zipper produced a soft staccato in the pregnant silence. It seemed to ripple down each vertebra of her spine, sending out a radiating shower of goose bumps as it went. In her mind, she could see him lower his jeans over the firm length of his legs, and then, with imagination so realistic that she could feel the heat of him, she saw the throbbing bulge of his manhood straining against his shorts.

Her resolve to remain indifferent fled. She could no longer ignore the need that burgeoned inside her. It was a hunger that only Colt had been able to completely satisfy. Desperate, she reached over and turned the radio on, hoping the soft music would cover the familiar sounds of his movements. She knew when he lowered himself onto his bed and pulled the covers over his long, lean length. She remembered vividly the feel of his body as it had moved against hers.

She turned her back to the sliding door and pulled the sheet around her face. Drawing her body into a fetal position, she hugged herself closely, seeking the warmth she craved, warmth that had nothing to do with blankets. She ached with the tight longing that lingered in her loins, and sleep was a long time coming.

Colt was awake with the dawn. He listened to the even rhythm of Fran's breathing for a few minutes, and then decided to get up without waking her. She looked so pale and tired every time he saw her lately. He had disturbed her sleep when he came last night and it would be a shame to awaken her so early.

Besides, he had a feeling this day could prove to be a long one. He had underestimated how difficult it would be to stifle his desire for her. The longer she slept, the less time he would spend being tormented by the arousal created by proximity. He let himself out the door and walked to the corral, where she kept the saddle horses. Automatically, he doled out a measure of feed for them, then after a brief hesitation, saddled up the bigger gelding and set out for a short ride.

Frank awoke at the usual time. She listened for the sound of Colt's breathing, and then finally peeked around the corner to see if he was there. Finding his bed empty, she drew back the sliding door and got up. As she slipped on her old terrycloth robe, she went to the door and looked out to see if he was anywhere in sight. When she didn't see him, she decided to dress and get ready for the day.

She was making their lunches when he opened the door. The first thing his eyes lighted on was her slender figure. She was wearing a soft blue plaid shirt and a pair of jeans that were looser than any he had ever seen her wear before. Her hair had been brushed and neatly braided, and the same light scent she always wore wafted in the air.

She turned to greet him with a smile. "Aren't you an early bird? Have you been riding already?"

"It was just a warm-up exercise. Do you have any idea how long it's been since I've spent a day in the saddle? I'll probably be as stiff as an old man by tonight," he said with laughter in his voice.

Chuckling, she asked him what he wanted for breakfast.

He frowned. "I told you I'd make breakfast."

"I don't want you stumbling around in my kitchen. So, what will it be? Bacon and eggs?" A few minutes later, when she handed him his plate, the usual nauseous reaction to the smell of cooking food had assailed her, and she was struggling to control it.

Colt noticed that her face paled considerably, and she seemed distant. "Fran, you don't look well; you haven't for weeks. Why don't I take you to a doctor today? We don't have to ride."

"No!"

"Something is wrong, no matter what you say. You've lost too much weight, and I'm sure you know it. I don't believe you're on a diet."

"Colt, will you lay off? You and Ollie are like a pair of old bantam hens with one lone chick. I'm all right. There's nothing to be concerned about. And I don't want to hear any more about it. I'll admit I've lost a bit of weight. But I had the flu for a few days. I'm sorry you don't like skinny women, but half the female population starve to look like I do."

Colt looked at her with a mixture of exasperation and concern, but he refrained from commenting further.

CHAPTER THIRTEEN

The day proved to be less tense than either of them had dared to hope. Once in the saddle and on the trail, they chatted amicably, and before either of them realized it, it was late afternoon. They headed back to the trailer, and Frank persuaded Colt to have a light meal before he left.

The bikers were on her mind while she washed dishes. Maybe she should have told Colt about them. She had started to several times during the day, but each time she had held back. They hadn't bothered her again. The whole thing was probably just an idle threat. Short of staying here with her, what could he do about them?

Later, she showered and washed her hair. It wasn't until she turned off the blow dryer that she heard the drone of motorcycle engines as they drew nearer in the darkness. Her first reaction was panic. Then she galvanized into action, dropping the dryer and running to the door to ensure that it was locked. Frantic, she dashed to the counter and hit the kill switch for the generator. The lights in the trailer extinguished seconds before the headlights of the bikes swept across the windows when they sped into the clearing.

Heart pounding, she felt her way to the closet where she'd put the gun. "Where is it?" she whispered fearfully as she groped in the dark. *God, please don't let me knock anything over*, she prayed. Her hand touched the cold smoothness of the barrel. She held her breath as she carefully eased it out of the small space.

She tensed, her breath bated and body rigid. An icy chill ran down her spine. Someone was turning the doorknob. *Please go away and leave me alone.* The thought was a silent, desperate cry.

"C'mon, mama, let us in," a coarse voice yelled and someone began pounding on the door. "We checked on you earlier today. Your old man's truck was here then, but we met him going out a few minutes ago, so we decided to stop in."

Frank felt sick as she listened to the speaker's suggestive laughter. "Why don't you open the door so we don't have to tear this tin can apart? We know you're in there. We saw the lights go out."

She stood, riveted to the spot, scarcely breathing. After they tried the doorknob again, they began to move along the side of the trailer, pounding and rocking it. She searched the top shelf frantically. Where were the shells? She groped again in the darkness and let out a long breath when her fingers touched the box in the far corner.

Found them! Now, I have to get this open. She tried to make her trembling fingers work. After what seemed to be an eternity, the box opened. *Come on*, she pleaded silently as she worked to coax a shell out of the box. Once she succeeded, it was an equally difficult task to get it into the chamber of the gun. The pressure mounted as her tormentors returned to the door.

She shivered. "I hate guns," she whimpered as tears of fear slipped down her cheeks. "I'm such a fool. Why didn't I tell Colt?"

Something smashed against the big window at the front end, and she heard glass break. She swung around and raised the gun in that direction, waiting, sick fear filling her.

Suddenly, the sounds outside changed. She heard muffled curses and the sound of running feet. The glare of the headlights swept across the front of the trailer, and the air was filled with the screech of brakes and the sound of tires sliding to a halt.

"What the hell's going on here?" a familiar voice bellowed, followed immediately by the noises of a scuffle and the thud of flesh against flesh. "Get the hell out of here before I change my mind and beat you to a pulp," Colt roared. "You filthy bastards, if you've touched her I'll hunt you down and kill you."

Faint with relief, Frank sagged against the wall, drained and weak. In the darkness, she could hear the bikers struggling to start their bikes. Then they roared off into the night, and Colt was outside the door, calling her name. She laid the gun down on the table and unlocked it with trembling fingers. It swung open, and she stood there facing him, her face white and her eyes swimming in tears.

"Are you alright?" he cried hoarsely. Then she was in his arms. Violent sobs shook her body as she clung to him. He crushed her against him, enveloping her in his strong embrace. His fingers tangled in her hair as he caressed her, murmuring soothing sounds. When she finally stopped sobbing, he bent his head and claimed her mouth. He came up for a breath seconds later and stared into her eyes. "They didn't hurt you, did they?"

She shook her head.

"I shudder to think of what they would have done if I hadn't come back. Have they bothered you before?"

"I met them on the road when I was riding home Monday night. They made a few suggestive remarks and I brushed them off, but I was worried that they might come here."

"That's why you were so spooked last night."

"I fell asleep, and I didn't hear you drive up. I was afraid it was them." She buried her face against his chest again. "What brought you back tonight? I was certain that I was on my own and I was terrified."

"You should've told me, Fran. Why didn't you?"

Tears filled her eyes. "I-It was a good chance they were making idle threats," she stammered. "I felt sort of silly about being paranoid. Besides, what could you have done?"

"I would've never left you here by yourself." His arms tightened around her.

"Why did you come back?" she asked again, drawing back and easing out of his embrace.

"I left my wallet here. It's on the counter. I was almost at Loch Levan when I realized I didn't have it. Everything's in it: my driver's license, SIN card, credit cards, so I decided to come back. Thank God, I did. I can't leave you here by yourself now. I'll spend the night and decide what to do in the morning."

"Thank you," she said softly. "I doubt they'll come back, but I don't want to take a chance. Let's turn the lights on."

"I'll do it." He moved to the switch and flipped the toggle. The electric starter activated the generator and light flooded the trailer.

"That's better. You look like you could use a good stiff drink. Have you got some whiskey here?"

"I think there's some in the cupboard."

His eyes rested on her slender form and she flushed when she realized how little she had on. She moved to the bathroom door and slid it open get her terrycloth robe off the hook inside. Colt watched while she put it on, then turned to the cupboard and took out the bottle.

"Would you rather have a hot drink?" he asked.

She grimaced. "I'd rather have a cup of tea."

"You look like you could use something stronger than that."

"No. I don't want anything else."

"Alright. But, you sit there and I'll make it."

She sank down on the cushion seat by the table and watched him. When he brought the steaming mug and sat in front of her, their eyes met and held for a breathless moment. Unconsciously, she slid the tip of her tongue along her top lip. Colt swallowed hard, then turned away abruptly, and poured himself a stiff drink. He belted it down before he looked at her again.

"You're tired. Finish that, and I'll tuck you into bed." He watched as drained her cup and then he put down his glass and moved to her side. He gently took her arm, helped her to her feet and guided her to the bed. Solemnly, he untied the belt of her robe and helped her take it off. Then he cupped her face in his hand and bent to cover her lips with a gentle kiss. "Sleep well, sweetheart," he whispered as he helped her to bed and drew the covers over her.

Sweetheart. The sweetness of the word lingered with her and a soft smile curved her lips when she fell asleep moments later.

Colt left the sliding door open. After he made his bed, he took off his shirt and poured himself another strong one. He sat on the edge of the mattress and drank it while he looked through the open door at her sleeping form. *If they had hurt her....* His heart twisted. He set his glass on the counter, turned out the lights, then took off his jeans and socks and slid between the sheets. Sleep eluded him for what seemed hours. He had slipped into a light slumber when Frank's terrified cries woke him. He shot into a sitting position, straining in the darkness to see what she was doing.

"No, no! Oh God, no! " She was sobbing. "Colt! Colt, help me," she cried frantically. She bolted upright in the bed, wild-eyed and disoriented, shaking violently.

He was at her side in an instant. "Fran, it's okay," he said quietly, as he slipped his arm around her shoulder. "It was just a bad dream. I promise I won't let anyone hurt you. Just lie down and go back to sleep."

"N-no... I can't... I don't want to."

"You need to rest." He hesitated, knowing he shouldn't do what he wanted to, but reasoned that she was afraid and it would sooth her. He told himself that he would just comfort her. He had no intentions of letting things get out of control, but he needed to hold her. He spoke softly. "I'll lie down beside you. You'll be safe. Okay?"

She hesitated, then nodded, and lay back on the bed. Colt slipped in beside her. She turned on her side, snuggling her back into his chest. He curled his arm around her waist and fitted her body to his.

As he lay there, he savored the feel of her softness and unbidden memories came flooding back. He remembered with clarity the hours they had shared at the ranch and the passion with which she had responded. He struggled to stifle his response, but the temptation was strong, and he was only human. His hands slid up to her breasts and caressed them gently. She had lost so much weight, but they seemed fuller than he remembered, he noted absently.

The thought was lost, when he felt her instinctive response. She pushed into him and he drew his breath in sharply. He let his hand slip to her hips and pull her tightly against his body. His hand eased to the hem of her short gown, and then, after pulling it up to her waist, moved down over the softness of her warm skin until his fingers slid along the lacy edge of her bikini panties and rested in the warm, moistness hidden there. When his finger slipped the bikini over her hips and down her legs, she didn't resist him. Instead, she moved to help him.

Frank floated in a state of drowsy limbo. She could feel the hardness of Colt's arousal, and she waited with expectation while he slipped out of his shorts. She pushed her body against his, as his hand slid down over her stomach and came to rest where his fingers could gently caress the soft triangle of curly hair that guarded her secret place. He probed gently, touching her sensitive spots.

Desire surged within her, becoming an ache, and she gasped with pleasure as she felt him seeking entrance to her soft warmth. She pushed against him, inviting him in. He dropped soft kisses at the back of her neck and then moved his lips to the lobe of her ear, nibbling softly. She drew her knees up to make it easier for him and his hips lunged forward, plunging into the welcoming opening, burying himself inside her. He made a raspy sound of ecstasy, and then with each strong, seeking stroke that followed, uttered primitive sounds of pleasure. Suddenly he tensed, holding his breath. "I'm sorry sweetheart!" It was a sharp cry of distress, made as he lunged again. He groaned, sagging against her. "I cheated you, but I lost it. I couldn't hold back any longer,"

"It's all right," she whispered, clasping his hand with hers. They lay; her back snuggled against his chest, legs entwined, for what seemed an endless length of time. Eventually, he stirred and nuzzled behind her ear, dropping soft little kisses downward along her neck to her shoulder. "I'll go get something to clean up with," he whispered.

In seconds, he was back with a towel. He stood by the bed, looking at her in the moonlight that filtered into the trailer. She gazed at him through lids that were heavy with contentment. Shyly, she relaxed her muscles, letting him touch her gently, lovingly. She watched him through half-closed lids, feeling her desire spiral again. She gasped when he leaned forward and dropped his lips to the musky inviting spot. She writhed as he explored her intimately, and a hoarse cry escaped her lips as she strained to escape an ecstasy too intense to be borne.

Her hands reached for his head, twining her fingers in his dark hair. "Please, Colt...," she whispered as she slipped into a world of sensation, losing touch with everything but the waves of desire that washed over her, building, building, until she ached for an explosion of release.

Colt raised his head, trailing his burning lips up across her stomach to her swollen straining breast, pushing up the softness of her gown as he went. He swirled his tongue around the darkened tips, sucking, teasing. Frank wrapped her arms around him, straining her smoldering, demanding body against his.

He was ready again, and he shifted his body on top of hers. She spread her legs, fitting his hips between them. "Please, now...."

"I want to make it perfect for you." Slowly he lowered himself to her, filling her exquisitely. He guided her surely, increasing tempo until his hard muscled body was pounding into her welcoming softness again and again. She cried his name as ripples of sensation surged through her. Violent spasms overtook her, and she clung to him desperately, small incoherent sounds escaping her lips. Colt followed her lead within a heartbeat, and with a rough exclamation, plunged over the precipice of desire into the blissful warm well of satiety.

For a time, they lay entwined in a languid oblivion, savoring the sweetness of their shared release. Then Colt shifted onto his back, sweeping her with him in the cradle of his arms. "My darling, Fran," he whispered.

When she woke the next morning, Frank disentangled herself from Colt's arms and sat up to watch him while he lay sleeping. Her eyes traced the shock of dark curly hair that rested on his forehead, then moved to the fan of dark lashes that shadowed his cheeks. Mentally, she traced the curve of his upper lip and touched the firm fullness of the bottom line. A familiar ache grew within her as she recalled the passion they had shared the night before.

Briefly, she allowed herself to fantasize that it could remain this way forever, the two of them and the baby. It felt so right, she thought. *"But it wasn't,"* whispered the voice of conscience. Frank tried to push it away, but it persisted, reminding her that Colt was engaged and that he must have made love to Shauna Lee many times, the same way he had made love to her. The thought sickened her, and she closed her eyes tightly, trying to shut it out.

"Fran, what's the matter?" Colt asked softly.

For a moment, she didn't respond. She hadn't realized that he was awake, and she was caught off-guard. "Nothing," she answered, anguish tinting her voice.

"What are you thinking?" he asked gently, as he reached out to caress her arm. "Whatever it was, it has upset you." He tried to draw her down onto the bed beside him, and when she resisted, he looked at her with a puzzled expression. Their eyes met, and he could see the pain and resentment she was feeling. "Tell me what's bothering you."

"We have no right to be here like this."

His hand tightened on her arm as he pulled her toward him, imploring her with his eyes.

"Don't, Fran. Neither one of us intended for this to happen, it just did. Don't spoil what we shared. It was beautiful."

"What about Shauna Lee?"

Colt looked at her for a long moment. "I explained how it is between us before. We're engaged now, but nothing else has changed. I won't tell her what happened last night. There is no need to."

"Colt, you must have some emotional commitment. Don't you sleep with her and hold her, and make love to her like you did me?" she blurted out in agony.

"Damn it, Fran," he said, closing his eyes. "I'm going to marry her. I've gone out with her for four years. Of course, I've held her, and yes, I've had sex with her. But no...." He spoke with a strangled voice, "it's not like it is when I make love to you."

Frank looked at him with a sick disbelief. "You're not an insensitive person, and I can't believe you're that naïve either. You must realize that if you share the everyday parts of your lives and have an intimate relationship with Shauna Lee, one, or both of you, will get involved emotionally.

"What have you done? Have you willfully ignored everything you don't want to accept and convinced yourself that you will be able to hide behind the security of a safe relationship, with no emotional ties, no risks involved? I suppose then you'll feel justified to gratify your sexual needs wherever and whenever the urge hits you. After all, since you don't have any emotional commitment, it won't matter if you simply don't tell her. Do you really believe that Shauna Lee feels that way? Well, I don't believe it, Colt!"

"Fran, you're being unreasonable. I didn't say anything like that. I don't plan to screw around. Last night was just ..."

"Last night was just what?" Pain tore at her. She scorned him, lashing out in her misery. "Just, another meaningless night of sex with the ranch hand?

"Fran, I could never feel that way about you. I..."

"Stop it! As far as I'm concerned, you're despicable. I can tell you one thing: you'll never satisfy your urges in my bed again. You'll never touch me again," she cried; anguish vibrating in every word and every line of her body. She jerked away from him and moved to the other side of the bed. "Please go."

"Fran! It's not like that." There was a sick look on his face.

"It is like that! You may be fooling yourself, but you'll never make a fool of me again. Now get out of my bed."

"You've got this all wrong," he protested.

"No, you've got this all wrong. Get. Out. Of. Here!" she yelled.

"You don't understand."

"I understand more than you think. Leave!" She pushed him.

"What a fucking mess...."

"You're right. That's exactly what everything that's happened between you and me has been."

He groaned as he flung himself off the bed. He put on his shorts, then reached for his jeans and pulled them on with stiff, angry movements. Without looking at her, he snatched his shirt off the counter. He bent to pick up his boots and carried them to the door, where he jammed his feet into them: then with his shirt in his hand, he stepped out into the morning air and slammed the door behind him with a violence that shook the trailer.

Frank sat in the middle of the bed, tears slipping down her cheeks. "I wish I'd never met you," she cried after his departed figure. "My whole life is a shambles. Why didn't I learn after the first time?" Collapsing onto the bed, she buried her face in the pillow and sobbed raggedly until the pain had eased out of her body and a curious numbness had set in. Then she stirred and got up.

When she went outside, Colt was sitting on an overturned water pail by the corral. His head lifted when he heard the trailer door shut. He stood up and walked toward her. Deliberately, Frank walked to the front of the trailer and inspected the broken window. She busied herself, picking up the broken pieces of glass while she waited tensely for him to join her.

"I've decided to move the trailer back to the ranch. I can't risk leaving you here alone again. You and Ollie can drive out to check the cattle a couple of times a week until we move them in. Go in and secure everything to travel. I'll take care of what needs to be done out here."

A new ache settled in Frank's heart as she worked. The trailer had become home to her. It had been her last refuge, and now she was losing that. *I have to leave the ranch as soon as possible,* she acknowledged regretfully. *I'm too vulnerable, and what happened last night could happen again, even if I think I wouldn't let it. I couldn't have any respect for myself if it did. Besides, soon it will be obvious that I'm pregnant, so the sooner I'm gone, the better.*

Ollie was surprised to see them that afternoon, but agreed it was the best move when Colt explained about the bikers. He invited them in for lunch, cautiously observing both of them and making note of the tension between them.

He knows something's wrong, Frank thought. I hope he doesn't question me.

While they ate, Colt and Ollie made plans to move the cattle in from the lease as soon as Colt finished harvesting. Frank withdrew into her thoughts and let their conversation flow over her. She decided she would phone her mom and dad and tell them that she was coming home. She was glad she had kept her apartment, and Dr. Winters had said she could come back to work at the clinic anytime. Hopefully, the offer still stood.

When she had finished eating, she gathered up the dishes and put them in the dishwasher. Then she moved her personal belongings in from the trailer. An empty feeling filled her when she realized that Colt had left without saying goodbye.

***

Colt sped away from the ranch. He felt like the devil itself was chasing him. "I am such a damn fool," he cursed. "I let that little witch get under my skin and I knew better than to let it happen."

He raged at Frank Lamonte. "That damn woman, I should have sent her packing that first night like I intended too. Instead, I let those big brown eyes suck me in, and my fingers itched to run through that thick mane of hair." He could feel her soft, inviting lips under his and his anatomy reacted to the feeling. "Lay down you stupid son of a bitch. You got me into this mess," he raged as he slid through the curve, his truck fishtailing on the gravel.

Suddenly the memory of a red pickup driving off the road into a snow bank came flooding back. He recalled the tall slender woman who had gotten out of the pickup and given him a tongue lashing about hogging her share of the road. Recognition flooded through him.

"That was her!" Anger surged through him and he pounded the steering wheel with his right hand. "Even then, I knew she was trouble. I should have left her there." Suddenly the truck was careening out of control, whipping on the gravel. He had to fight to get it back on track, and then he pulled over on the side of the road and stopped. His heart was pounding, and his legs were shaking. He laced his hands together and held on to the top of the steering wheel. He rested his forehead against them.

Suddenly he was assailed by the sick fear he'd felt the night before when he'd found the bikers at the trailer. It melded into Frank's screams that had awakened him during the night, and then the sweetness of her body, the passionate way they had made love.

He'd wanted to hold her like that forever. But, this morning she had rounded on him. She kicked him out and called him despicable, and told him that he'd never lie in her bed again.

"And I won't. I'll make sure of that." He took out his phone and called Shauna Lee. He could hear the smile in her voice when she answered, and she welcomed him to her bed. *We have to get married soon*, he thought. *I'll talk to her about it tonight.*

"Maybe not tonight," he reflected. "Tonight I'll work that red-haired witch out of my system. Shauna Lee knows how to distract me. His heart was pounding, and his legs were shaking. I'll put last night behind me. And we'll push the wedding date up, so I'm not tempted to do anything stupid again." He started the truck and pulled out on the road. His mind was still on Fran. "Not that there's any danger of that happening. I'm not going anywhere near her again."

That night he was insatiable. He and Shauna Lee had hot, desperate sex, but when she curled her back into his chest and fell asleep, dark brown eyes, fiery glints in a mass of auburn hair and a mouth that burned under his, haunted him. He groaned as he felt heat rise in his groin, knowing Shauna Lee would never be able to extinguish that flame.

Three weeks went by before he parked the combines and harvesting was done. Colt had only talked to Ollie twice. He'd been busy, but deep down he knew he didn't want to hear anything about Fran. He was trying to block her out of his mind.

He had persuaded Shauna Lee to set a date for the wedding. As far as he was concerned, the sooner it happened, the better. They could even elope, but she'd said if she was actually going to get married, she wanted to have a wedding. She couldn't see what the big rush was, but Colt had kept at her to make plans.

Finally, he knew he couldn't put off the inevitable any longer so he made arrangements for the cattle liners to arrive at the pastures to pick up the cattle and then he phoned Ollie.

***

During the weeks since Colt had left, Frank chafed to be gone, but she felt obligated to stay until they moved the cattle. Every day she realized how attached she had become to Ollie and the ranch. She knew that leaving was going to cause a painful gap in her life for a while. Each day was like a goodbye in her heart, and she hated prolonged goodbyes.

She waited for Colt's arrival with trepidation. It would be

awkward working with him, even for a few days, after what happened. He had been cold and aloof after he had stormed out of the trailer and in spite of the fact that she deplored the choice he'd made, and what had happened between them, it hurt to feel so distant from him.

She was tense with anticipation, wondering how he would react to her. To her relief, he was pleasant, if guarded and impersonal, and once the roundup started, there was no time to be awkward or wary in his presence. Everyone was too busy to let personal feelings interfere.

Three days later, all the cattle were back at the ranch and the calves were weaned and sorted. Colt had gone back to the farm right after dinner that evening. Frank went to bed early. She found she tired more easily now, and she needed more rest. Sleep didn't come quickly. She ran her hands over her stomach and memories of the brief time she and Colt had spent in that very bed flooded through her. *This baby was conceived right here,* she thought. *Not out of love, but out of lust and passion. Love came later and I was the only one foolish enough to embrace it.* She caressed the small bulge that she'd begun to notice. *But I'll always have you as a result of it, my little one. I'm grateful for that.*

A painful lump of emotion was lodged in her throat. The time had come now. She had honored her decision to stay until the cattle were rounded up and the calves were ready to be sold. Now there was only one thing left to do and she would take care of that in the morning.

The next day, Frank and Ollie sat quietly, enjoying a cup of tea after breakfast.

"Ollie," she said nervously, breaking the silence. "I'm not going to stay on for the winter. I hope it doesn't put you in too much of a bind, but it's time I got on with my life."

Ollie sat for a moment, his eyes focused on the floor while he digested her words. "I've sensed a lot of tension between you and Colt ever since you moved back from the lease. I suspected you'd be leavin'." He looked up at her. "I'm not goin' to deny I'd like to see you stay. You know I've grown right fond of you, and I like the way you work, but you have to do what's best for yourself. Have you told Colt about your plans?"

She shook her head.

Ollie grunted. "There's so much damn foolishness goin' on

between the two of you. You're more than half in love with him, and I swear he feels the same about you. But he's so busy fightin' it, he won't admit it. I wish he'd get his head together. I don't understand his gettin' engaged to Shauna Lee and from what he told me while he was here this time; they've pushed up the wedding date. He isn't a fool about most things. How can he be so stupid about this?" he demanded, obviously frustrated.

"Still, there is something else that's botherin' me even more. It's none of my business, but I can't help but wonder...." He looked at her keenly. "Have you told him about the little one you're carryin'? He is the father, isn't he?"

Frank felt the blood drain from her face. She looked at him in stunned silence, wanting to deny the truth.

"I was beginning to wonder what was going on earlier," Ollie continued. "You kept sayin' you had the flu and you got so thin. Then I got a phone call here one mornin' from a doctor's office in Calgary. You had been there and filled out some forms, leaving this number as a contact. Then you rushed out of the waiting room and disappeared without seein' him. They were concerned about you.

"I knew then. When you came back here, I tried to put out feelers and get you to talk to me. But you cut me off at the pass." There was compassion in his face as he stopped speaking. "It's only speculation, but I figured you were plannin' to tell Colt about it at the barbecue. That's why I tried to warn you about him and Shauna Lee. I'd heard a rumor about them gettin' engaged, and if it was true, I didn't want you to get caught by surprise. I was shocked to hear he had told you about her. I know you well enough to realize that you were pretty upset by the announcement of the engagement. That was why I decided to come home that night. I thought it would be near impossible for you if we stayed."

Frank closed her eyes and pressed her hand against her forehead for a moment. Then she opened them and sighed. "It's true, Ollie. I am carrying Colt's child. The two of us becoming lovers was simply spontaneous lust. Afterward, he told me that he would never let himself fall in love again, and if he ever did get married, it would probably be to Shauna Lee. I didn't think it mattered then. In the first place, I never thought I'd get pregnant. Aside from that, I didn't plan on getting involved with anyone. What had happened between us was out of character for me and I just wanted to put it behind me."

Frank squirmed in her seat. She felt uneasy telling Ollie such intimate details of her life. She pushed back her chair and stood up to walk over and look out the window.

"It wasn't very long before I realized that I cared too much for him. Then I discovered that I was pregnant. I was a mess. I didn't want to force him into a marriage because of the child. Besides, I'd never get married for any reason other than love. I went to Calgary to have an abortion, but when it came right down to it, I couldn't bring myself to do that. I decided to tell him about the baby and let him play a role in its life if he wanted too. But I was going to raise it. At least, I thought that's what I was thinking," she added bitterly.

She turned to look at Ollie. "After he announced his engagement to Shauna Lee, I had to admit that I'd been hoping he'd tell me that he loved me and we would get married and become a family. That's no longer a possibility, and I'm not going to tell him now.

"I want this baby. It may be the only child I'll ever have, and certainly the only part of Colt that will ever be mine. He is going to marry Shauna Lee. They can have their own family. I have a good career, so I'll be able to provide for the child and I have lots of love to lavish on it. There are a lot of single-parent families now. Coming as I do, from a close family, it's certainly not what I would have chosen to give my child. Still, it's better than setting us all up for a lot more heartache later on."

Ollie leaned back in his chair and looked into space for a few minutes. Then he cleared his throat and sat up straight. "I understand how you feel, and I'm not sayin' you're wrong. But have you ever thought that withholdin' the fact that you're gonna have his child, could be withholdin' the very information that would make him stop and realize that he's set on a course that could be the biggest mistake of his life? Even bigger than the one he made when he married Sharon?"

"Ollie, Colt is very aware of what he is doing. He admits that he doesn't love Shauna Lee. He respects her, he enjoys her company, and he has told me bluntly that as far as he's concerned that is the best basis for a marriage. 'No romantic fantasy,' he said."

Ollie shook his head sadly. "How soon do you want to leave?"

"I want to go as soon as I can without putting you in a bad spot."

"Have you given any thought to what you're gonna do or where you're goin'?"

"Dr. Winters persuaded me to keep my apartment when I left

Stettler, so I have a place to go too. He also told me I'd have a job there when I came back, no matter how long it took. And Mom and Dad are home now."

"How will your parents feel about all this when they find out?"

"I know I can count on their support." Her eyes filled with tears of regret. "They'll be shocked, and no doubt a bit disappointed, possibly even a bit ashamed, but they won't condemn me and I know they'll stand behind me."

"Well, it's the end of the month, so I guess you can leave anytime you want. I hate to see you go, but I understand why you feel you can't stay."

Tears of gratitude filled her eyes. "I'm going to miss you, Ollie."

"I'm gonna miss you too, girl. Let me know when that baby arrives. And keep in touch. I'm not much of a letter writer myself, but I'd sure like to hear from you."

The next morning she hugged the man who had become so special to her. "I will never forget you, Ollie. Take care of Cypress Jade and give him a few extra flakes of hay for me."

"Count on it. You have any message for Colt?"

"No," she said unhappily. "And Ollie…about the baby and my feelings for Colt; I told you that in confidence. I trust you won't betray it. I don't want him to know."

"I know that, girl. I won't tell him, but I can't promise that I won't encourage him to find you when he finally comes to his senses. Once you're gone, I'm bettin' he'll never marry Shauna Lee."

CHAPTER FOURTEEN

Colt phoned his cattle buyers and made arrangements to sell the calves. Then he sat at the desk and doodled on a piece of paper. He was no artist, but the strokes of the pen took on the resemblance of a woman.

The irritation that had plagued him since he'd left the ranch the previous evening bubbled to the surface as he stared at it. She had long hair and big dark eyes and a sad look. "Shit," he exclaimed as he crumpled it in his hand and threw it into the wastebasket. "I can't escape that woman. I'm getting married to Shauna Lee in three months, and here I am, drawing pictures of Fran." He sighed. "Getting married was supposed to get her off my mind. I'd never have steamrolled Shauna Lee into marriage otherwise. Things were great without making any changes."

He closed his eyes. "I wish she'd just pack up and leave. I can't fire her because she pisses me off. Ollie would kill me. But it would solve everything if she just packed up and took her hot body and her sexy mouth out of here. She's not irreplaceable. We'd find another hand."

He phoned Ollie to let him know about the arrangements he'd made with the buyers. Just before he was ready to hang up, Ollie cleared his throat. "Ahhh… you'll have to get Shauna Lee to start looking for another ranch hand."

Colt felt his chest constrict. "What are you talking about?"

"I'm talking about Frank leaving. This morning she told me that she won't be staying for the winter. She's leaving tomorrow morning."

"What the hell happened? I thought you two were a match made in heaven."

"She and I are still good and I hate to see her go. But sometimes things just happen. Anyway, she's leaving, so we have to find someone new. We'll probably need to get two men to replace her."

"She's not irreplaceable, Ollie."

Ollie snorted. "Time will tell."

When he ended the call, Colt twirled a pen in his fingers as he stared at the top of his desk. He was reeling from the news. "She's leaving? Just like that?" He sat there, remembering her face, her eyes, her fragrant hair, and her soft body as it moved under his. "Damn it," he cursed as he snapped the pen in his hands.

He pushed back his chair, stood up and turned to stare out the window. He couldn't believe how much it hurt to know she was leaving. He would never see her again. Then he gave himself a mental shake. "Well, this is what I wished for this morning. Now I'm getting what I asked for."

***

Frank spent the first night back in Stettler at her Mom and Dad's place. The long drive had exhausted her physically. Her tumultuous thoughts had exhausted her emotionally. It was soothing to be in the comfort of her parents' home, knowing they weren't far away.

The next day her mom went with her to open the apartment. They dusted and aired it out, so Frank could move back in. Rayelle Lamonte loved her daughter with all her heart, but Frank had never been one to talk to her mother about her feelings. Rayelle was startled by her thinness, and she sensed a deep pain underneath the surface, but she didn't know how to broach the subject. And as usual, Frank guarded her secrets carefully.

She came to her parent's house often during the following week, sometimes just to stop in for breakfast. One morning, Rayelle watched Frank wait for the kettle to boil. "I can't get used to you drinking tea in the morning. You always loved your morning cup of coffee. In fact, you were hardly civil until you had it."

Frank looked at her parents for a long moment. Then she took a deep breath. "Mom and Dad, I don't quite know how to tell this to you. I've been home for a week and I've been waiting for the right moment, but probably no time will seem right, so I guess now is as good as any. You are going to be grandparents."

Frank winced inwardly as expressions of blank astonishment washed across their faces, to be followed by a fleeting moment of shocked disbelief. Tears of regret filled her eyes as she held her breath and waited for them to break the silence.

The moments seemed to drag endlessly before her mother spoke. "Are you sure, sweetheart?"

"Yes, Mom. I know when it happened. I'm sorry. I realize this must be a terrible shock. If I were only sixteen, it might be more easily excused, but here I am, coming home pregnant and unmarried at twenty-six. I know you would've preferred to see the ring, the confetti, and rice, and a husband first. Believe me, so would I." Her voice wavered. "I always wanted my child to be raised in a loving home like I was, with both parents, but it isn't possible this time. When I first realized I was pregnant, I was sick about it. I agonized over it until I realized that I had become so stressed that I was ready to fall apart again. I didn't think I could handle a baby on my own, and I decided not to have it. I went to Calgary to make arrangements for an—"

"Frank! You didn't!" her mother interrupted with a horrified gasp.

"Yes, I did, Mom. I felt desperate. But when I got to the doctor's office, I knew I couldn't do it. I left without seeing him and went back to the ranch. I was beating myself up for having been foolish enough to get into this predicament and scared to death about the future, but a week or so later, something happened to me. It was like a light went on and suddenly I realized how much I wanted this baby. I knew then that everything would be okay. It's given my life a sense of purpose that I haven't had since Martin left me. I started to dream and make plans. Now, I'm excited and I can hardly wait to hold it in my arms, to share my life with it."

"When are you due?"

"I haven't been to a doctor yet, but if my calculations are right, it'll arrive in early March."

"Who is the father, Frank?" Her father spoke, finally, breaking his silence.

"It doesn't matter, Dad. He doesn't want to marry me."

"Would you want to marry him?"

Frank sighed and looked at him. She could see the hurt in his eyes. "If you mean, do I love him, yes I do. But, Dad, I didn't love him when this happened. It was just a case of...." She hesitated, closing her eyes against their questioning looks as she searched for the right words. "What can I say? At first we clashed every time we got near each other, but then circumstances threw us together, and in spite of the fact that we rubbed each other the wrong way, there was a strong physical attraction between us. Things just got out of hand.

"Maybe you can't understand that. I swear, I don't make a habit of going to bed with guys, but it did happen that time. Neither of us thought about prevention. We hadn't planned to get involved. After it was too late, I did a rough calculation and thought everything would be all right. I didn't even give the possibility of being pregnant another thought, until weeks later when I started having morning sickness."

"Did you tell him?"

"No, Dad, I didn't."

"Then how do you know he doesn't want to marry you?"

Briefly, Frank related what Colt had told her regarding his feelings about love and marriage and his subsequent engagement to Shauna Lee. "It's best left just as it is. I want this baby. I can support it, and I can lavish all my love on it. It may be the only child I'll ever have, and it'll certainly be the only part of Colt that I'll have."

"You said Colt. Wasn't he your boss?" her father asked.

"Did I say that?" she asked, startled. Her face flushed softly. "Yes, the father of my baby was technically my boss, even though I didn't work with him. He owned the ranch," she admitted. "Dad, I can tell you are hurt, and I'm sorry if you're ashamed of me."

"Frank, it isn't that. I'll admit, this isn't an easy thing for me to accept, but I'm not ashamed. There are lots of unmarried mothers these days. It's just that being a single parent isn't an easy task. I always dreamed...well, I always wanted something better than that for you. The father does have some responsibility in the matter. He should've been told."

"I'm not going to tell him. He's engaged to someone else now, and he got engaged after he knew me, after we were together. If he'd been interested, he would've pursued our relationship. To tell him now would be a form of blackmail, and I'm not going to do it. Even if he did break his engagement and want to marry me for the sake of the baby, I don't want marriage on those terms. Other than that, he could fight me for custody of the child. And if he's married, who is to say that a judge wouldn't rule in his favor? I can't take that risk. I am going to have this baby and raise it by myself," she said emotionally.

"Don't get upset, dear," her mother pleaded. "Dad was only thinking about your future, but we understand. And you know you have our love and support, no matter what. You should go to the doctor soon."

"I'm going to. I'll make an appointment today. I'm going to see Dr. Winters too and see if he can use me at the clinic again. He promised there would be a job there when I came back, and I'm counting on that."

"Martin and Coleen still both work there, honey."

"That doesn't matter, Mom. In all honesty, Martin did us both a favor. By the time he left me for Colleen, our relationship was no more than a comfortable habit. I suspect I suffered more of a blow to my ego than any real heartbreak. I didn't realize it until I fell in love with Colt. There's a very real difference."

"Doc will probably be happy to have you back if you can convince him of that."

"I'll have to tell him I'm pregnant. It wouldn't be fair not to. It won't be long before I can't hide it anyway. Then, the news will get out and everyone will start speculating and gossiping. Will that bother you two very much?"

"Probably a bit, but nothing to worry about," her father replied with characteristic honesty. "As usual, it will only cause gossip until something new comes along. That probably won't take long," he added with a smile.

"Ollie guessed about the baby. He asked me how you would take the news," she said with tears in her eyes. "I told him it would be a shock, but I knew you would stand by me. Thank you, Mom and Dad. You'll never know how much easier it makes everything, knowing I have your love and support. " She rose to walk around the table and hug them both. "I know I'm twenty-six, but there are times right now when I feel uncertain enough to be only sixteen."

"Being grandparents sounds like fun, now that I'm past the initial shock. I mean it was so unexpected. If you'd been married, we'd have been waiting impatiently for you to make this kind of announcement. This way, it was just a bit of a surprise," her mother said as she hugged her close.

Later that morning, Frank drove to the vet clinic. She parked, then studied the familiar building and sighed. "Back to square one," she said softly. "I know Dr. Winters will take me back on staff." She covered her eyes with her hands. "But what will he think of me? Coming home pregnant and unmarried isn't the greatest testament to my character. I hope he won't be too disappointed." She opened the pickup door and stepped down onto the pavement and walked to the front door.

Colleen Nutlatch was sitting behind the reception desk when Frank walked through the door. She was busy talking to a customer on the phone, but her shock was obvious when she looked up and saw Frank. She momentarily lost her composure and color rose up her neck and flooded into her cheeks.

By the time she concluded the conversation, she had collected herself. "Frank! How nice to see you. Have you come home for a visit?"

Frank smiled. "I've come home to stay."

"Ohhh…"

"Is Doctor Winters busy?"

"He's in his office. I'll tell him you're here for a visit. Things aren't too crazy this morning. I'm sure he'll make time to see you."

Frank smiled as she watched the receptionist dial Dr. Winters' line. He appeared almost immediately and his face was covered with smiles. "Frank! It's good to see you." He opened his arms to embrace her. "Come to my office and tell me what you've been doing."

When he closed the door, he gave her a fatherly looking over. "You've gotten too thin, but other than that you're looking good. Are you visiting, or have you come home to stay?"

"I'm home to stay."

"How are you managing the depression?"

"I took medication for three months and then I gradually decreased the dose, the way the doctor instructed me. I still have blue days once in a while, but I know the difference now and I assure you, I won't let it creep up on me again. I have to thank you for putting me on a leave of absence. Being away has definitely given me a new perspective. I'm totally over Martin and I wish him and Colleen nothing but the best."

"So you're ready to come back to work?"

She smiled. "I'm hoping there's still a place for me here."

He grinned. "You know there is, girl. Aren't you glad you kept your apartment?"

"I owe you a lot and you can't know how much I've appreciated what you did."

"So when are you ready to start? Is tomorrow okay?"

"There is something I need to tell you first." She looked uncomfortable.

"Yeah? You're looking pretty serious, girl."

"This is serious. I'm pregnant."

"Pregnant?"

"And I'm on my own, so I'm really counting on this job."

"You're on your own? Why?"

She blushed. "I-I got caught up in a moment. Can we just leave it at that?"

He shook his head. "Frank, Frank..."

"I know."

"Are you okay now?"

"When I first realized what had happened, it really threw me. But now I'm really happy about the baby."

"Where's the father?"

"He's totally out of the picture. I make terrible choices when it comes to men. But I'm done with them now. I'll have my baby and I'll make a good life for us."

"Well, have a chair." He walked around the desk and sat down. "Let's talk about you coming back to work."

CHAPTER FIFTEEN

Frank glowed with happiness when she drove into her parents' driveway later that day. The aroma of frying chicken met her when she stepped into the house. "How did you make out with Dr. Winters?" her mother asked as she finished setting the table.

"He's happy to have me back at the clinic. He really needs someone to look after the small animal end of the practice so he and Martin can be free to deal with the large animals and the outside calls. He said I could start work tomorrow if I wanted to."

She leaned against the kitchen counter as she watched her mother put the crisp golden pieces of chicken into an ovenproof dish.

"Uhm, that smells wonderful mom. " She reached over to pick a crumb from a piece. "Anyway, looking after the small animals won't be that strenuous. It will be just right for me at this time. He seemed really pleased when I took him up on it. Naturally, he was surprised when I told him I'm pregnant, but he assured me that taking a leave of absence to have the baby would not present an insurmountable problem."

"How did Martin react, or does he know that you're coming back yet?"

Frank looked thoughtful. "Dr. Winters took me into the surgery and told him I was coming back. He seemed a little surprised, but that's only natural. He'll get over it once we start working together again." She smiled happily. "It's a relief to know that I have no residual feelings for him. I was certain that I was over him, but today, I found myself wondering what I'd ever seen in him in the first place."

"Did you make an appointment with Dr. Scott?"

"Yes, I see him tomorrow afternoon."

Her visit to Dr. Scott confirmed what she had already known; she was indeed pregnant.

***

Colt Thompson was miserable. Everyone noticed the change in him. His usual happy nature had turned sullen and morose.

Shauna Lee was getting ready for the marriage he had insisted on having. She was having fun planning the wedding, but the closer the date came, the more desperate Colt felt. Thoughts of Fran Lamonte haunted him daily.

Each night he lay in bed remembering her softness, her passion. Her leaving had not given him the relief he'd expected. Instead, he felt as if a hole had been ripped out of his heart and time did nothing but make it feel bigger and rawer.

When he thought back to the end of his marriage to Sharon, he realized that his feelings had been entirely different. He'd been angry with her for cheating on him, but the ultimate betrayal had been the abortion. For him, there had been no going back after that and by the time they'd signed the divorce papers there was no love left; only a deep-seated rage.

Now he was faced with a commitment to Shauna Lee and he knew it was the wrong thing to do. She was his friend and they shared a sexual relationship. She wasn't interested in his lifestyle, and she'd never pretended to love him as anything other than a friend. Even now, as she planned the wedding, it was just an event that she was putting on.

And worst of all, now he was haunted by the fact that they didn't love each other the way a couple should if they were making such an important commitment. He'd seen what his parents shared and somewhere out of the blue, it became important to have that in his own life.

He acknowledged that he hadn't known Fran very long; in fact they'd spent very little time together. But she had found her way into his stubborn heart and he couldn't seem to shake that hold. He realized that he had disrespected her in many ways and she probably felt nothing but contempt for him. *You're despicable,* played over and over in his mind.

But heaven help him; he loved her. And he had no idea where she was and if Ollie knew, he wasn't dropping any hints. In fact, sometimes he felt that Ollie was almost enjoying his discomfort and sitting back, waiting to see if he would actually marry a woman he didn't love.

Two weeks before Christmas, Colt went to see Shauna Lee at her office. He intended to talk to her then, but when she started telling him about the wedding plans, he lost his courage. She asked him to come to her place for the night, but he said he wasn't feeling good and went home.

He spent a sleepless night, beating himself up for not being upfront with her. The next day he went to her office again and asked her if they could go to her place at lunchtime.

She agreed. Something was wrong. She had watched his misery grow and it puzzled her. She didn't know what to do. He was the one who had insisted on getting married, but about a month after she agreed to the ridiculous idea, she noticed a change in him. His demeanor had become increasingly despondent.

When they went inside her apartment, he sat on the couch and just looked at her. "I'm so sorry," he said. His green eyes suddenly filled with tears.

Tears! She thought. The depth of his emotion shocked her. She sat beside him. "You're sorry about what?"

He sobbed raggedly. "I'm a first-class ass and you don't deserve this."

Shauna Lee was stunned. She took his hand and rubbed his fingers softly. "Colt, we're friends. You can be an ass at times, but for the most part you're a wonderful man, so tell me what you think you're doing that I don't deserve."

He looked at her through tear washed eyes. "Shauna, I hope you'll forgive me, but I can't go through with this wedding."

She was silent for a moment. "Alright. It was your ridiculous idea in the first place. I've always told you, I'm not the marrying kind."

"I don't want to embarrass you and you've already made so many wedding plans. It's just that as much as I love you as a friend,

I don't love you the way a man should when he's getting married."

She nodded. "I've always known that. So tell me, what has changed for you? I'm not blind, I've seen what's been happening, and I just didn't know how to fix it."

"I'm in love. And God help me, I certainly didn't intend for *that* to happen. I fought it tooth and nail, but I just can't get her out of my mind, and now the joke is on me. She's a real lady and I treated her like any other asshole would. She probably won't want to have anything to do with me now."

"What did you do to her?"

He sighed. "I've done so many things, but the thing that really topped it for her, was the night I went back to the trailer to get my wallet. We'd been riding that day and I'd left it on the counter. When I got there, some bikers were harassing her. It scared the hell out of me. She was terrified. I couldn't leave her alone so I stayed. In the middle of the night, she had a nightmare, and I got into bed with her to comfort her. I didn't plan for it to happen, but we ended up making love. The kicker was, you and I were already engaged. The next morning, she was sick about what we'd done. She ordered me out of the trailer after she told me I was despicable and she never wanted to see me again."

"Jeez! Was that Frank Lamonte?"

He nodded. "You know, I prayed that she would leave. Then when she did, it was like someone tore my insides out. I'm empty. I have no idea where she is and her memory haunts me every single day."

"So you were scared shitless of your feelings for her when you insisted that we get married?"

His look was pained. "I knew you couldn't hurt me the way she could because while I love you as a friend, I'm not *in love* with you. I was desperate to protect myself. I thought if we got married it would make me immune to her. But what I've learned is that I didn't have to be afraid of her. I had to be afraid of me."

"You really are an ass, Thompson." Shauna Lee punched him in the arm. "Don't worry about the wedding plans. I'll give my staff and friends the best New Year's Eve party they've ever seen."

Colt shook his head. "I'll pay you for what you've spent on it. You bought a dress and spent money you never would have otherwise."

"It's a tax write-off, Colt; remember I'm an accountant. "

"But your dress…"

"Did you ever imagine I would wear something traditional? Not likely! I'd hardly have dared to wear virginal white. It's a pale blue and it's classy and elegant, perfect for New Year's Eve. If we don't find Frank, you can be still my escort, just not my groom."

She squeezed his hand. "Now we need to see what we can do about finding the love of your life. I have her application form on file." She smiled wickedly. "Frank Lamonte. Imagine calling your daughter that."

"They knew she'd be their only child, and her dad named her after her grandfather." He was thoughtful. "I'm not certain she would have gone back to Stettler. She had a lot of painful memories there."

"You need to go see Ollie. He'll know where she is, if anyone does."

Ollie was surprised to see Colt when he arrived at the ranch that afternoon. "What brings you out here this late in the day?"

"I have to talk to you about Fran."

Ollie shrugged his shoulders. "What's there to talk about? You're getting married and she's gone."

"Do you know where she is?"

Ollie shook his head. "Can't tell you."

"Can't or won't."

"Both."

"Look man—"

"Look man, yourself." Ollie bristled. "It's time *you* manned up, Colt. I love you like my own, but these past few months, I've wanted to plant the toe of my boot in your ass. You are not the only man who's had a marriage go sour. Sharon was a bitch and that was rough, but a lot of time has passed since then. Instead of looking ahead and building a future, you've been whoring around with Shauna Lee, taking the easy way out." He snorted. "Friends with benefits as you call it."

"This summer you had the perfect chance to connect with a decent woman who cared about you, and what the hell did you do? You turned tail and got yourself engaged to a female who fills one need in your life. She's not interested in anything else you do, and even worse, you don't love each other. What is effing wrong with you, man? If you married the right woman, you'd have all the fringe benefits you could want, as well as a partner. Frank would've been happy to work side by side with you on the ranch and at the farm. As far as I could see you two fit like a glove, but you were too chicken-shit to step up and at least try to make it work."

Colt swallowed an angry retort and spoke calmly. "I'm not getting married to Shauna Lee."

Ollie shook his head again. "I'm afraid that's too little, too late and sadly you are the biggest loser. Anyone with half a brain could see how Frank felt about you, but you treated her like shit. I have no idea what happened when you rescued her from those bikers, but the happiness just disappeared out of her, and you acted like she didn't even exist after that.

"I wasn't surprised when she told me she was leavin'. I thought you'd finally be happy, but you've been moping around like a dying calf. I guess that's what happens when you cut off your nose to spite your face. It was obvious that you were half in love with her, but you drove her away."

Colt's face flushed. "I'm guilty of all of that. Now, I realize what I let slip through my hands. I want to find her and see if I can make it right."

Ollie stared at him for a few seconds. "I promised I wouldn't tell you where she is."

"Will you give me a hint?"

"You've been such a fool. I hope she gives you another chance because under the circumstances it's the right thing to do, but I hope she brings you to your knees before she does it. All I'll say is her roots are deep."

"Her roots?" Colt smiled for the first time in weeks. "Stettler?"

"I'm not saying any more. If you want to find her, you're gonna to have to put some effort into it."

***

For Frank, time passed quickly. Suddenly it was December 17 and Christmas was just a week away. She finished the last bit of shopping that afternoon, and she had brought the last parcel into the house when the phone rang. *That'll be Mom*, she thought, smiling as she pulled her boots off and ran to answer. "Hello," she sang happily.

"Is that you, Fran?"

An icy coldness seeped into her veins, spreading through her body, numbing her. She leaned against the wall, trembling with weakness.

"Fran?"

"Colt!" Her voice faltered. "How did you get my number? Why are you calling?" The words became a whisper when she asked "Where are you?" She was panicked, suddenly afraid that he might be in town. Her voice was thick with shock and emotion.

"I'm at the farm. I need to talk to you, Fran."

"Well, I don't need to talk to you. I want you to stay away from me. Do you hear me? Just stay out of my life." She disconnected the call and stood staring at the phone for a long moment before she went to sit in a nearby chair. When it rang again, she ignored it. Why did he have to call? Everything had been going so smoothly. She had reached a point where she could think about him without so much pain and now, with a single phone call, he had crowded his way back into her world.

Frank didn't sleep well that night. She couldn't escape the sound of Colt's voice, and for the first time in several weeks, her bed felt cold and lonely. She hugged herself, pulling her knees up as close to her chest as she could with her bulging midriff. It was futile because she sought comfort and warmth that couldn't be provided by a cozy quilt. It was the kind of warmth that only Colt had given her.

Two days later, Dr. Scott scheduled her for an ultrasound to determine the baby's development. As she watched the screen with him, she was filled with a sense of awe and disbelief when he pointed out two fetuses. "I suspected this last time, but I didn't want to mention it before I was certain. You're having twins, Frank," he said with a wide grin.

She stared at him in stunned silence. "Twins!" The word echoed through her mind. She didn't know what emotion she felt most: her uncertainty at the prospect of having double the responsibility or her joy at having been given a double blessing from Colt's passion. Tears sprang to her eyes.

"It's a shock. I never dreamed... there are no twins in my background. It must be—" She stopped speaking, and tears began to roll down her cheeks.

"What's wrong, Frank? There's nothing to be afraid of," he said gently. "Are you worried about the added responsibility?"

"No... yes... I don't know, maybe a little. I can't help but think how wonderful it would've been if-if things were different," she said in a muffled voice. "He phoned me a couple of nights ago. I thought

I was getting over him, but just hearing his voice... I know I'm not." She brushed the wetness from her cheeks impatiently.

The doctor leaned back in his chair and surveyed the young woman in front of him. He had known her since childhood. In fact, he had delivered her. He didn't know what had led up to the situation she was in now. What was obvious was that she was in love with the man who had fathered her babies, and he wondered why she was facing the prospect of parenthood alone.

"Frank, I don't want to pry. You said he phoned you the other night. Does he know that you're pregnant?"

"No," she said, biting her lip.

"Why haven't you told him?"

She sniffed into a tissue before she lifted her eyes to meet his. "He doesn't want to marry me. He might if he knew I was pregnant, but I'm not willing to marry anyone just to give my babies a father. Anyway, he isn't available now. He got engaged to someone else after he was...after we were together."

"He still should know, Frank. He has a moral right to know and a financial obligation to you and the babies, if nothing else."

"I don't want him involved in my life." She sniffed as she worked the tissue nervously with her fingers. "I want to get over him."

"I'm not pushing you, Frank, but I wish you would give it some serious consideration, for your sake and his, as well as the babies."

Frank left the office in a daze. She should have gone back to the clinic, but she was in such a tizzy, she decided to drive to her parents' place instead. *Twins! I still can't believe it*, she thought. By the time she reached their home, she was smiling uncontrollably through her tears.

Her father answered the door. "What are you doing here, Frank? Aren't you supposed to be at work?"

"Where's Mom?" she asked as she sailed past him.

She's in the bedroom. She'll be out in a moment," he answered as he looked at her curiously.

She couldn't control the tears that glinted in her eyes or the smile that sparkled on her lips. When her mother joined them, she looked at her with surprise. "Hi there, honey. You're glowing. What's up?"

"Mom and Dad, hold onto your buttons! I just came from Dr. Scott's office. I'm going to have twins! Can you believe it? Now there'll be one for each of you to spoil."

"Twins," they both shouted. They laughed with happiness when they joined hands and drew Frank into their arms. The three of them clung together in a loving embrace.

Her mother was bubbling with joy. "Frank, just imagine how wonderful it will be if you have a boy and a girl. This is so exciting!"

Her father became very quiet. Frank brushed the tears from her cheeks and looked at him questioningly. "What is it, Dad?"

"I still think you should tell Colt Thompson; even more so now. He has a right to know, honey."

Frank turned away. "He called me the other night," she said slowly.

"What did he want?" her mother asked curiously.

"I don't know. I was shocked to hear his voice...at first I was afraid he was here in town, but he was at the farm. He said he had to talk to me. I told him I didn't want to talk to him and I wanted him to stay out of my life. I hung up on him," she said, squeezing her eyes closed against the memory. "I thought I was getting over him, but hearing his voice again, I realize I still love him. But I will never settle for second best. I won't do it."

CHAPTER SIXTEEN

Christmas came and went. Frank tried hard to keep thoughts of Colt out of her mind, but as New Year's approached, she found herself wondering if he and Shauna Lee were married yet. The thought was disheartening.

It snowed heavily on New Year's Eve. Frank worked until noon and then spent the afternoon with her parents. When she drove home that evening, she took childish delight in the big fluffy flakes that floated to the ground. *What a winter wonderland*, she thought as she parked and went inside.

The first thing she did, after taking off her coat, was light a match to the fireplace. She had set it up before she left that morning, and she sighed with contentment while she watched the flames lick along the logs until they became a full-fledged fire, crackling in the silence of the room. She put her favorite CD in the player and went to run a bath.

Half an hour later, she stepped out of the tub and rubbed her body dry. She surveyed her distended figure in the mirror and wondered what the babies would be like. "How wonderful if they are a boy and a girl. Can I be so lucky?" she wondered out loud.

Humming softly, she dried her hair and brushed it until it fell around her shoulders in a silken, fiery cloak. She sprayed herself with a light mist of perfume, slipped an emerald green velour lounging gown over her head and adjusted the cowl neck so it framed her face softly. Her parents had given it to her for Christmas, and she loved its richness. She paused for a moment as she observed her reflection in the mirror. Lately, she had begun to gain a bit of weight and her skin had taken on a new glow. Now, it was obvious that she was pregnant and it suited her.

"That's a good thing," she said as she turned toward the kitchen. "Seeing that I'm doubly so." She hummed to herself while she prepared a salad. She was getting a piece of chicken from the fridge when the doorbell rang.

Who can that be? she wondered as she shut the fridge door. The bell rang twice again in rapid succession. *Someone in a hurry*; she was smiling when she opened the door.

"Hello, Fran."

"Colt." The word was a strangled sound. She felt the blood drain from her face, and the smile died on her lips. She stared at him, stunned into immobility for an instant. Alarms started going off in her mind, and she moved to shut the door against him. He was too quick and too strong for her.

"No, you don't. I have to talk to you. I didn't drive all this way to have you slam the door in my face." He pushed his way inside and shut it behind him. His eyes never left her face. They clung to it, devouring it as if he couldn't get enough of her.

"Why are you here? I told you—"

"I know what you told me, but I had to come, Fran. I couldn't let you get away so easily. Invite me in, because I'm not leaving until you hear me out."

With resignation, she turned to lead the way into the living room. She didn't realize that he hadn't followed her until she heard his strangled voice say "What the hell!" When she turned to look at him, she found him staring at her, his face ashen.

"You're pregnant," he said hoarsely. His eyes blazed with anger. "You are a fast worker, aren't you? You told me you wouldn't let me use your bed to *satisfy my urges*, but it's obvious that you didn't hesitate to share it with someone else almost immediately after that. I guess my first impression of you was more accurate than the rosy picture I began to paint in my imagination later on." His voice was harsh with pain. "Tell me," he taunted "why hasn't the guy married you?"

"Because, he got engaged to someone else," she shot back, stunned by the stab of pain his question inflicted.

"Did you tell him you wouldn't share his bed anymore?"

Frank stared at him numbly. "Please leave," she begged.

He stood statue-like, glaring at her, the muscle in his jaw working with suppressed emotion. He swore vehemently and then strode out the door, slamming it violently behind him. She listened to the tires spin on the snow when he roared out of the driveway.

She was trembling when she sank into a chair and buried her head in her hands. Tears coursed down her cheeks and ragged sobs shook her body as she gave in to the raw, drained feeling the assault of his words had left. *At least he doesn't realize that he is their father. He automatically assumed that it was someone else.* She sobbed bitterly.

She was wiping her tear-streaked face with a tissue, when she heard a knock at the door moments later. She froze, filled with dread at the thought of facing anyone. Maybe they would go away if she didn't answer.

There was another knock, louder and more insistent. This time, it was accompanied by the frenzied ringing of the doorbell.

She dried her face and ran a hand through her hair. Her eyes were red and puffy; her face blotchy. She looked a mess, but she didn't see how she could avoid answering the determined summons. The ringing of the doorbell reminded her of how Colt had rung it earlier. But he had just walked out that door. Why would he come back? What could he possibly want? Reluctantly, she went to the door. "Who's there?"

"Let me in!" Colt demanded. Her tormented mind filled with questions. The possible answers frightened her. One thing she did know was that she didn't want to see him again.

"Go away!"

"Let me in, or I'll make such a scene that all your neighbors will be stepping outside to see what's going on. I won't stop. I'll break down the door if I have to. I am going to talk to you and you are going to listen."

"Please go away. There is nothing more to talk about."

"Like hell there isn't, lady! Let me in, or I'm going to start yelling the place down. I want some answers and I intend to get them. If you don't open this door, I'll stand out here and share our dirty laundry with all of your neighbors. I'll wait to hear what you have to say; and so will they."

She knew he would carry out his threat. She unlocked the door and opened it, then stood aside so he could enter.

"Why did you come back? You had your say. Wasn't that enough?"

He whirled on her, backing her against the door as she closed it. "When I left here, something Ollie said started running through my mind. He said he hoped you gave me another chance because *under the circumstances it was the right thing to do*. I hadn't reached the corner before I realized it's only been three months since you left the ranch. It's seemed like so much longer, that I didn't pick up on it right away. That only means one thing, Fran. That's my baby." He trembled with emotion as he confronted her.

Tears filled her eyes once more.

He reached out and grabbed her by the shoulders. "Isn't it?" He spoke in that chilling, velvety tone of voice that barely masked the steel edge of anger.

"Get your hands off me." She pushed him away and walked past him. When out of his reach, she turned to face him and touched her belly. "These are my babies, Colt. I'm having twins, but they are my babies. Not anyone else's. Do you understand?"

"Fran!" His voice rose. "It's my baby too. You didn't conceive it by yourself." Then he stopped in shock. "You said twins?"

She nodded.

He made a strangled sound. "You shouldn't have been alone. I should've been with you. It was my responsibility. Damn it, it was my *right*. I had a right to be with you. I had a right to share the changes in your body with you. I had a right to share the thrill of their first movements, the first doctor's appointment, and all those little things." His face was pinched and pale. "Damn it, I had a right to take care of all of you, to look out for you. You shouldn't have been working. You needed rest. You needed to take care of yourself."

"You are engaged to Shauna Lee."

He shook his head in denial and would have spoken, but she cut him off.

"I didn't need your help, Colt. I didn't need your money. Not then, and not now. I don't need you. I've gotten along just fine on my own—"

"Only because you wanted it that way," he interrupted angrily. "You cheated me. You knew how much I wanted a child. You knew you were pregnant long before you left the ranch. It all fits together now. That's why you weren't feeling good, why you got so thin, why your breasts seemed so much fuller that last time in the trailer. Damn it! You must have gotten pregnant the first time we were together and didn't you tell me."

"I didn't realize I was pregnant until after the first week in August. I was going to tell you the weekend of the barbecue, but you announced your engagement to Shauna Lee before I had a chance to. I couldn't tell you then. Besides, you'd made it plain that you didn't want me. I suspected you might be willing to marry me for the babies' sake. But, Colt, I could never settle for second best, and I would never marry without love, not even to give my babies a father, a family, and a name. I've decided to have them on my own and raise them by myself. I have a good job, and I can give them enough love for a dozen people."

"Do you realize how self-centered and selfish you're being?" he demanded. "You would deprive me of my family? You would deprive our children of a home with both parents? Every kid needs a mother and a father if it's at all possible." His eyes burned angrily in his pale face. "I have some rights as far as these babies are concerned. I got cheated out of a family once before. I won't let you do it to me again," he yelled. "I'll fight you for them if I have to, but I'm not going to let you shut me out of their lives."

Frank cringed. His anger frightened her. "What do you want?"

"I want my family. I want to marry you and give our babies my name. I intend to help raise them. We have a choice. Either we get married and do it the way it should be done or I'll fight you for custody."

"I can't marry you," she cried in anguish.

"Why can't you?"

Tears filled her eyes. "I won't marry for the sake of propriety, Colt. I want my marriage to be based on love. I want my babies to grow up in a home filled with it. For us to marry for any other reason is crazy. Look around you. Thousands of people who marry because they think they are in love are getting divorced every year. They don't stay together because of the children they've created. What chance would a marriage that is made because of the kids have if there was never any love? I want more than that. When I get married, I want it to last a lifetime."

Colt looked at her for what seemed an eternity. He spoke softly. "Fran, you can't deny there is an attraction between us. Given time, it could grow into love if it's encouraged."

"I can't take that chance."

He reached out to her, his eyes pleading. "Fran, I'll teach you to love me if you give me a chance."

"You'll what?" she exploded. "How could you teach me to love you? You'd have to love me first, and if you loved me, you wouldn't have gotten engaged to Shauna Lee."

He quickly closed the distance between them. Grasping her by the shoulder, he pulled her toward him. One hand reached out with gentle firmness to tilt her face to his. He looked deep into her tear-washed eyes. "Fran, the sad truth is that's exactly why I got engaged to her. I was scared to death of what I felt for you and I knew she couldn't hurt me because I wasn't in love with her."

His hand moved along the line of her jaw until his fingers twined in her hair. He cupped the softness of her cheek against his palm, and his thumb brushed against her lips sensuously.

"I tried so hard not to love you. I hoped I'd be able to put you out of my mind if I made a commitment to Shauna Lee." He gave a mirthless laugh. "It didn't work. I still wanted you. There were times when I wished you'd leave." He shook his head. "Then you did, and I felt like I'd been gutted.

"Finally, I stopped fighting and admitted that I loved you. I knew I couldn't marry Shauna Lee. It would've ruined our friendship and our lives, but most importantly, I realized that I couldn't marry someone I didn't love."

He slid his other hand along her shoulder and up her neck to cradle the other side of her face. His fingers brushed the remaining tears from the corner of her eye before they moved to twine restlessly in her hair. He looked intently into her wide eyes, willing her to understand and believe him.

"I felt guilty about it. She'd already started making plans for the wedding, and she certainly didn't deserve such shoddy treatment. I expected her to make a scene when I told her how I felt about you. Instead, she admitted that she'd known for a while that something was bothering me, but she didn't know what it was or how to fix it. She reminded me that getting married was my idea and the only reason she'd finally agreed to go through with it was because I had been so insistent. She encouraged me to find you and work things out."

Tears welled in Frank's eyes again.

He shook his head. "Don't cry," he whispered as he gently wiped them away. He pulled her against him, and his hands slid to her shoulders, kneading them gently as he continued. "I went to the ranch to see Ollie and he tore a strip off me. He said he'd wanted to plant the toe of his boot in my ass for months, and it was time I manned up. He told me a few other unpleasant truths too, including what he thought of the way I treated you.

"I phoned you right after I got home that day, and you hung up on me. I was as miserable as hell."

His hand tightened on her shoulders. She could see the uncertainty in his eyes. "All the way here, I was scared to death you would slam the door in my face. I knew I deserved that, but I didn't know how I could face your rejection then. I know I can't face it now." His grip became painful and everything in his being reached out to her.

"Fran, don't you understand? I love you. I know I told you that I'd never allow that happen again, but you snuck into my heart in spite of the rigid walls I'd put up. This relationship got off to a terrible start, and I know you're afraid of getting hurt. So was I, until I realized that my life wasn't anything without you anyway. I've come here to ask you to marry me. "

Frank stared up at him. She was confused. So much had happened. Her mind rioted with conflicting desires and fears. She wanted to believe him. Swaying toward him, she closed her eyes and wet her lips with the tip of her tongue.

He groaned. Then he was kissing her with a desperate hunger. Love and desire surfaced at his touch, and she found herself responding with an unquestioning passion.

He lifted his lips from hers and cradled her again. "I was afraid I'd never hold you again. My life has been a mess since you left." He held her away from him so he could look into her eyes. "Say yes, Fran. Just give me a chance. Give us all a chance, sweetheart," he whispered.

Warmth filled her, releasing the tension. Sobs of relief swept through her, and she clung to him as they gathered force, shaking her body.

"Don't cry, sweetheart. I know how badly I screwed up my

chance with you at the ranch. I promise I'll get it right the second time around."

"I know," she answered with a hiccup. "It's just that, deep inside, I've been so miserable. I couldn't deny my feelings for you, but I didn't think you loved me. I convinced myself that the babies would fill the gap. They gave me a purpose in life, someone to love, and someone who needed me. I thought I could devote my life to them, and the love they gave in return would make up for the lack of an adult relationship.

"When I saw you on the step tonight, I was sure that Ollie had told you I was pregnant. I was afraid you would try to force a marriage without love so you could have the babies or worse yet, try to take them away from me. To hear you say that you love me...."

"Never doubt it, sweetheart. Say you'll marry me. I need to hear you say it, Fran."

"My name is Frank."

"You'll always be Fran to me, so get used to it, because I plan to call you that for the rest of our lives if you'll just say you'll marry me."

Her heart filled with love and compassion at the uncertainty she still saw in him. "I'll marry you, Colt."

She heard him draw in his breath sharply. He swept her up in his arms, carried her to the loveseat that faced the fireplace and sank down onto it. The motion was made awkward by her unaccustomed bulk. He grinned as he cuddled her close. "They'll definitely come between us for a while, won't they?"

"I'm afraid so. These last two weeks I seem to have ballooned. I can't imagine what I'll look like by the first of March."

"Is that when they arrive? There is so much I don't know. Tell me everything."

They cuddled and talked while watching the flickering flames, happy that they were together at last. Colt got up to throw more wood on the fire. He took off his jacket and tossed it on the floor, then returned to sit down beside her and pulled her against him again.

He heaved a sigh and kissed her forehead. "It feels so good to hold you like this. If I ever lost you now, I'd be an empty shell." His arms tightened around her. "I'm trusting you with everything that I am, everything that matters to me."

Frank realized how difficult it must have been for him to break down the wall of anger that he had fortified for so many years and admit that he loved her. It had to be equally hard to overcome his fear of hurt and rejection and offer that love to her, knowing the power he was giving her.

"If I ever hurt you, I'll be hurting myself," she whispered as she slipped her hand up along his arm and over his shoulder to caress his cheek. Her fingers traced along his jawbone until they reached his chin. Then they feathered up and gently traced the outline of his lips. Grasping her wrist, he buried his lips in the palm of her hand, kissing it with intensity. He turned his cheek against it and pressed it to him.

"It's almost hard to believe that I'm here beside you and you're telling me that you love me. I want to marry you right away."

"Whenever you want," she whispered huskily against his shoulder.

"Tomorrow?" he asked.

"We can't do it that fast."

"Well, as soon as possible. If we can't rush to the courthouse tomorrow and get hitched, then I want the real deal. I want to see my bride looking radiantly happy in a wedding gown. And we'll have a wedding cake and flowers and all the trimmings. We'll have a photographer too." There was a smile in his voice.

"Colt! I'm as big as a house."

"I don't care. You're big with my babies, our twins! And I'm as proud as a man can be. Maybe this wedding is a few months late coming, but it's just as significant and just as special to us. I want to look back at it like that in every way," he said fervently. He brushed his lips against her cheek. "You are beautiful to me," he whispered.

"You even make me feel beautiful, and these days I can use all the help I can get. I have never felt so big and so awkward in my life."

"You'll always be beautiful to me," he whispered as he bent to drop a light kiss on the corner of her mouth. "And I'll always love you." He cradled her in his arms, resting his head against her hair. Silence stretched comfortably between them until the bell in the neighboring church belfry rang at the stroke of midnight, welcoming the New Year.

Colt kissed her thoroughly. Then he sat up suddenly. She looked at him, puzzled. "I almost forgot! I have something for you in my jacket. So much has happened at once tonight, I just..." Grinning, he stood up and went to pick up his jacket. She watched him unzip the inside pocket and take out a small box.

"I had serious intentions when I came here." His face was solemn when he sat down beside her. "I still do," he said gravely as he lifted the lid.

Frank gasped. A magnificent diamond sparkled in the firelight. "Oh! It's stunning." Tears flooded her eyes again.

"No more tears."

"But these are happy ones, Colt."

He reached for her left hand. "You've already said yes, so is it okay if I put it on your finger?"

"Please do."

"It may have to be sized. I had to make a guess at this—I had no way of knowing if it would fit, but I wanted to have it with me. I didn't want to leave anything to chance."

"Colt, it's perfect, maybe slightly loose, but not much." She stretched out her hand and admired it. "You really did set out to impress me. I love it, but really, all I needed was to know that you loved me."

"This, my darling, is a symbol of that love. But yes, I did want to impress you with the fact that I love you; that I was serious about it and I wasn't going to let you get away. I was terrified you'd say no." He kissed her gently. "Instead, you have given me your love and our babies. I could never have dreamed of all this."

They kissed long and passionately again. Then he pulled away gently. "I have to call my parents and wish them the best Happy New Year they've ever had! They knew I was coming here and they knew I had gotten the ring, but they'll never guess the rest. A wedding right away and twins! They'll be beside themselves."

"And we have to call Ollie and tell him the news." Frank's eyes lit up as she smiled. "It will make his day, even if we wake him up!"

"He said he hoped you made me get on my knees before you gave in."

Frank laughed. "He'll be disappointed that I was such a pushover."

***

Bob and Serena Thompson were ecstatic. They liked Frank and were relieved to know that she had been willing to give Colt another chance—but the prospect of grandchildren—twins none the less! That was almost beyond their comprehension. They were so excited; it seemed that they would have talked all night. Finally, Colt told them he had to make another call and said goodnight.

Then they called Ollie. The phone rang several times before he answered. "I don't go for this Happy New Year's crap. This had better be good news if you are waking me up in the middle of the night."

Colt laughed. "I've just gotten up off my knees, old timer."

"What're you talkin' about?"

"Pour yourself a drink, Ollie. We have some celebrating to do."

"I take it you found Frank? I was hoping she'd make you squirm for a while."

"Fortunately, she was more forgiving. I take it you knew about the babies?"

"I knew she was pregnant. I tried to get her to tell you before she left, but she's as stubborn as you. She swore me to... did you say babies? Like more than one?"

Frank took the phone. "Yes, Ollie, we're having twins."

"Holy shit." Ollie started to chuckle. "You're really gonna have your hands full. I love you, girl and congratulations." He was laughing. "Now I really do need that drink. I'll never get back to sleep tonight." Then he sobered. "Let me talk to Colt again."

Frank handed the phone back to Colt and he grinned as he listened to his old friend.

"You're gonna to marry her, right?" His tone was protective.

"I brought the ring with me. I wasn't letting her get away again."

"So when is the big day?"

"I'd marry her tonight if it was possible. But she says we can't do it that fast. Now that I think about it, I want the whole nine yards, but I want it to happen as soon as possible. Will you be our best man?"

"I'd be damned mad if you didn't ask. But I'll have to find someone to do chores while I'm gone."

"Call the Kowalski boys."

"I'll do that. Let me know when I have to be there. I wouldn't miss this for the world." Just before Colt ended the call, he heard Ollie let out a big whoop of joy in the background.

Colt chuckled. "We made his day!"

Frank smiled. "I guess we could call my mom and dad, but they'll be in bed, so I think we should just drop by in the morning and introduce them to the newest member of the family. They are so excited about the twins. Now they'll have the wedding they would have hoped for in the beginning. Mom will be right into helping with the planning. She'll be thrilled!

"And Dad will be so happy!" She studied the ring thoughtfully. "It'll mean a lot to him, you know; that you brought the ring with you. It'll reassure him that you love *me*, that you wanted to marry *me* and that you're not just doing the right thing. He wanted me to tell you that I was pregnant all along, especially when I discovered I was carrying twins."

"He probably thinks I'm a real jerk."

"No, he knows how stubborn I can be."

CHAPTER SEVENTEEN

Frank clung to Colt's hand when they walked up the steps to her parent's home. She smiled as she rang the doorbell; not once but twice and then again, just as Colt had rang hers so insistently the night before.

Rayelle Lamonte peeked out the window and saw a large dark blue diesel pickup parked in front of their car garage. "Someone's here, dad. I don't recognize the truck, but whoever it is, they're impatient." She hurried to the door. "Okay, okay," she fumed as she eased it open. She was confused when she saw Frank standing there.

Her eyes focused on her daughter's face. Rayelle frowned. "Why didn't you just come in?"

"Happy New Year!" Frank and Colt sang in unison.

When Rayelle heard the second voice, her eyes moved to the tall man beside her daughter and she noticed that they were holding hands. Her mouth fell open. Then she yelled for her husband. "Cameron! Come here. Cameron! Get out here."

Frank's face was splitting with a happy grin when her father came running. "Happy New Year, Dad."

Cameron didn't miss the tall man behind her. "Who is your friend?"

"Let us come in and I'll introduce you."

Rayelle and Cameron stepped back into the entry, and the happy couple stepped inside. Frank turned to Colt and smiled. "Mom and Dad..." Her eyes brimmed with happy tears. She lifted her hand and flashed her ring. "I want you to meet Colt Thompson. He's the babies daddy and soon to be your son-in-law."

Rayelle let out a squeal of joy. "Oh, thank you, God," she murmured as she hugged Frank."

Cameron's gaze was focused on Colt. "Is she wearing that ring because you love her?"

Colt extended his hand, his expression open and sincere. "She definitely is, sir. I love your daughter and after she left the ranch, I knew I didn't want to live my life without her. I came here with honorable intentions. I had no idea that she was pregnant until I arrived at her door. It was a shock to me."

Cameron's hand clasped his. "I'm glad to know that. I wanted her to tell you about the babies, but she's got a mind of her own. She swore she'd never marry you because you didn't love her. I'm relieved you two have worked that out. Those babies deserve a loving home and both parents."

"Sir, if I had known, I would never have let her go. I love her and I've wanted a family for years."

Cameron looked thoughtful. "Maybe its best things turned out this way. Now she'll have no doubt that you loved her before you knew about them."

Colt's gaze met the older man's. "She told me you'd feel the same way, sir."

Cameron smiled. "She's right. I spent a lot of years protecting her, but in the end I couldn't protect her heart when Martin Cole broke it. Some things in life just have to work themselves out, I guess."

Rayelle hugged Colt and then looked at the newly engaged couple. "God works in mysterious ways. Sometimes we just have to trust that everything will lead to the place where we are supposed to be."

Cameron turned toward the kitchen. "Come in. Mom is making waffles for breakfast."

The four of them spent the morning talking about the upcoming nuptials. Rayelle was delighted that Colt wanted a real wedding. Her mind was teeming with ideas and Frank gave her absolute freedom with the planning.

Later that afternoon, Frank phoned Dr. Winters and asked if she could come over. Sadie answered the phone and welcomed her.

When they arrived, Frank rang the doorbell the same way she had at her parents place. Dr. Winters was frowning when he opened the door. "Frank! Why the impatience?"

She smiled and lifted her ring finger. "Jason Winters, I am here to introduce my fiancé, Colt Thompson." She leaned her head into Colt's shoulder. "And the father of our babies," she added with pride.

Dr. Winters' gaze met Colt's. "Well, I can only assume that you've convinced her that you love her young man, because I know her well enough to know that she wouldn't be standing here with you if you hadn't." He reached out to shake his hand. "Congratulations."

Then he turned to Frank and pulled her into his embrace. "He didn't beat you into submission did he? Cause I may be an old man, but I know people who aren't."

She laughed and hugged him back. "No, I have no bruises, mental or physical. He had no idea I was pregnant when he arrived at my door with the ring in his pocket." She looked at Colt and smiled. "His initial reaction verified that." She chuckled. "He was livid and he stormed out, assuming I was with someone else. A few minutes later, after he'd had time to realize that I'd only been gone for three months, he was back at my door. And he wasn't taking no for an answer. When I saw how sincere he was, I was totally convinced. So you don't have to beat him up for me."

"I'm glad to hear that. And you can't know how relieved I am to see you with the daddy of those babies. The situation has been eating a hole in my gut."

She kissed his cheek. "I know."

***

After the weekend, Rayelle and Frank drove to Red Deer to shop for a wedding dress.

After visiting several bridal shops, Frank was ready to give up. "We should just buy a tent," she said ruefully.

"Nonsense," Rayelle shot back. "There's a dress out there that's perfect for you."

"I wish we'd have gone to a marriage commissioner and quietly gotten married."

"I'd have had a hard time forgiving you if you'd done that.

You've always been your father's girl. You can't imagine how much it means for me to have the privilege of planning your wedding."

Frank groaned. "But Colt wants a photographer too, and I'm huge."

"Nonsense," her mother retorted again. "A good photographer will take pictures in a way that you'll only see the beautiful bride you are. You are not the first pregnant woman to get married. I love that my new son-in-law wants to do this right."

Frank sighed. "Becky said the same thing. She's excited about being my bridesmaid."

"Who's going to be the best man?"

Frank smiled. "Ollie Crampton. He's the ranch manager that I worked with. He's thrilled. He was so good to me and he's known Colt for years."

"When is he coming?"

"Bob and Serena are bringing him with them. You'll like them. They're good people."

Rayelle and Frank came home with a beautiful gown that evening. The dress was so beautiful that she didn't worry about her burgeoning belly.

That night when they went to bed Colt asked her what it was like.

"I can't tell you that," she said indignantly. "What I will tell you is that I truly do feel beautiful in it, and that's something I couldn't imagine happening. By the time we found it I was ready to buy two white sheets and sew them together, but my mother was a woman on a mission and she wasn't quitting until we found the perfect one."

"I like the way your mom thinks."

***

Ten days later flowers and candles filled the church that Frank's family had attended for years. The minister who performed the marriage ceremony had baptized her.

Ollie Crampton stood beside Colt. When he had arrived with Colt's parents, Frank hadn't recognized him for a moment. He had cut his hair and shaved off his beard for the occasion; it was amazing how much younger he looked.

Becky Freemont walked down the aisle and took her place at the front where she waited for Frank to join her. Cameron Lamonte walked his daughter down the aisle and happily gave her hand to Colt.

Serena and Bob Thompson and Rayelle and Cameron Lamonte made an instant connection. They shared similar ideals and interests and enjoyed a comfortable friendship; both families were pleased to know that their children had been raised with similar moral values and work ethics. Dr. Winters and Sadie were in attendance as well. Becky's husband, Russ Freemont, was busy snapping impromptu pictures. Rayelle knew the professional photographer she hired and she had explained that Frank felt uncomfortable about how big she might look. She asked him to do his utmost to position everyone so that the bride's very pregnant state would appear as inconspicuous as possible. He was creative and took beautiful pictures that Frank appreciated later on.

After the ceremony was over and the pictures taken, everyone gathered at a local restaurant for a private reception. Toasts were made; tears of happiness were shed, congratulations and best wishes given. A single tiered wedding cake was cut and Frank and Colt fed it to each other in the traditional way.

Frank was relieved when the evening was over. Tiredness was a companion that she'd become familiar with, but during the past two weeks she hadn't been getting enough rest and on the night of their wedding, she was exhausted.

Colt took her back to the apartment and put her to bed. He lay with her in his arms, realizing that life had dealt him a winning hand the second time around.

Everyone who attended the wedding met at the Lamonte household for breakfast the next morning.

Before they went back to the farm, Bob and Serena Thompson took the newlyweds aside and announced that Bob was going to retire. They would be moving into an apartment in Regina, leaving the farmhouse available for Colt and Frank. Colt was relieved to hear that his dad had chosen to step out of the business, knowing it was best for his health. Also, the decision quickly resolved the housing crisis for Colt and Frank.

It was tempting to go to Saskatchewan right away, but Frank's Alberta medical insurance was still active and her doctors were familiar with her pregnancy. The newlyweds decided to stay at the apartment in Stettler until the babies were born.

Rayelle and Cameron went to Saskatchewan and worked with Colt's parents, using colors that Frank and Colt had selected to decorate the nursery. They picked up cribs and furniture that had been ordered online and the two grandfathers worked side by side, putting them together. The grandmothers had fun buying diapers, blankets, tiny onesies and sleepers for the expected twins.

Frank's doctor kept close tabs on her and he decided she should go to a Calgary hospital for a safe delivery. The date was set for a C-Section, roughly two weeks before the expected birth date. Frank and Colt stayed with Becky and Russ Freemont until the delivery.

A week after Sam and Serena Thompson were born, the family traveled to their new home in Saskatchewan. Chaos reigned in the household for a few weeks while everyone adjusted to new demands and schedules. Fortunately, Frank and Colt's parents provided a lot of support.

Colt was a proud, hands-on father and husband. Love flowed from him, encompassing the twins and Frank.

Working together, they established a routine during the inevitable late night feedings. Colt took the first baby that had nursed and cuddled it in his arms until the other one was satisfied. Then he would place it in the crib that had been moved into the master bedroom for the first few weeks, because both parents found peace in knowing that the babies were within arm's reach. Next he would take the second baby and cuddle it while Frank cared for her nipples. When their mother was ready to go back to sleep, he placed it next to its sibling and tucked a light blanket over them before he returned to her side.

He was not a church going man, but every night he thanked God for his blessings and that he'd gotten it right *the second time around."*

***

Thank you for taking time to read *The Second Time Around*. **Few people realize how gratifying reviews are to an author and how important they are to the success of a book**. Reviews are read by potential readers, who will value your opinion of a book and may decide to buy it (or not) based how on your experience with it.

Writing a review can seem intimidating, but *please do not feel that you can't do it*. Think about how *you felt* about the characters, *what you liked* (or disliked) about the book, and *how you connected* with the story when you were reading it. *Then write it down in simple words.* That is what really counts. Fancy words *do not* replace simple *honesty* and *enthusiasm*, which are the most compelling ingredients in a review.

Connecting with readers is a heartwarming experience, for an author. It reaffirms the value of what we spend hours doing in solitude. *I would love to hear from you and learn a bit about your life.*

If you enjoyed this book, I would be delighted if you could leave a review at any one of the following sites: Goodreads.com, ePrintedbooks.com, Amazon.com, Facebook, Twitter, or my website at **http://www.gloriaantypowich.com** If you could post your review on several sites, I would be absolutely thrilled!

Facebook: Gloria Antypowich Author, (Please stop by and like my page!)

Twitter: @gantypowich

Website/Blog: Gloria Antypowich-Romance and Love Stories at http://gloriaantypowich.com/

Email: gloria@heartsatrisk.com

I look forward to hearing from you!

FULL CIRCLE, Book Two of the Belanger Creek Ranch Series, will be available on Amazon and ePrintedbooks.com very soon.
ISBN 978-0-9939166-0-1 (pbk.).
ISBN 978-0-9939166-1-8 (ebook)
Here is a peak preview. I hope you enjoy it!

BOOK TWO CHAPTER ONE

Shauna Lee Holt stared out the window in her office. A knot of frustration formed in her gut. She sighed as she looked back at her desk, her eyes resting on the folder in front of her. Thompson Holdings: Belanger Creek Ranch and Cantaur Farms. She flicked a loose staple with her long, brightly colored fingernail, then absently tapped the keys on her computer keyboard.

COLT THOMPSON—the name popped up on her screen. She stared at the door he had just exited. "Why did I let him go so easily?"

But, she knew why. When he had asked her to marry him four years ago, neither one of them had professed to be in love and there were no unrealistic, romantic notions. They were mature adults... friends, companions. He came from an esteemed family in the area. He was good looking and treated her with respect, was a great dinner companion and someone to go to high profile events with. They had vacationed in Mexico once, even though he was totally out of his element. And... he was great in bed.

Yeah—he was great in bed! She pushed her chair back and stood up, scooped up the file on her desk and carried it down the hall to the senior accountant that the client had been assigned to.

Then she walked back to her office and grabbed her jacket. Stopping at the reception desk, she told Christina Holmes that she was leaving early. As she pushed through the door, she took out her cell phone and quickly dialed a familiar number. She smiled when the deep, masculine voice answered. She knew he had read his call display when he said "Hi sexy, how about dinner tonight?"

"Why did it take you so long to ask? I'm available, willing and ready!"

Josh Kendall laughed. "Alright sweet cheeks, but if you're available, willing and ready, I'm definitely going to need some nourishment first. We could grab a bite at The Steakhouse on George Street. Then we can head on over to your place."

She gave a throaty laugh. "That works for me; I'll meet you there."

Shauna Lee pulled up in front of the restaurant and parked. She surveyed the parking lot but didn't see Josh's car. She hesitated for a minute, running her fingers through her blonde hair, which was cut in a curly shoulder length bob. She looked in the rearview mirror and big, blue eyes reflected back at her. They were her most notable feature, wide and luxuriously fringed with sweeping dark lashes that she had inherited from her mother.

A quick glance showed that her mascara and subtle application of eyeshadow were still in place. She took a slim stick out of her purse and applied fresh lipstick. Josh still hadn't shown up, so she decided to go inside and get a table and order a glass of wine for herself while she waited.

She picked a table against the wall, midway down the dining room. After ordering a glass of wine at the bar, she carried it to the table. She sat down, smoothed her stylish dress and stretched her legs while admiring her high heeled shoes. She sipped her wine and looked around the room.

People were coming and going. She watched them idly. Suddenly, she heard a familiar laugh. She was instantly alert. It was Colt. He came into the dining room with another man; someone she didn't recognize. Her heart leaped. What was he doing there? She thought he would have been back in his happy home by now. He had left her office an hour and a half ago. He hadn't said anything about staying in town.

She watched him intently, willing him to look at her. There was a time when he would have instantly been aware of her, but today he sat down at a table, absorbed in conversation with his companion.

Irrationally, she felt slighted. If she went to the washroom, she could go right past his table. She got up and walked by, tossing her hair and swaying her hips. He didn't notice her. Neither did his companion.

She went into the ladies' room, fluffed her hair and retouched her lipstick. Then she sashayed out and up to his table. She feigned surprise when she stopped by him. "Colt," she purred. "You didn't mention that you would be in town tonight."

He looked up at her, surprised. "Shauna Lee! I didn't expect to see you here." He didn't ask her to join them or give her any indication that she was welcome.

"I thought you'd be home by now."

He motioned to his companion. "We're going to an agriculture seminar at the Best Western tonight. Have you two met?"

They shook their heads, so Colt introduced them. "Shauna Lee Holt, this is Brad Johnson. Brad has set up a business here in Swift Current. He owns Windspeer Energy. He's giving a presentation about small wind energy generated turbines at tonight's seminar."

He looked at his companion. "Shauna Lee owns Swift Current Accounting and Bookkeeping Services. Her firm has managed our accounting for years."

She looked at Colt's companion: tall, well-toned, dark brown hair, gray eyes. He was a long legged, good-looking guy wearing blue jeans, a soft shirt, a western cut denim jacket and cowboy boots. His Stetson sat on the table. He was definitely a real country boy.

She gave him an intimate smile and she didn't miss the spark of interest that flashed in his eyes. "How nice to meet you, Brad. Are you new to the area?"

"Yes. I'm from British Columbia; Dawson Creek, to be exact."

"If you need someone to show you around, I'm free and over twenty-one." She flashed him a smile as she reached into her purse for a business card and handed it to him. "My number is on the card.

"If you need accounting services, my firm is the best." She winked. "And, I'm good company too, aren't I, Colt?"

Colt had been watching the exchange with amusement. Her question startled him. What the hell was she up to? "Oh... yeah... I guess you are."

"Colt," she chided him. "You guess? Have you forgotten already?"

She glanced up when the restaurant door opened. Josh Kendall walked in. He sauntered up to them.

"What's this sweet cheek? I'm late, and you're checking out the competition already?" He winked at Brad. "She's mine for tonight, so you're out of luck this time, buddy." He slid his hand familiarly around her waist, letting it rest on her hip, with his fingers trailing down toward her pelvic bone. "Sorry, I'm late, babe. I got hung up at the last minute."

His words sent a flush of anger through her and she felt color rise in her cheeks. Then Josh tightened his arm around her waist and suggestively rubbed against her. She was suddenly embarrassed.

When Josh and Shauna Lee moved away, Brad looked at Colt and raised an eyebrow. Colt just shrugged and the two men resumed the conversation they were having before they'd been interrupted.

Shauna Lee led the way to the table where she had left her glass of wine. They sat down and Josh ordered a drink. While he downed it, he kept up a commentary about what he would do with her during the night ahead of them. It was a conversation they had shared before, but tonight it wasn't working for her. Before the waitress came to take their food order, Shauna Lee realized that she had lost her appetite; for food, for Josh, and the distraction he offered. She had initiated the evening, but it had been a knee-jerk reaction to Colt's indifference to her. Josh was primed and ready for a night of sex, but his words gnawed at her. *He made me sound like a prostitute... or a common whore.* Embarrassment twisted in her stomach. Then anger surged through her. She would show him who was out of luck!

She set her wine glass on the table. "Josh, suddenly I don't feel very good. I'm going to pass on tonight. I'm just not into to it."

He looked at her in surprise. "What do you mean you're not into it? You're always into it." Then he laughed. "Are you playing hard to get?"

He reached across the table to caress her hand. He raised an eyebrow as she pulled away. "Come on, sweet cheeks. We both know that you're never hard to get. In fact, I'll bet you're hot and wet right now, and I'm ready to go." He reached for her hand.

"I'm serious, Josh!" She stood up, avoiding his touch. "I shouldn't have called you. I'm going home now, and I'm going alone."

"Like hell you are! You think you can tease me and get away

with it? I'll be at your door, right behind you." He stood up and grabbed her arm, trying to pull her with him.

"Josh Kendall." She had raised her voice and heads turned. "Take your hands off me. I said NO!"

His face turned red and he let go of her. He swore as he turned and went to pay his bill. Then he strode outside.

Shauna Lee finished her glass of wine. She looked out the window and saw that Josh was still standing outside, waiting for her. Damn him! She cringed when she saw Colt look her way, and she decided to escape to the washroom. She avoided his table on her way.

Ten minutes later she thought it would be safe to leave, certain that Josh would have left by then. Colt and Brad Johnson were paying at the till when she slipped out the door. She had started toward her car when Josh stepped around the corner of the building.

"Thought you'd ditch me, eh?" He grabbed her arm. "What the hell's gotten into you? I don't appreciate being embarrassed in public."

"And I don't like having you talk about me like I'm a common whore."

"Funny, you never seemed to mind acting like one before. What's got you so high and mighty now?"

"You bastard!" She slapped his face.

Colt and Brad witnessed the scene when they came outside. Colt quickly realized that the situation could get ugly. In an instant, he made a decision and stepped into the angry tableau.

"Alright, you two; it's time to cool off." He looked at Josh. "It's none of my business, but she clearly said 'No' when you were in the restaurant. You'd be wise to walk away for now. Both of you need time to rethink things and work out your problems when you're calmer."

Josh's face flushed. "Damned right it's none of your business and aren't you one to talk! How many years did she screw the balls off you?" He laughed harshly. "Why aren't you home with that wife of yours instead of here defending her? Don't tell me you've still got the hots for our Shauna Lee!"

"That's enough!" Colt spoke with steely calm. He reached into his pocket, took out his cell phone and flipped it open. He pushed a button and waited while it rang. Then he spoke. "I'm calling to report a problem brewing in the parking lot at The Steakhouse on

George Street. I'd appreciate it if you would send someone down here to diffuse the situation before it gets out of hand."

He waited for a couple of seconds. "I'm Colt Thompson. Yes, I'll wait here to fill you in and I'll give you a statement."

His hard, green eyes pinned Josh as he closed the phone and put it back in his pocket. "Don't ever question my love and loyalty to my wife. Shauna Lee is my business associate, and I still view her as a friend! That's it, period!

"But I won't stand by and watch any man force himself on a woman. The fact that she and I had a relationship in the past makes no difference now. That is in the past."

They heard a siren blip twice and the flash of red and blue lights could be seen coming down the street. Josh swore violently as he turned to his truck. "You'll pay for calling the cops on me. I know people in high places." He laughed. "Hell, I know a guy at the cop shop that's screwin' her, too. Good luck, bitch!" He slid into his truck, started the engine and gave Colt 'the finger' as he eased past the patrol car that was pulling into the parking lot.

Shauna Lee covered her face and wished she could disappear. She had been insulted by Josh's attitude and his lack of respect for her. Now she was humiliated. Colt had come to her rescue, but he hadn't defended her honor. In fact, he had left no doubt about where she fit in his life. There were no lingering feelings of attraction there. What a fool she was; and now she had to go through all of this hassle with the police.

Two officers stepped out of the patrol car. Colt stepped toward the one nearest to him. He extended his hand. "Colt Thompson, sir. I made the call." He introduced Shauna Lee and then briefly sketched out what had happened.

Brad Johnson stood back, not wanting to get involved. He was grateful that Colt hadn't drawn him into the situation, even though they were together. He was surprised by this steely, calm side of Colt Thompson. Clearly he was a man who didn't stand for much nonsense. He thought about the way he had made that call, knowing it would involve him in an awkward situation.

His eyes moved to the woman standing by Colt. She was clearly someone from his past; he had left no doubt about that. She was good looking. It would seem that she was pretty hot too. Josh Kendal was probably ten years younger than her, and he had left little doubt that their relationship was all about sex. She was definitely trouble;

the kind of woman a smart man would steer clear of.

Colt walked over to Brad. "I'm sorry about this, but I have to stick around for a few minutes. Go ahead and get set up. I'll get there as soon as I'm finished here." Brad nodded and walked across the street to the Best Western.

Twenty minutes later, Colt came into the small meeting room, followed by a subdued Shauna Lee. Brad had saved a seat at the front for him and he was surprised when Colt ushered Shauna Lee into it. "The place is packed. I'll find a spot against the wall at the back," he said softly as he stepped away.

Brad scarcely looked at Shauna Lee, but he could sense the tension in her body as she sat next to him. Shauna Lee shifted uncomfortably in her seat, and he couldn't help but notice the way the slim skirt of her dress rode up on her thigh, or the curve of her ankles and the slender length of her legs. She was petite and delicate looking.

He had set up his laptop when he had first arrived, so all he had to do now was turn it on and start his PowerPoint presentation. He fidgeted, waiting for his turn; wanting to get up and move away from Shauna Lee. He was uncomfortably aware of her.

He had been an onlooker in the parking lot, but he couldn't push aside everything else that had happened; like the way she had smiled at him when Colt had introduced them. He had recognized the invitation. Then she had baited Colt and that had thrown him. Colt's cool, disinterested response had piqued his interest. Then Josh Kendall had shown up and the whole picture had deteriorated.

Brad gave his presentation about the innovation of wind energy and its potential for use in agriculture. He didn't miss the change in Shauna Lee's demeanor as he spoke. She became alert, with unfeigned interest. She watched the slides and listened to the questions from the audience and paid attention to his answers.

The seminar broke for coffee after he finished and people started circulating around the room. He fielded several questions about his company's wind-energy program. Eventually, he noticed Shauna Lee standing at the edge of the group listening and talking with the others. He noticed the professionalism in her manner and the respect in their demeanor as she conversed with people. She was all business. There was no sign of the coquette he had seen earlier.

He had to wonder. Who was the real Shauna Lee Holt?

After the meeting, Colt joined Brad and helped him pack up his presentation. He looked directly at Brad when they were finished. "I need to ask a favor of you."

"OK."

"The cop said that Shauna Lee shouldn't go home right away. He wanted to have a talk with Josh and tell him to back off, but he wasn't sure if Josh would show up at her place before he tracked him down.

"I suggested that she come here with me. I told him that I'd make sure she got home all right after the meeting. I hate to ask you, but would you come with me? I'd rather not go there on my own. Do you understand?"

Brad sensed the tension in Colt. "Yeah—I think I do."

"It won't take long. She doesn't live far from here. I just want to make sure that she gets in the house all right. Then I'll bring you back to your pickup and I'll head home to my wife and kids."

***

Shauna Lee sank onto the couch in her living room. Colt had been a perfect gentleman. He'd followed her home in his truck, walked her to the door and made sure she'd gotten safely inside.

She couldn't ignore the emptiness in her gut. What the hell was wrong with her? She couldn't get Colt out of her mind. It was insane. He was married and nauseatingly happy with Frank and had the family he never thought he would have. Even though she'd never seen him exclusively, she and Colt had been 'friends with benefits' for four years before he'd gotten married. She'd watched him change into a wonderful, loving husband and father, and she'd began to regret that she'd let him slip away.

She winced. She had made several subtle advances to him throughout the past year, but he was so involved in his own happiness he hadn't even seemed to notice.

And tonight... she cringed remembering how he had made it very clear to Josh that she was part of his past.

She stood up and walked into her bedroom. She threw her purse on the chair, stripped out of her clothes and went into the bathroom. She turned on the shower and let uncomfortably warm water sluice over her, feeling the burn, wanting to wash away the humiliation that Josh's words had left with her.

She stepped out on the mat and gave herself a brisk rubdown, then quickly blew her hair dry. She didn't look too closely at her reflection in the mirror, unwilling to meet her own eyes.

As she turned to step back into her bedroom, she muttered Screw him, as she flipped the switch to turn off the bathroom light.

Her eyes lit on the bed. She laughed with irony. That's exactly what he planned to be doing; right there on that bed, just like they'd done how many times before? She felt a flush of disgust. She wasn't certain how many times they had wrinkled the sheets there.

She sat on the edge of the bed, thinking. He'd been a voracious sexual companion. She hadn't asked for love. But he didn't respect her. *What do you mean; you're not into it? You're always into it.* His words played a loop in her mind. *We both know you're never hard to get.*

She cringed remembering his response when she had told him she didn't like having him talk about her like she was a common whore. *Funny, you never seemed to mind acting like one before. What's got you so high and mighty now?*

Anger washed through her, followed by embarrassment. *Hell, I know a guy at the cop shop that's screwin' her, too.* Her breath hitched. He had to have meant Jim Wiley. She had been with him a couple of times. Had they compared notes? Revulsion washed over her.

She buried her face in her hands. "How did I get to this place?" she groaned.

She turned back the covers and shut off the light on her night table. She lay down, pulling the sheets up under her chin. She tried to force the tension out of her body and relax, but her mind would not shut off. She could hear Josh's voice saying, S*he's mine for tonight so you're out of luck this time, buddy.*

What had Colt and his friend thought? Not that it really mattered but damn it, it did matter to her. She turned the light back on, then went to her dresser and pulled out a pair of cotton pajamas. Usually, she didn't wear anything to bed, but tonight she felt naked and she needed something; as if the pajamas would cover her humiliation.

She went to the bathroom. She opened the medicine chest and took a sleeping pill, then after a hesitation, swallowed a second one to ensure the oblivion of sleep; a respite from the devil that beleaguered her mind.

BOOK TWO CHAPTER TWO

Frank Thompson tiptoed into the nursery to peek at the three-year-old twins who were sleeping soundly in their beds. Selena's dark curls were tousled on her pillow. Her 'blankey' was clutched tightly in her fingers, tucked up under her chin and pulled up against her cheek.

She was a combination of both her mother and father. She had Colt's dark curly hair and Frank's dark brown eyes. Her cupid bow lips were parted softly and a slurp of drool ran out of the corner of her mouth and onto the pillow. She was a wisp of a child; pixie-like, but determined and feisty.

Sam was curled up in the other bed, his back to her, moonlight spilling softly over his sheets. She could hear the slurping sounds he made as he sucked his thumb. He was as sturdy as a linebacker; quiet and unexcitable. He had inherited his mother's auburn hair with the same fiery glints, but his eyes were calm blue ponds like those of his namesake, her grandfather, Frank Samuel Lamonte.

Her hand moved to the subtle roundness of her tummy. "I hope you have your daddy's green eyes," she whispered as she turned and eased out of the room silently, closing the door gently behind her.

She went downstairs and into the living room and walked over to the bay window. Pushing aside the ruffle of the gauzy white Priscilla curtain, she looked out past the veranda, her eyes traveling down the tree-lined driveway that lead into the farmyard from the gravel road.

She glanced at her watch, noting that it was nine-thirty. Colt should be getting home any moment. He had gone to Swift Current earlier in the day. He'd had an earlier appointment at the accountants and then later in the evening he was attending a meeting that the district agriculturist was hosting at the Best Western Hotel.

Restless, she wandered over and turned on the electric fireplace, then sank into a deep armchair and watched the artificial flames flicker in the darkness. A few minutes later, she heard the crunch of tires on the driveway.

Colt bounded up the steps onto the veranda and was opening the screen door as Frank opened the inside one to meet him.

"You had a long meeting!" she said with a smile, as she clasped his hand and pulled him inside. She shut the door behind him as he pulled her into a warm embrace.

"Yeah, it was interesting—not just the meeting!" He released her, took off his hat and put it on the rack, and then turned to her.

"What else happened?"

"Oh, Shauna Lee..." He shook his head. "She was at the restaurant where Brad and I went for supper before the meeting. She came by and said hello and made a hit on Brad right off the bat!" He grinned and shook his head. "That girl never changes. Then Josh Kendall came in. I don't know if you know him."

Frank shook her head.

"He's a young high roller who works in the oil business. He has an office in town. I guess they had arranged to meet there. When he arrived, she was talking to us. He got territorial and let Brad know that she was his for the night.

"I think she was embarrassed by the way he said it. She got pretty red. They went to their table, and I have no idea what happened, but obviously the evening didn't go as planned. They got into a disagreement and she told him 'no' loud enough for the whole restaurant to hear. He was pissed off. He paid his bill and stormed out.

"She stayed at the table until he went outside. She waited a few minutes and then she went to the washroom. I think she was giving him time to get out of there. She must have slipped outside while

Brad and I were paying for our meal.

"When we went outside, Josh was still there and they were going at it again. She slapped his face and he grabbed her. It was getting ugly. I thought I could diffuse the situation if I just stepped in and got them both to cool off."

He looked at her sheepishly. "It didn't work. He just got uglier and made her sound like the town tramp. Then he got personal about it with me, by bringing up the fact that she and I had been together in the past and suggesting that I still had a thing for her.

"I set him straight on that score, but his attitude really put me off. I called the cops, and then he was really pissed off. He threw some more insults at Shauna Lee and sped out of the parking lot just as a cop car arrived."

"Colt!"

"He won't be a problem. He was embarrassed as much as anything. I suspect he was planning to spend the night at her place, but she plainly told him 'no' and he was trying to force her into the situation. When the cops came, I told them what I'd seen and they talked to Shauna Lee."

"Where was Brad when all this happened?"

"He stood back and watched the whole mess unfold. After I called the cops, I told him to go set up for the meeting and I'd meet him there when I was finished. He left right away. I'm sure he was relieved."

"I wonder what he thought."

"He didn't comment. But after Shauna Lee talked to the police, they said she should wait for a while before she went home, so they had a chance to track Josh down and warn him to leave her alone.

"I ended up taking her to the meeting with me. After it was over, I asked Brad to come with me, and we followed her when she drove home. I made sure she got into the house and heard her turn the deadbolt. Then I took Brad back to his truck and came home. That's why I'm so late."

He put his arm around her and pulled her back into his embrace, kissing her deeply. "I love you," he whispered. "I can't begin to tell you how much I appreciate having you in my life."

She nibbled on his bottom lip. "Let's go to bed." They turned off the lights as they moved through the house and up the stairs, stopping at the nursery to check on the twins.

"Little angels," Colt whispered as he looked at them, smiling.

She chuckled. "They look like angels when they are sleeping," she whispered. "But sometimes the halo needs a little polishing when they are awake."

He led her into the bedroom, where he began to unbutton her blouse as he kissed the corner of her lips. His fingers gently brushed her skin as they slid down to undo the tiny clasp between her breasts, releasing her bra. His mouth followed the same path, dropping soft feathery kisses all the way down her throat, over her shoulder to where the bra strap had lain, then down along her breast, coming to rest on her full nipple.

She moaned and pushed against him. Three years of marriage and the birth of the twins had not dimmed the fire that his touch stirred in her. The flames leaped hungrily as they helped each other undress. They tumbled on the bed and lost themselves in the ageless ritual of sexual fulfillment.

Exhausted and satiated they dozed, Frank lying in the circle of Colt's arm, her cheek against his chest. An hour later, they stirred and moved to pull back the sheets and get into bed. Colt was quiet.

"What are you thinking?" Frank whispered.

"About how wonderful my life is; you and me, the twins, and in a few months our new baby is arriving." He reached over and rested his hand on her belly. "When I think about where I was stuck before, in my anger and bitterness; all I would have missed if you hadn't come along...."

"That goes for me too, Colt. When you told me what happened with Shauna Lee tonight, I had to feel sorry for her. I wonder if she'll ever find what we have."

"You know, I'm not sure what she's doing these days, but if any of the stuff Josh was rattling off is true, I'm concerned about her. He made it sound like she is pretty promiscuous. When I was with her, she was definite about not wanting to get into a real relationship.

We spent a lot of time together over those four years, but when I asked her to marry me, she wasn't very keen on it. If I hadn't been so insistent, I doubt if she would've agreed."

"What is she running from, Colt? Obviously, it's not sex because she seems to gravitate to that. So what has hurt her so much?"

Colt sighed. "I know her dad was an alcoholic. Shauna Lee had a brother quite a bit younger than her and she worshiped him. He died in an accident on the farm when he was three or four."

Frank groaned. "It makes me sick to think of that. How could any of them deal with it?"

"I think that is part of her problem. It was like the straw that broke the camel's back. From the little she said, her dad just buried himself deeper in the bottle. Her mother slid into depression. Shauna Lee was about thirteen when it happened. She had no support at home.

"Her dad eventually left them and I think her mom died. She moved in with a local guy when she was really young. I don't know if they ever actually got married. I have no idea what happened after that, but eventually she was on her own again. She's got guts. She pulled herself together, finished her education and got her CA."

"I wish she could meet someone she would truly be happy with."

"I doubt if she'll meet that kind of guy doing what she seems to be doing now."

"Do you think it would help if you talked to her, Colt?"

He frowned. "I'd really have to think about that. It bothered me to hear the insinuations that Josh made tonight. That's why I asked Brad to go with me when I followed her back to her place. I don't want to do anything that could be misinterpreted. I don't want to put us at risk."

Frank snuggled close. "I'm not worried about that. We're solid."

***

The phone rang at six-thirty the next morning. Frank was pouring coffee when Colt answered it. The conversation was brief.

"That was Ollie. He's wondering when we're going to bring the cows and calves in from the lease."

"I want to go with you this year. I'd enjoy a few days in the saddle again!"

Colt frowned. "Will that be okay? You know; for the baby and all?"

"I'm not sick! I'm pregnant. That's the oldest condition in the world and I'm as strong as a horse!" Her smile was radiant. "I was riding range when I was carrying the twins and it didn't hurt me. I've missed being on the roundup the past three years, but I really couldn't go while the twins were so small.

"They're old enough to leave with your mom now if she'll look after them. It would be great if your mom and dad would come out to the ranch and watch them there. Then we could give them a kiss goodnight and tuck them in. What do you think?" Excitement sparkled in her eyes.

Colt thought for a moment. "Ollie would sure be happy to have you there. He still swears you are the best ranch hand he ever had." He reached out and took her hand, pulling her onto his lap. He nuzzled the curve of her neck. "And I'd love to have you with me. We made some wonderful memories out there."

She turned her face to settle her lips on his. Their kiss deepened and she could feel him harden as she rested against him. He shifted and turned her to face him, his hand moving to her breast. Fire leaped in her groin.

"Do we have time?" he whispered. She nodded and he swept her up in his arms and carried her up to their bedroom. They tore off their clothes and fell onto the unmade bed that they had left little more than an hour before.

Fifteen minutes later they lay together, panting and sweaty. Colt ran his fingers through the tips of her hair. "You're still so hot, woman!"

"And you're still so horny!" she said with a laugh. "We'd better get up and have breakfast. The coffee will be cold and the twins will be up in half an hour. Quickie time is over!"

He sighed. "You're right. While you make breakfast, I'll call Mom and see if they'll come out to the ranch and watch the kids."

Colt was frowning when he came to the kitchen after he'd called his parents. "Mom can't come; she and dad already have plans. She suggested a nanny that one of her friends knows. The woman was an elementary teacher. Her husband died ten years ago and her kids are grown. She retired and the last couple of years she's been a nanny for Mrs. Chapman's daughter. Mom says she comes highly recommended. We could check her out. What do you think?"

"I don't know. We don't know her and the twins don't know her. I'm not sure if..."

"We could meet her and see how we feel about her. If it feels right, we can bring her out here and see how it works with her and the kids. I've been thinking about this for a while... I want to get someone to help you. You handle everything so well, but sometimes I'm just blown away by all you do. I see how much work the twins are, and now with you being pregnant again, I'd like to get someone to give you a hand."

"Colt, I don't need help—"

He laid two fingers across her lips. "I have a selfish motive in this, too. I'd like you to be able to come to a meeting, like the one last night. Or go with me to a horse race when I go, and you could come out to the ranch for a day without having to worry about the twins. You should have a bit of time for yourself. I didn't marry you to keep you barefoot and pregnant. I wanted you to be my companion as well!"

"I... all right, we can check her out. When are you moving cows?"

"Ollie and I decided next week will work best, so we'd better get on this nanny thing right away. I want you to be on the roundup this year."

"Did your mom tell you her name?"

"Ellie Raines. Mom is going to call back with her phone number."

"Does she know if she's available now...?" Her keen senses detected a whimper upstairs. "That's Selena! The kids are awake!" Frank whirled and went flying up the stairs to the nursery. Colt shook his head. She was so in tune with the twins that it amazed him.

He could hear her crooning to their daughter. Selena would be rubbing her eyes with her little fists, her face all scrunched up on the verge of tears, protesting grumpily as she shed the drowsiness of sleep. Sam would be sitting on his bed, calm and wide-eyed. They were as different as night and day.

The phone rang. Colt answered it, ignoring the call display. He didn't recognize the callers' voice.

"Could I speak to Colt Thompson?" a youthful sounding female voice asked.

"Speaking."

"This is Ellie Raines. Connie Chapman talked to your mother this morning. She said you were looking for a babysitter next week."

"We are. Of course, we need to meet you first."

"I could drop by any time today."

"That would be great. Do you know where we live?"

"Not exactly; Connie said you lived on a farm near Cantuar, but I don't know your exact address."

Colt gave her directions to the farm and she said she would be there around eleven that morning. Then he bounded up the stairs to tell Frank and the twins.

***

Ellie Raines was punctual. She drove down the tree-lined driveway and parked her silver colored compact car in front of the older two-story house. She noted how well-kept the house and grounds were. As she stepped out of her car, she looked through the tall trees that formed a dividing line between the lawn around the house and the equipment yard.

She looked with interest at the huge, modern combines parked in front of a large machine shed. Experience told her that harvesting was finished. The weather had been good for harvesting. She noted the large metal grain bins lined up. The little tell-tale piles of grain on the ground in front of each one told her that grain had been augured into them and they were probably all full.

She turned as she heard the house door open. Her eyes met a tall, good-looking man with the greenest eyes she had ever seen. She decided he was probably in his late thirties or early forties. She smiled as she sized him up.

"Hi. I'm Ellie Raines. I was just looking at the combines and the grain bins. My husband and I had a mixed farm near Chitek Lake. Our kids weren't interested in the farm and it was too much for me to handle, so I sold it after he died. But, I've always loved harvest time."

Colt smiled as he watched her walk up the sidewalk. She was dressed in comfortable brown chino slacks and a fresh-looking pink blouse. She was probably about five foot four, pleasantly rounded and motherly looking; not fat, but definitely not thin. He guessed that she was in her early sixties. Her hair was a warm brown with golden highlights and a few threads of silver showing up in the temples. It was cut in a smart style that suited her well. Her eyes were a cool gray; warm, open and friendly. His first instinct was that he liked her. He reached out to shake her hand and invited her in.

"Fran," he called. "Ellie Raines is here."

He heard her answer from upstairs. "I'll be right there. I'm changing Selena's clothes. She spilled a glass of milk on herself. Will you make a fresh pot of coffee? Oh, and watch where you step by the table. I didn't get the milk all wiped up."

Colt motioned for Ellie to follow him into the kitchen. He pulled some paper towels from the roll and turned toward the table. Ellie reached to take them from his hand. "Let me clean up the spill while you make the coffee. I'm dying for a cup." She smiled as she took the paper towels from his hand and nimbly bent down to wipe up the spill.

Frank and the twins came down the stairs, and smiles of unfeigned delight wreathed Ellie's face. Colt introduced her to Fran and each child in turn. Selena ran to Ellie, open and accepting and Ellie stooped and picked her up. Frank and Colt watched the immediate connection between them and looked at each other with mutual understanding.

Ellie moved slowly toward Sam, speaking to him softly as she knelt down in front of him. She gently stood Selena on the floor beside her, cradling her close to her as she held her hand out to Sam. She spoke to both of the children, letting Sam make the next move. At first he clung firmly to his mother's legs, but he gradually relaxed as Ellie gained his confidence and reached out to touch her fingers.

She looked up at Colt. "Well, daddy, is that cup of coffee ready?" She took both children by the hand and followed Frank and Colt to the kitchen table. As they drank coffee, Ellie produced her credentials and references. She told them she was looking for full-time work and asked them to phone her past employers, particularly the family where she had last worked. She was no longer needed there because the mother had been laid off, but she had been sad to leave. She said she loved working with small children.

She left, giving them time to make a decision and assuring them that she could be available immediately. That evening, after they had checked her references and talked to her former employers, Colt phoned Ellie and confirmed that they wanted to hire her for two weeks. If the five of them worked well together, he assured her there was a good possibility that they would want her to stay on full-time.

She was thrilled and agreed to be there the next day.

"Where is she going to stay?" Frank asked.

"Well, she could stay in the spare room."

Frank wrinkled her nose. "Not enough privacy. That cuts out early morning activities like this morning." She grinned as she arched her eyebrow.

"We can't have that! What else can we do? We don't have anywhere else to put her."

"Could we buy a mobile home; something that's not too big, yet roomy enough for her to be comfortable? Then she would have her own place to stay. She'll have enough space to do whatever she wants, and we'll have our privacy too."

"That is a great idea. We'll have to figure out how to get power and water and sewer hooked up for it right away."

BOOK TWO CHAPTER THREE

Shauna Lee struggled to consciousness. Her thinking was fuzzy, still affected by the extra sleeping pill. She stretched out and rolled over onto her back, pushing the covers away from her face. She squinted against the light that streamed in through the bedroom window and then looked at the clock on her night table. "Ten o'clock. Jeez, I simply died!"

She swung her legs off the bed and sat up. Her pajamas were uncomfortably twisted around her slender frame. Her head was still foggy. She rubbed her eyes and yawned, thinking that a cup of coffee would bring her back to the world of the living.

She stood up and wandered into the kitchen. After she had set up the coffee pot, she wandered over to the front window and looked outside. Idly she watched a couple strolling hand and hand down the street, enjoying the beautiful September morning. Another family came into sight; a husband and wife and two small children.

The girl swung on her father's hand. The little boy was about four years old. He was running ahead, then spinning back and charging toward his mother. He stopped just beyond her reach, eluding her as she smiled and leaned forward to catch him. Then he ran back up the street again, laughing as he went.

Shauna Lee's eyes fastened on the boy. She bit her lip as she watched him. Feelings she had buried twenty-one years ago bubbled to the surface. She shook her head, pushing them away, but she couldn't seem to tear her focus away from the child. Tears filled her eyes, blurring her vision, then escaping down her cheeks. She turned from the window, dashing them away with the back of her hand.

She stumbled to the table and sat on a chair. Sobs racked her body and she cried uncontrollably until she was exhausted and drained. Then she sat, staring out the kitchen window, her emotions numb.

Ben would have been twenty-two now; the son she had loved with all her being and the son whose father, Dave Trutcher, wouldn't accept because he had been born with a physical deformity that revolted him.

Shauna Lee couldn't hold back any longer. She ran to the bathroom and vomited the bitter acid that roiled in her stomach. It burned her throat and lingered sourly in her mouth. She hadn't eaten anything since late the afternoon before. The coffee she had made sat in the thermal carafe on the counter.

She was cold and sick. She filled a glass with water and rinsed her mouth, then crawled back into bed and huddled under the sheets, willing her thoughts to go away. Gradually the exhaustion of her emotions claimed her in sleep.

She awakened later in the afternoon. Her watch showed it was four-thirty. Her head hurt and she knew she needed to eat. She went to the kitchen and poured herself a cup of coffee. The carafe had kept it lukewarm. She sipped it mindlessly and opened the fridge to look inside. Nothing looked appetizing. She closed the door, uncertain what she would do. She knew she needed something, but what? She looked like hell and she was definitely was not leaving the house. Pizza? She could order in. She reached for the phone and then hesitated.

In her mind, pizza was meant to be shared. Suddenly she realized that she couldn't think of anyone to share one with. At one time, she would have called Colt. In the years since then... well she'd seldom had lonely weekends. Men like Josh hadn't been hard to find for company.

What the hell had happened this time? It was as if Josh had opened Pandora's Box with his crude remarks and things just kept tumbling out. She had been forced to look at her life, like Scrooge at

Christmas time, but she wasn't Scrooge and it wasn't Christmas. However, as it had been for Scrooge, it was difficult for her to accept what her life had become.

She picked up the phone and ordered a pizza. She decided to have a shower while she waited for it to be delivered. She would eat it by herself while she watched TV and escape reality until she got back on track.

Shauna Lee woke up crying at four-thirty on Sunday morning. She had been dreaming about the night Ben had died. The horror of it clung to her as she fought off the cloud of sleep. Dave's rage hung in the room, so real she could feel it.

She lay there thinking about that soul-destroying time in her life. She hadn't told anyone about Ben, not even Colt. What had triggered those memories, making them come to the surface now?

She got up and went to the bathroom. She was still wearing her pajamas from the day before, and they were creased and damp with sweat and tears. Glancing at the clock, she noted that it was only five in the morning.

What day is it? she wondered. She went into the kitchen and turned on the soft light under the microwave that was installed above the stove. Automatically she emptied the thermal coffee carafe and set up a new pot of coffee. She poured herself a bowl of dry cereal, splashed some milk over it and added a sprinkle of sugar.

Then she sat down at the table. She ate mindlessly, purposely pushing her clamoring thoughts aside. It must be Sunday... it'll be another long day to get through. What am I going to do? I can't just sit here and drown in my memories.

She sighed and got up to pour herself a cup of coffee. "Maybe I should go for a drive, but where would I go?"

She wandered over to the couch and turned on the TV, but there wasn't much that interested her at six in the morning. She surfed through the channels and clicked on a program about small wind turbines. She listened with idle interest as the spokesman explained to the interviewer how the new small wind turbines were helping the environment by replacing dirty grid power with free, clean, green, wind-energy that was economical and affordable too.

When he introduced their newest dealer, she became alert. She recognized Brad Johnson. She heard him say "Years ago the landscape of western Canada was dotted with windmills that were mainly used to pump water out of the ground."

The rich timbre of his voice and the smooth way he delivered his words caught her attention. Its cadence captured her. She watched his expressions and the way he moved his hands as he talked, shifting slightly on his feet from time to time. He was confident and sincere, an earthy, unpretentious, solid individual. She'd been aware of that Friday night, but now she was really struck by it.

She picked up his words again... "and eventually I can see this type of landscape recreated again with our small power-generating wind turbines popping up on farms and ranches across the country. They are highly efficient, require very little maintenance and are simple to install. A truck or a tractor will easily pull the assembled tower into place."

The sound of his voice washed over her. She studied his physique. He was tall; over six feet she was certain. And she'd bet he didn't get those muscles pumping iron in the gym. He probably got them from throwing bales or wrestling calves.

He was wearing blue jeans again, and a western shirt that accentuated the gray of his eyes. He wasn't wearing a Stetson today, and his rich brown hair was ruffled by the breeze. Did he have cowboy boots on? She watched closely as the camera moved back. "Yes!" she murmured "And nice ones, too. He is a hunk!" She watched him dreamily until the camera shifted away to show a wind turbine being installed.

"And... I'm sure he thinks I'm the town tramp.... He probably wouldn't come near me." Then reality hit her like a punch.

Discontent washed over her as she surfed through the channels a few more times, then stood up and turned off the TV. She dropped the remote on the coffee table and glanced at her watch again, debating what she should do. It was only eight-thirty. She sighed deeply. "This is going to be a long day. Well, I have laundry to do. That will take up some of my time."

As she gathered her laundry from the hamper in her bedroom, she wondered what had happened to her. *Why haven't I made friends? Right now, I wish I had someone to talk to—maybe a girlfriend. But I've never had a real girlfriend*, she thought as she dropped a load of whites in the washing machine.

The phone rang as she was closing the lid. She turned the washer on and ran to answer it. Glancing at the call display, she hesitated, trying to recognize the name. It was from the Country

Lane Inn in town.

Who the heck? she wondered as she answered. "Hello?"

"Shauna Lee, this is Mitch...."

"Mitch...?" There was a question in the word. Who...?

"Mitch Wagner from Saskatoon."

"Oh, Mitch. It's been a while. You caught me by surprise."

"I'm in town. I have a meeting tomorrow, but I was wondering if you wanted to get together today. I think the Eliminators Car Club has its show and shine at Riverside Park. We could stop and check it out if you like."

"Hey, I'd love to get together. I'm just sort of kicking around here on my own!"

"All right, I'll drop over in an hour or so to pick you up. It'll be great to see you again!"

"I'll be waiting," she said with a smile. *Mitch, you're a wish come true. You've rescued me from myself. Thank you! Thank you!* She quickly shut off the washing machine and ran to the bedroom. She opened a dresser drawer and selected a sexy, lacy set of matching panties and bra. She dashed into the bathroom and turned on the shower.

She washed her hair and lathered her body quickly and then reached for her razor and shaved her underarms and legs. As she rinsed off she ran her hands over her skin. Smooth as silk, she thought with a smile.

She blew her hair dry, applied her makeup and added a light spray of seductive perfume. Then she slipped into her bra and panties and checked out the closet to decide what to wear. After some thought, she selected a silky, bayou blue top that closed with a crossover tie and showed a lot of cleavage. It brought out the color of her eyes.

She picked out a pair of stretchy jeans that fit her like a glove and grabbed a long, tweedy blue sweater. She rifled through her sock drawer, grabbed a pair of white ones and then slid her feet into a pair of running shoes. She was ready. She went into the kitchen and tossed her purse and house keys on the table. She poured herself a cup of coffee, just as the doorbell rang.

She had slipped into predator mode without even thinking. She waited a minute and then strolled to the door. *Can't appear too eager*, she mused as she opened it. She smiled coyly at the tall blonde man that stood in front of her.

"Mitch, imagine seeing you again!" She stood aside and let him step in, then closed the door behind him. She looked him over from top to bottom, then slid her arms around his neck and pulled him to her.

He smiled as he bent his head to kiss her gently. "It has been a long time," he said softly.

She nestled her head against his shoulder. "It has." She slipped her hand into his and led him into the living room, pulling him down onto the couch beside her. Her hand slid to rest on his thigh. "You're looking handsome," she said, smiling into his admiring eyes.

"And you're still gorgeous! You never change. How long has it been; three or four years? What's been going on in your life? I heard once that you were engaged to a farmer. That surprised me!"

"What surprised you; that I was engaged or that I was engaged to a farmer?"

He laughed and raised her hand to his lips, nibbling on her fingers. "Both. I couldn't picture you with a farmer; or for that matter, one guy. You always said you never get married."

She gently pulled her hand away. "And I didn't."

"I heard something to that effect."

She stood up. "So what are we going to do?"

He raised his eyebrows and looked at her quizzically.

"Hey, cool your jets boy! We've got the whole day ahead of us." She playfully punched him in the shoulder. "I at least expect a nice dinner and a good glass of wine," she said, laughing as she walked to the table and picked up her keys and purse.

"It's just that you're looking so hot...."

"I'm sure I heard you say something about going to the Eliminators Show and Shine." She walked to the door and stood waiting for him. "I thought they usually had that in August."

"There was a change in schedule this year." He grinned as he pushed himself up off the couch and walked over to join her. He pushed the door closed and pulled her against him, kissing her deeply, his tongue slipping into her mouth, dancing with hers.

She could feel the bulge in his crotch as he rubbed against her and fire leaped in her groin. She moaned as he ravaged her mouth. Then he swung the door open, pushing her out in front of him. "We'll do it your way for now; then we'll do it my way tonight!"

It was a beautiful, fall day and there was a large crowd at the show. Shauna Lee smiled for the first time in two days. She loved looking at the hot rods and old classic cars. She knew a lot of the people there; several of them were her clients. She stopped and chatted with them as she moved through the rows of cars with Mitch.

Mitch met a man he knew and stopped to talk business, so she kept wandering down the line. A hopped-up old truck caught her eye. She wandered closer to look it over. "Sweet!" she said softly as she trailed her finger along the polished grill.

"It's well done," a deep rich voice commented from behind her. Shauna Lee jumped and whirled around, almost losing her balance. She stared into a pair of warm gray eyes that widened in surprise. Brad Johnson was standing there.

Her heart stood still momentarily. "Oh... you... I didn't hear you come up behind me."

She looked so shocked, so defenseless, he couldn't help but smile. He reached out and touched her shoulder in a gesture meant to steady her. "I didn't realize it was you."

She flushed. *Or you probably have gone the other way,* she thought. "Isn't this a cool old truck," she babbled, trying to hide the fact that seeing him had thrown her off balance. She slid a caressing hand along the bright red fender. "It's a 1949 model!"

"It's custom built. These guys rebuild old cars and trucks for a hobby, and it's an expensive one!" He touched his toe against the spokes of the chrome tire rim. "Look at these wheels, and did you notice the chrome stacks behind the cab?" He rubbed his hand along the top edge of the box. "This baby never looked so good; even when it was new."

They fell into step and moved along the line to the next vehicle.

"Oh! I saw you on TV this morning."

He looked puzzled and shook his head.

"Yes; you were being interviewed about the wind turbines."

"Oh, I see." He smiled and her heart missed a beat. "They recorded that last week. So you saw it this morning?"

"I don't know what channel it was on. I was surfing and I happened to hear a guy talking about the wind turbines. And then, there you were. Actually, it was quite interesting. Listening to you today and having seen your presentation the other night, I can see where there is a lot of potential, especially in the outlying areas for farmers and ranchers."

"The potential is incredible, and not just in the rural areas. Hydro isn't as expensive here in Canada, as it is in other parts of the world. The manufacturer is a forward thinking guy and most of his market is overseas now. But hydro costs will eventually go up here, too. Then people will be looking for the opportunity we offer. It's just a matter of time."

"I can see where a few of my clients could be interested in them; especially ranchers and farmers. So many of the smaller places have amalgamated into the larger ones; in some areas you travel miles without seeing an active home site."

Brad looked at her, seeing the intelligent businesswoman he had gotten a glimpse of on Friday night. They stopped and inspected a bright yellow Ford Fairlane. Brad ran his hand along the front fender. "My dad owned one of these fifty years ago."

Conversation flowed easily between them, and neither of them noticed that an hour had passed before Mitch caught up with them. He came up behind Shauna Lee and slid an arm over her shoulder.

"Sorry for leaving you on your own. I ran into a client and I needed to talk to him."

"Not a problem. I ran into Brad. He markets and installs wind-powered turbines. He gave a powerpoint presentation on them the other night, at a seminar that the DA put on. They are a fascinating concept."

She turned to Brad; she could see the speculation in his eyes. *Jeez,* she thought fiercely. *What must he be thinking?* "Brad Johnson, this is Mitch Wagner. We've known each other for several years. He's from Saskatoon, but he's in town for a meeting tomorrow, so he looked me up this morning."

The two men shook hands and made small talk for a few seconds before Mitch reached into his pocket for his cell phone. She saw him frown as he turned away and answered. His face blanched. "I'll be right home. No; forget about the meeting. I'll reschedule. You just hang in there! I'm on my way."

He turned to Shauna Lee. "I have to go home."

"Is something wrong?" she asked with genuine concern.

"M- my son, Kyle. He was playing baseball and got nailed in the head with a bat. They're taking him to the hospital right now."

Your son? "How old is he?" she asked, her voice choked.

"Eleven... I've got to go." He looked at Brad. "Look, I'm sorry to do this, but could you give Shauna Lee a lift home?"

"Don't worry about me, Mitch. Just go... your son needs you and you should get home as soon as possible. I'll have no problem catching a ride. I know a lot of people here."

"I'll take her home," Brad said. "Just get on the road, man! I hope your boy is okay."

"Thanks, guys. I'm out of here."

Shauna Lee watched him run through the cars. *That bastard! He's married and has a family. A few hours ago he was trying to get in my pants.*

Brad touched her arm, mistaking the reason for the troubled expression on her face. "All we can do is hope that everything is all right. Getting hit in the head with a baseball bat is rough. It's hard to say how bad it is until the doctors examine him."

"Poor kid." *You have no idea!*

"Look, it's four o'clock. Are you in a hurry to go home?"

"Brad, you don't have to worry about me. I'm a big girl. I can take care of myself."

"Hey, your friend asked me... and honestly," he chuckled as he looked her over from head to foot, "you don't look like a very big girl to me. If you're in a hurry to get home, I'll take you straight there. If you're relaxed about it, we could go have supper somewhere and then I'll take you home."

"Well..."

"Look, we both need to eat sometime. Company with supper would be a nice change for me."

"Well, when you put it that way, I have to admit you're right. We can go anytime you like."

"We could swing by The Steakhouse. How about it?"

She nodded. They turned and walked back to the parking lot. She felt disappointed when he didn't reach for her hand or curl his arm around her waist and draw her close against his side. It would feel good to snuggle against his shoulder.

The restaurant was busy, but they found a table in the corner where it was a little quieter. Brad asked her what she would like to drink. She opted for red wine; he ordered rum and coke and when their drinks came they slipped into easy conversation.

"How long have you lived in Swift Current?" Brad was looking down at his drink, swirling amber liquid over the ice as he spoke.

"I've been here for thirteen years. After I had got my CA, I came here to work for the previous owner of my business. I worked for him for three years. He had a good clientele, and I'd worked with him long enough to earn their confidence. He wanted to retire so I bought the business from him."

She caught her bottom lip in her teeth and then sighed as she released it. "I'd worked hard through the years; in fact, I did little else but work and study." She twirled the stem of her glass between her thumb and index finger. Then she looked up to find him watching her intently. "I'd saved enough to buy the business. He did give me a break though; he was happy to have me take it over. It's done well over the past ten years."

"You can be proud of what you've accomplished. What about your family? Didn't you have support from them?"

"I don't have any family." She decided she needed to shift the conversation away herself. "Now tell me about you? The other night you said you were from B.C.?"

"I'm from Dawson Creek."

"Where is that?"

"More northern; if you drew a line from North Battleford across to Dawson Creek, you would find that they are pretty close in latitude. I took the Wind Turbine Maintenance Program at Northern Lights College and that got my toe in the door. Experience got me here."

The waitress came to take their food order and Brad checked with her to make sure that it was alright before he ordered another drink for each of them.

"So were you born there?"

"Yeah, my dad owns a bulk station in town. He handles diesel, gas, oil and grease. Mom's retired now, but she was a teacher."

"Do you have any brothers or sisters?"

"We're the 'perfect' family; there are two of each of us."

She smiled. "So what did you do for fun? Did you play hockey or football?"

"The truth? Neither one, but I like to watch both. As far as football goes, I'm a Saskatchewan Rough Riders fan now, but it's hard for me if they are playing the B.C. Lions. I still cheer for the Vancouver Canucks when they play hockey, but I like junior league hockey as much as the NHL. They are young and full of piss and vinegar. They usually deliver a good game. Are you a hockey fan?"

Shauna Lee shrugged. "Not really, but I've never actually checked it out. I've seen games on TV in the bar, but I wasn't actually concentrating on them. But, tell me more about you; what do you do for R&R? Somehow, I don't think you're a couch potato."

He grinned. "No; I'm an outdoors guy. I like to hike in the mountains. Dad and I hunted together from the time I was a kid; we used to pack in with horses. We would ride back into the mountains where you seldom saw anyone else. I loved doing that. I also rode bareback in the high school rodeos."

Her eyes sparkled. "Wow! A real cowboy; sexy."

"Don't get carried away. I wasn't big time or anything like that. I loved to ride and I still do. Give me a horse and turn me loose and I'll be happy for days."

"You are Colt's kind of guy; you both like cows and horses."

"I like Colt. I think we have a lot in common."

"So," she said leaning across the table toward him. "Are there any women in your life?"

He raised an eyebrow. "Are you always so direct?"

"Well, you're a good-looking man. I'm just curious."

"How many guys are there in your life?"

She blushed. "Touché."

The waitress brought their meals and they ate in silence.

When he was finished, Brad put his utensils onto the plate and pushed it aside. "Are you ready for coffee?"

"I am stuffed. You could take me home and stop for coffee. It would give me half an hour to digest the steak."

He looked at her for a long moment. Her heart accelerated as she wondered what he was thinking. "If you'd like to do that, we could," he said soberly.

"Sure, let's go. I might even offer you some dessert."

Brad paid for their meal, and then held the door open for her as they exited the restaurant. His hand touched the small of her back as they walked to his truck. The touch sent a hot tightening into her belly and down into the heat of her femininity. He opened the door and helped her up onto the passenger seat. He was smiling when he got in on his side. "These trucks are so high. It's quite a stretch for a shorty like you to get your little tush up onto the seat."

"Now, a gentleman wouldn't have noticed," she said with a sexy little giggle.

"I guess I'm not a gentleman then because I did notice."

When they pulled up in front of her house, he got out and came around to open her door so he could help her get out. Shauna Lee felt giddy with anticipation as they walked along the walkway to her house. She smiled as she opened her front door and stepped inside, standing aside to let him in.

"You can leave those beautiful boots on the mat." She spoke over her shoulder, as she moved into the kitchen and tossed her keys and her purse on the table. "Just grab a spot to sit and I'll put on the coffee."

Brad looked around the open kitchen and living room area. It was beautifully decorated, but he noted the lack of personal things. There were no pictures of family or friends and no books: all she had was furniture and a top-of-the-line TV and stereo system.

He eased his long frame down onto a kitchen chair. "Nice place."

"It works for me," she said with a warm smile. "Do you want a tour of the rest of the place while the coffee pot does its magic?" She smiled at him, raising an eyebrow. "There is a laundry room, bathroom and a bedroom with a queen-sized bed."

"I just got settled here. Why don't we just sit down and chat until the coffee is ready." It wasn't a rebuff. It struck her as meaning that there would be plenty of time later. As they talked, her eyes registered an unspoken invitation, her inherent sexual essence oozing out.

Brad smiled, accepting the cup of coffee she gave him. Her fingers brushed his softly, lingering with promise. When their cups were drained, he leaned back in his chair and looked at her, his gray eyes cool and intent.

"Shauna Lee, I told you I'm a hunter. I have hunted cougars in the wild. That is where I like to keep them: in the wild, with me doing the stalking."

Her face went scarlet. "Are you calling me a cougar?" she asked, indignantly.

"I think the description fits you fairly accurately. You're no teenybopper getting her first hormone flushes. If you were looking for a wedding ring, you'd have one. You're successful, and I'm not blind; you're hot.

"I'm not stupid either. You're on the prowl for sex. You've been stalking me all evening. I could take you to that queen-sized bed that you mentioned earlier and do it justice. But I seldom hunt where everyone else has been working the territory."

He stood up. "I enjoyed your company today. I enjoyed having supper with you, but I'm not into playing this game. I'm not willing to be another one of your boy-toys." He walked to the door and opened it.

"I'm sure you don't want my advice, but I'll throw it out there anyway. Figure out who you are before it's too late. You've got a lot more to offer than sex, but you'll never find that out if you keep running from real intimacy. Bed hopping with your 'nothing serious, no strings attached, no risk attitude' is never going to get you there. One day, you'll wake up and find yourself old and alone."

He stepped out and closed the door.

She stood immobile for a second, stunned. She grabbed his cup off the table and flung it against the door. It shattered into pieces, but she didn't even flinch. "Who the hell do you think you are, Brad Johnson?" she raged. "A shrink? Well, I don't need one."

She kicked the leg of the chair he'd been sitting on. "I've got news for you. I know just who I am. I've been old and alone since I was eighteen years old."

***

Also, watch for *The Hand of Fate* (Book Three) and *A Second Chance* (Book Four) in the Belanger Creek Ranch Series.

ABOUT THE AUTHOR

Photograph by Suzanne Englund

Gloria Antypowich grew up on a farm and most of her married life has been lived on a ranch. Human relationships fascinate her. Ideas for stories can be found everywhere; over-heard conversations in a public place, a couple fighting in a restaurant, a story in the news, even a chance remark in a conversation with a friend. She is enamored with the power of words and she loves to use them to paint images of characters that become so real, they feel like they could be your next door neighbor.

Gloria is an avid reader of several different genres and listens to a wide selection of music. A good game of cards, sharing a laugh with a friend over a glass of wine and spending time with her family are a few of her favorite things to do. She loves to write and says her husband was her inspiration for the heroes in this series of books. He was a cowboy, a rancher—and a lover. Gloria lives with her husband, in the central interior of British Columbia, Canada. They are retired now, but they still have "chemistry".

Made in the USA
Charleston, SC
09 October 2015